Being Magic
A Journey to Wholeness

Michael Ellison, Ph.D.

with Melanie Stinson

Published by Space Cadets Studios

For more sci-fi/fantasy content, visit
spacecadetsstudios.com

ISBN: 979-8-218-11194-6

DEDICATION

To the dreamers and the seekers...
May your own journey help you appreciate and value the present
moment, even as you search out and embrace new possibilities in your
quest to be more of who you are capable of being.
Lots of blessings!

And to my mother, Ellen, who always encouraged me to follow my
dreams and claim my own sense of wholeness.

CONTENTS

ACKNOWLEDGMENTS..i

Preface..1

1. Down the Drain..2

2. Upheaval..12

3. Sinkhole to Solaba..24

4. Unsettling In..31

5. The Space Between..38

6. Thanton, the Adventure World..47

7. Challenging Reality..59

8. Navlys, the Air World..62

9. Vergon, Home to Felagor..74

10. The Kermuffles..86

11. Riding Kermuffle Waves..104

12. The Clearing..112

13. Astara, the Healing World..119

14. Sleenaje..134

15. Recovery..140

16. Life in Astara..148

17. What Price Safety?..157

18. Welcome to Erinmar..167

19. Life in Erinmar..176

20. Painting..186

21. Connections..200

22. Facing Felagor..214

23. Welcome Forward..225

ACKNOWLEDGMENTS

As with any work of this magnitude, there are an enormous number of people to thank. First and foremost among these is Melanie A. Stinson, whose beautiful, powerful artwork is included here. The first seeds of the ideas that appear here actually grew a few years ago from a book of collages Melanie shared with me. The imagery was so powerful, I remember remarking, "I think you have the ideas for at least three shows here." We got together after that and within a few months created a twenty-eight-page treatment for a Cirque du Soleil – inspired show called Being Magic: A Journey to Wholeness. Shopping that around we got some very positive response, yet no one was quite sure what to do with it.

After working with Melanie in numerous ways, creating playful empowerment workshops and encouraging/challenging each other to grow, I got the bright idea to turn that treatment into a book. Melanie repeatedly warned me that would be a mammoth undertaking, which it certainly has been. The time and care it has taken to flesh these characters out and bring them to life has been at times overwhelming. Yet she stuck with me every step of the way, serving as a guide, a sounding board and an editor who inspired me to clarify the voices of these characters and make the journey more active. Melanie, I can't thank you enough for the time you invested, your terrific insights and all the rewrites you shepherded me through, not to mention your wonderful artwork. There is no way this journey would have been possible without your inspiration, support, and hard work.

I am delighted that you, the reader, get to enjoy some of Melanie's incredible artwork and the evocative ways she illuminates the journey of our lead character.

Once we had a working version of the book, we shopped it around to various friends to get their insights. Many thanks to Carolyn Agosta, Connie Neufer, Retha Karnes, Cherie Anderson, Liz Cope and Pamela Stinson for taking the time to read the fourth draft and share your feedback.

In addition, young audience author Bill Konisberg offered invaluable insights which impacted the final product. Thank you so much, Bill.

Michael Wilson, thank you for sharing your reactions to the work on so many levels, including how you see my own journey reflected in the book. Thank you for seeing me so deeply and so clearly.

Cynthia Running-Johnson, much thanks for your very careful and thorough reading of a draft of the book and your extensive feedback.

Special thanks to Cherie Anderson for inspiring the "License to Follow Your Dreams."

Finally, Brent Winzek, I cannot begin to thank you enough for your generosity on reformatting the book and plowing through it with me page by page for a close to final edit.

The book you are holding (or reading on your electronic devise) is unusual in several aspects. Author Bill Konisberg commented, "It's certainly a fun and interesting juxtaposition of contemporary fiction, self-help, and fantasy. I've never read anything quite like it."

That amalgamation of elements is certainly the most challenging aspect of this book – and also my favorite thing about it. My hope is that the preface helps to introduce various ways you might interface with this book.

May it prove to be an enjoyable and enlightening journey for you!

-Michael Ellison, Ph.D.

As artists and energy practitioners, we are committed to exploring ways the arts can be utilized to inspire and support people in claiming their own magic and celebrating who they are.

-Michael & Melanie

PREFACE

There are many ways in, many ways through any journey.
There are even a few different ways to interact with this story.

In addition to the recounting of the tale of our heroine
you will find here the magical artwork of Melanie Stinson.

ENJOY THE JOURNEY!

1. DOWN THE DRAIN

She opened her mouth to scream, but nothing came out. She was freefalling – plunging through the darkness. *Oh, my god!* she thought, *What's going on? Where's the ground? I just keep falling. Oh, no! It's a sinkhole.* Down. Down. She kept expecting to crash into solid ground but kept falling and falling. And she couldn't breathe. She kept gasping for air, terrified that dirt would pour in.

When she bolted up in bed, the air rushing into her lungs startled her as she looked out into the darkness. It took her more than a moment to get her bearings – to register that she was safe. *I'm just here – in bed. No sinkhole.*

"It's all right, Pro," she told herself. She had long ago gotten used to the nickname her college roommate Ali had given her. The irony was not lost on her. Kathryn Proscher felt like anything but a pro.

It was just another nightmare about sinkholes. She tried to laugh it off, thinking, *It's just the world caving in, what's the problem?* But no matter how hard she tried to dismiss how shaken she was, the cold sweat that made her shiver told another story. *Damn! I thought I was done with that. It's been weeks since I had a dream like that.*

Catching her breath, she thought of the first time that she had that dream – months ago. The day before she had seen some YouTube videos: one of a young woman who just fell through a hole that opened in the sidewalk and another of a couple whose car got swallowed by a hole in the highway that suddenly appeared. They all died.

Sinkholes are a real thing. She had thought that then, and now, this morning, too. *A bizarre real thing, but a real thing. Oh, yeah! Sinkholes feel like far too real a thing. Perfect evidence that life is arbitrary, and you never know what might happen. Like we need more proof. Lord! That's MY LIFE.*

The dream had really rattled her. *Why now? Another sinkhole. Another dream of doom? I thought I was doing better. I just need to calm down. Maybe some warm milk?*

The warmth of the mug of hot almond milk with vanilla and honey was soothing. Pro moved out of the kitchen and into the living room, then found herself in the alcove that served as her painting studio.

She stared at the blank canvas — and it stared back. In its own way the white canvas felt just as frightening as the darkness of the sinkhole — just as empty — just as foreboding.

Is it judging me? Taunting me? I haven't been able to paint since Ash - not my own painting, anyway. Well, okay, fine, yes — I've thrown paint on the canvas, or at the canvas. But nothing has stuck. Nothing means anything.

What do you expect, Pro? That your art could, what? Save the world? Well, I guess, yes, in a way. At least that's what it felt like in college. That's what I loved about my art classes — what Professor Tilson drilled into us.

"Art is not just putting some vague impressions on a canvas. It's about meaning", she would say. "What do YOU have to say that is uniquely yours?"

But, Professor Tilson, what if I DON'T have anything to say? What if life HAS no meaning? How can anything have meaning when you feel like you're sleepwalking through your life?

Okay, heavy stuff for three-thirty in the morning. Bathroom. Teeth. Bed.

If only the bed didn't seem so empty now. I can't look at it without remembering our second anniversary, when Ash had strewn it with rose petals and orchids. What a wonderful night that was!

For a while after Ash left, painting had served as a distraction, but that rapidly faded. She was more successful at burying herself in her work as a graphic designer— which was still art, of sorts, but hardly "Art with a capital A."

It's commercial art with a capital C, she thought as she brushed her teeth. *If it sells to the client, it's good, if not — no matter how beautiful it is or how much I have poured my heart into it – it is virtually worthless. Which is exactly what most of my work has felt like lately – worthless. Utterly devoid of meaning. Sorry Professor Tilson! Sorry I wasted your time.*

Are you done? It's three-thirty-seven. You need to sleep.

Pro snuggled back under the covers.

I just need to focus on something pleasant.

She brought her mind round to the class she taught at The GridLine last Thursday after work. The eight-to-twelve-year-olds she taught were so excited to be showing off their paintings of nature projects. She had told them, "Every one of you did such a great job. Your use of color and line is bold and fun. I am really proud of all of you. You know, you are wonders of nature, too! Just like your paintings. Give yourselves a big hand."

The youngsters applauded and whooped and hollered for themselves and each other and Pro whooped and hollered right along with them. "Ok, that wraps up class for today. Let's get all of our materials picked up and put in the storage closet. I'll see you next Friday."

She brushed her long brown hair out of her face. Her hazel eyes sparkled.

"Thank you, Miss Proscher," Beatrice said, giving Pro a big hug.

Shy little Fen came up to her – well - not so little. He was ten and at five-foot-seven he already stood eye to eye with Pro. The black eye he had come in with the week before had broken her heart. She was glad to see it was healing. "You're the best," he said with a tentative high five.

The moment their hands touched Pro plunged back into the abyss of the sinkhole – falling, falling down, down, alone – and doomed.

Noooooooooooo, Nooooo, NOOOOOOO. The screaming woke her up, but it took her a moment to realize that the screams were hers. Sweat poured down her face and she hugged herself hard – holding on for dear life. But she couldn't stop shaking.

Was that all just a dream?

No, the class happened. That was just a few days ago. I haven't completely lost it. But what do you do when the earth opens up and swallows you? Give up? Try to claw your way out?

4

I am not losing my mind. I am NOT losing my mind. I am not LOSING my mind. Pro hugged her knees and rocked back and forth.

"You are doing just fine, Pro," she could hear Dr. Lamdowski's soothing voice, "You are doing just fine."

F-you, Dr. Lamdowski, she thought, *I am NOT doing "just fine." Oh, I hold it together at work and while I am teaching at the GridLine. It's just the rest of my life that's in shambles.*

Fighting to control her tears, she tried not to think about Ash – which, of course, only insured she could think about nothing else. For weeks, she had kept hoping he would call – that they could work things out and get back together. But – no call. She had resigned herself, hadn't she? For a moment she was tempted to cave in, to fall into a sinkhole of failure and despair.

NO! I am NOT going there. Shower. Work. GO!

Pro made sure she looked sharp in comfortable dress pants, a light blue button up blouse and her favorite navy-blue jacket. She had always dressed up for work, but she'd found herself putting in more effort since Ash left.

Why shouldn't I look good? One last look in the mirror for good measure.

Okay, I have lost a couple of pounds, but at least I've been working out at lunch three times a week. I'm not completely falling apart. And off we go!

She would be at work extra early, but that was fine. It was better than sitting in the apartment by herself. Taking care to lock the door, since she had been so absent-minded lately, Pro headed for work.

She had just emerged from the subway, traveling on autopilot, when her phone startled her into the present. *Who would be calling this early in the morning,* she thought as she fished her phone out of her purse. *Oh! Of course!*

"Hello, Mother. Is everything all right?" Pro said.

"Well, yes and no," her mother replied.

Cryptic as ever, Pro thought. "I can't talk long," she said aloud. "On my way to work. What's up?"

"Well, have you seen the newspaper this morning?"

"No, you know I never read the paper. I check the news online to grab the headlines when I have time, but usually it is so depressing I don't bother."

"I forget. You really should read the newspaper you know, just so you know what is going on."

Leave it to my mother, Pro thought to herself, *she's always ready to tell me exactly what I ought to be doing. Say something, Pro. Tell her off. Why can I never shut my mother up? Or Patricia? Or Ash? Why do I let them railroad me? I'm such a pushover. Ugh!*

"Well, at any rate, you might want to pick up one this morning," her mother said, "but I am glad I caught you first."

"What's going on?"

"I looked at the society page this morning – and there was a picture of Ash and his new bride to be."

Pro stopped in her tracks. She felt like she had been punched in the stomach.

"Are you sure it was Ash?" Even as she asked, she knew it was true.

"I am certain there can't be too many Ashley Harrison Simpson III's who look just like him," her mother asserted. "There he was larger than life with his new fiancé. I guess he must have been seeing her when… I told you - you should have fought harder. That should have been you. It would have been you if you had played your cards right."

The roar in Pro's ears was deafening. Absentmindedly she said, "I have to go, Mother. Bye."

"Of course, Kathryn. Call us if you need anything."

Pro ended the call and tried to get her bearings. She couldn't breathe. Her head was spinning.

This can't be true. It's only been three months since he left, she thought. *Okay, I have to stop and shake this off. I will deal with this after work.*

She shook her head to clear it and forced herself to press on toward work. When she saw a street kiosk, however, she immediately stopped and bought a paper. Then she refused to open it. Her heart was racing.

Pro looked at the paper in her hand like it was a snake about to strike. When she started to move and lost her footing on a curb, almost toppling, she realized how shaken she was. She was hyperventilating. She retreated to a wall to steady herself, as a nauseous feeling in the pit of her stomach made her realize she needed to stop and just hold on for a few moments to get her wits about her.

Darkness lapped at her ankles, creeping up around her. The earth quaked under her feet, as it threatened to open up and swallow her. She was tempted to give in and let that happen. *Just fall into this sinkhole of despair – why not?*

Clinging to the cold stone for support, she thought, *Whoa! Hold on! Wow, I must really be losing it. Get a grip, Pro,* she told herself. She tried to breathe, but her chest felt like it would explode. *Okay,* she thought, fighting to be lucid in the wave of fear that was welling up inside of her. *What can I do?*

One thing at a time, I have to get to someplace that feels safe – or at least familiar, before I lose my mind. Just get to Starbucks. But I have to look at that announcement, she argued with herself. *Get to Starbucks, get your drink, then we will sit down and look at the newspaper,* some other part of her seemed to counsel. *Okay, I can do this. One foot after the other. It's only three short blocks.*

When she got to Starbucks, she stuffed her desire to bark at the hustle and bustle around her. She was good at that, stuffing down her feelings. She got her regular, a tall vanilla chai latte with almond milk, and then bolted out the door.

Okay, where to now? She thought to herself. *You could go to the office. Are you kidding? There is no way I won't read that announcement before work, and there is NO WAY I am going to sit at my desk – or in the damn bathroom for that matter – to read it.* It struck Pro that she was not only arguing with herself but referring to herself in second person.

Dr. Lamdowski would be so proud, she thought with more than a little sarcasm.

"You are finally giving voice to the war going on inside of you that you fight so hard to pretend is not there," he would say.

"Aaaarrrrrrgggghhhh!" she growled out loud. A woman in a grey suit jumped at the sound and scurried past her, her eyes wide with terror.

She's probably afraid I might start foaming at the mouth.

Pro resisted the urge to take a few steps toward her and snarl *That's right, lady! I am a force to be reckoned with. Watch out!* And, for just a second, the thought amused her.

For God sakes, pull yourself together, Pro. Just go down the street to Mercy Park. You can find a place to sit there.

Thankfully, Mercy Park was only a half a block away, and directly across the street from where she worked.

At Mercy Park she found a bench and plopped herself down. Pro forced herself to take two sips of her chai latte before she rifled through the paper to find the society page. There on the front page of section D was Ash. There was no mistaking that dazzling smile and those perfect teeth.

Her mother was right, of course. The article with the big picture boldly announced his engagement to Madeline something or other. The article informed Pro that the bride-to-be was a former Miss Massachusetts, a title she won while she was attending Harvard. Her father was apparently a senator from Connecticut, hence the front-page billing, Pro figured. It struck Pro that Madeline's smile was every bit as dazzling as Ash's. In addition, she was practically as tall as Ash, while Pro was almost a half-foot shorter. They were the perfect power couple.

Oh! They met at the law firm where they both work. How nice for them, Pro thought. *Three months! It was just three months ago that he moved out. Five years together – all gone.*

"How could you do this," she shouted. It was only the startled reactions of passers-by that made her realize the shout was not just in her head. And she didn't care. Her head was reeling.

So, obviously, she admitted to herself, *he must have been seeing her – Miss Massachusetts - for God knows how long when... Ah! Those long late nights after he had joined the firm were...* Pro couldn't finish a sentence. *Wow!* she thought – *a coward AND a liar.*

She remembered the voicemail Ash had left her when he ran away. *Another phone call on the way to work,* she thought ironically. He had timed the call so her voicemail would pick it up while she was on the subway. She remembered receiving that call like it was yesterday. She had even saved it and listened to it repeatedly. She had relived that moment over and over and over – as she did now.

"Pro, I'm sorry." His voice pierced through her head.

What? she had thought. She had recognized Ash's voice, but *What?*

"I can't do this anymore," the voicemail had continued.

Do what, Ash? What are you talking about? she had thought, as if he could hear her.

"I'm just not ready... to... you – us – it's just not working for me! I'll have my things moved out by the time you get home."

That Ash had chosen to leave a voice message rather than talk with her in person was mind-numbing – then and now.

"I'm sorry, Pro." were the last words he said.

Oh yeah! Some pro I am.

Kathryn Proscher sat on the park bench numb as Ash's words reverberated through her and multiple images of Ash flashed through her head. "I'm just not ready. I'm just not ready. I'm just not ready."

Pro felt all of the old emptiness well up inside of her once more – a gaping cavern - as the thought bowled her over, *I guess he was ready, just not for us – for me.*

Did I do something wrong? Why wasn't I the one he was ready for? She couldn't tell if those questions were hers or her mother's.

Okay, I never had his confidence – his driving ambition, but who does? Uh! Apparently, Miss Massachusetts does. As the thoughts knotted up in her stomach, Pro tried to pretend it didn't matter.

I have to get to work. But how can I go to work like this? Can I even focus?

Hearing Ash's voice again, she felt the betrayal like a tightness in her jaw and the back of her throat.

She wasn't sure if she was just being a glutton for punishment, forcing herself to listen once again to that message, or if she simply couldn't help herself from going there – to that last connection to Ash.

Hell, I miss his voice. His warm, deep, reassuring voice. Ha! Reassuring? Maybe not. She played his message again – for the umpteenth time and refused to cry.

I suppose I am just being self-indulgent, Pro thought. Immediately, she heard her mother's voice. "You know that is just a waste of time and energy, Kathryn. Why do you do that to yourself?"

She shut her eyes tight and bit her lip to keep from crying out across the canyon of loneliness that yawned open inside her. She felt… hollow – drowning in an ocean of endless darkness. Alone.

She kept hearing his voice, "You – us – it's just not working for me. Just not working."

I guess a part of me had been hoping, even after three months, she thought, *that maybe we could work things out. Humpf! I guess NOT!*

Pro had to admit to herself, the breakup had been coming for a long time. It had been clearer with every passing day since his big job offer that Ashley Simmons III's fast track, as he liked to call it, left increasingly little space for her.

But apparently there was enough space for Miss Massachusetts, Pro thought. *But why? Okay, I'm not a beauty pageant winner with a pedigree from Harvard. We were never going to be that power couple that jumps out at you from the cover of a magazine. I knew he liked to be the center of attention and I was fine supporting him in that, celebrating his success by staying in the background. But I guess that wasn't enough.*

What's wrong with me? Why do I even take that on? Why do I feel responsible for someone else's happiness when I don't have a clue how to find my own? Especially now.

Uuuuuhhhhh! The emptiness inside was getting deeper – burrowing inside her. Part of her was slipping away. She felt like screaming and bursting into tears, but she couldn't. She wouldn't. She really just wanted to chuck everything – run away, hide, and sleep – sleep forever.

That would solve everything, she thought. *Just crumple to the ground and lie there until they take me away, to some place where everyone will leave me alone – my own Willy Wonka Land. Yeah, like my parents would ever pay for that, even though they're rich as sin. Okay, back to reality. What am I going to do right now?*

The thought that she couldn't just go back to the apartment and simply "feel better" landed in the pit of her stomach with a dull thud. Something was stirring – burning, like a wound opening up inside – festering.

She was about to go back and listen to Ash's final voicemail once again when she stopped herself and forced herself to erase it – and then immediately cleared her box of deleted messages, so it was permanently gone before she could change her mind. Pro felt a fleeting moment of triumph.

So there! she thought, *that'll show him.* Then her next thought rebounded, *Oh, yeah! How very junior high of you.* She tried to smile at her own childishness. Laughing things off, she found, was often the best medicine. *Pretend things don't matter and they go away.* At the moment, that was impossible.

She was shivering. Even though it was already warm out, she had broken into a cold sweat as betrayal and abandonment welled up inside of her again — even worse this time. Pro pulled her blazer tighter to her body.

So, what now? she thought, *Call in sick and go get drunk? Not a great way to start the week. Run away? Get lost in a movie sitting in the dark? Just bury your feelings in the actors on the screen. Sometimes that's worked.*

She could hear her mother's voice again, "Kathryn — get to work. Feeling sorry for yourself never solved anything." And even though the imagined advice came from her workaholic mother, a practical part of her thought it actually was the best thing for her to do. She would soldier on.

Kathryn "Pro" Proscher choked back her tears and pulled herself up. "That's right Mother. I'm not a baby. There's work to do," she said aloud, but not too loudly. She forced herself to focus on the work that lay ahead. "I need to take care of the Littlekins account. Mr. Atkins is depending on me — and I won't let him down."

Besides, she needed to get somewhere where she felt safe. *The familiar surroundings of the ad agency. That will work. Just get there.*

2. UPHEAVAL

Pro was more than an hour early when she entered the building and headed up to her cozy cubicle, on the eighth floor.

Atkins Advertising had been in existence for three generations and though she knew it was only the illusion of solidity, somehow the wood paneling along with the staid, old-world environment gave Pro a sense of stability. The portrait of Grandfather Atkins that dominated the front entrance was a testament to the staying power of the firm. Even as she rushed into the office, she took a moment to pause and look at that strong stoic reassuring face. Ever since she was hired three and a half years ago, she had always felt like this was a place where she was safe. She would do her graphic work, keep her head down and all would be well.

Pro sat down, sipped her chai latte, and tried to clear her head. *This is not the end of the world! This is NOT the end of the world,* she kept telling herself – more to drown out the sound of Ashley's voicemail and her mother's voice reverberating through her head than to convince herself. Just sitting in the familiar surroundings helped her get her bearings. *Thank God I work independently, instead of with a team of designers like they have at some firms. I'll focus on my work and get through this.*

Then she burst into tears. The tears came in waves. Pro ran to the ladies' room and sat in one of the stalls to pull herself together, as her mother would say.

When she had calmed down, she worked her way back to her desk. She got settled into her cozy cubicle and brought up the Littlekins file on her computer. Soft, rich colors filled the screen as she looked at her preliminary ideas for Littlekins to the Rescue, the second film in the series. Okay, it was cheesy, but Pro also found the mega-adorable characters kind of endearing. The movie company had liked her graphic designs on the original Littlekins film enough that they agreed that she should continue with the series. The sense of pride she felt in that accomplishment lasted almost an entire day, until she shared the news with her parents and her father said, "That's good, Kathryn. That's job security. Just don't let it go to your head." She did her best, now, to escape parents and Ashes and lose herself in butterflies and jewels.

When she found tears welling up, she would push them under the surface and refocus on her work. She tried to dredge up some excitement for how the ideas were coalescing, then her mind drifted off – to Ash, and failure and doom. She forced herself to work right through lunch, as she sometimes did when she actually felt inspired. Today that was necessary. The last thing she needed was time to herself – time to think, time to consider how extra empty the apartment would feel when she got home.

She managed to get through the day, though butterflies and jewels seemed to mock her at every turn. That night, her sleep was fitful. Every time she closed her eyes, falling into the earth as the ground gave way, Ash and Miss Massachusetts came dancing through – laughing. It was a rollercoaster ride.

Somehow, she made it through the night and forced herself to trudge to work. It wasn't until midafternoon that she noticed an uneasiness around her. There was almost a deathly quiet. Then it seemed like she was hearing whispering all over the office.

"He finally did it."

"Yeah – that door is closed."

"Well, who would stick around?"

Do they know that Ash, who just broke up with me three months ago is now engaged? Pro thought. Can they really see how broken I feel? Stop being paranoid. It's probably just my imagination.

But she heard more whispers.

"Let's face it – the ship has been sinking for a long time."

"Yeah, she's going down the drain all right."

The hushed whispers swept through her.

Am I about to lose the Littlekins account? Has Mr. Atkins lost faith in me? Pro didn't know whether to scream or cry.

She tried to focus on her work, but her hands wouldn't stop shaking. She rushed once more to the ladies' room. She almost didn't recognize the face that stared back at her, colorless and gaunt.

She was splashing water on her face when Elaine came in. With her three-piece pinstripe grey suit she was the epitome of professionalism. An outspoken redhead, Pro's office manager, Elaine, had been the first friend she made when she came to Atkins Advertising. Under her guidance, Pro had learned so much. When her confidence flagged, Elaine was right there to bolster her up. "I see a spark in you, Pro," she had said, "Let's do something with it. Get out of your own damn way."

Elaine was her staunchest supporter and just being around her gave Pro confidence. She was straightforward to the point of being blunt and Pro loved her self-assurance and her wry sense of humor. As their friendship grew, Pro began to feel Elaine was actually more like a sister to her than her own sister Patricia.

Usually very composed and sure of herself, today even Elaine was in a flurry as she said in amazement, "Well, it's happened."

Fearing Elaine was referring to Pro's personal dilemma, Pro feigned ignorance. "What?" she asked, trying not to shake.

"You haven't heard?" Elaine shot back, "it's been charging through the office like a stampeding herd since lunch. It's official – old man Atkins has sold the firm."

"Wait, what?" Pro said, "That can't be… You're kidding, right?"

"I wish I was, Sweetpea. But it is happening, and FAST. The old man has been having a lot of health issues – you know that. He finally caved in and sold – to Clive Bennett Advertising Associates, of all people. The inside scoop is that 'Clive' has been pursuing the sale for a long time, but Atkins always called him 'that young anarchist' and refused to 'tarnish the good name of Atkins

Advertising by selling out to a young revolutionary who has no respect for decades of tradition.'"

Her imitation of Atkins was so spot-on Pro laughed in spite of the dire news.

Elaine went on, "Well, no one knows WHAT is going to happen, but apparently 'Clive' is taking over SOON. So, look out. Everything is up for grabs. I'm guessing we are in for a roller coaster ride. Is your seatbelt securely fastened?" She flashed her wry smile.

"I think I need a new one," Pro retorted. "Lately, I seem to be flying out of my seat – well, falling out. And even forgetting I actually bought a ticket to the damn amusement park." Pro tried to smile. Elaine laughed and took Pro by the shoulders. "That's my girl. It'll be okay – I promise. You'll be okay." Elaine finished freshening her makeup and headed back to her office, tossing back over her shoulder, "Hang in there, Sweet Pea – talk later."

That afternoon, Atkins made the official announcement. "By now you have probably already heard the news, but I wanted to make an official announcement and take a moment to thank all of you for your dedication to this business that has been in my family for so very long. And it is time to let it go. Starting next week, Clive Bennett Advertising Associates will be taking over. There will be a period of transition. Clive assured me there would be no layoffs for at least a month. And, of course, those who are let go will receive severance packages." Old Atkins was getting choked up, fighting back the tears. "Thanks to each and every one of you for all of your hard work through the years. I will miss you." With that he retreated to his office; his employees burst into a buzzing bustle of fear and confusion.

That night Pro dreamt of rollercoasters that plunged down into all too familiar sinkholes, then launched her into the sky as she held on for dear life.

The following Monday, just as Elaine had predicted, the real rollercoaster ride began. Clive Bennett Advertising Associates, the CBAA, took over in a flash. The portrait of Grandfather Atkins was taken down that very afternoon. Pro felt like she had lost an old friend. The empty space on the wall was a gaping abyss, like the wound inside her.

The next month was one nightmare after another. The new boss blazed in with an army of flamboyant makeover artists he charged with "breathing life into 'this old dinosaur of an Agency.'"

"Welcome to the 21st Century!" was his way of graciously warning everyone in the office that there was no longer any such thing as business as usual.

Because Clive wanted the renovations to happen as swiftly as possible, crews worked slavishly through the night. As a result, every morning at the office was a new jolt to the system.

Pro vacillated between crying jags and angry outbursts because her shaking made it impossible to even draw a smooth line at times. She made a concerted effort to shove her emotions down, but sometimes it was just a losing battle. Every night, lying in bed alone, Ash's lies: "Big case, lots of extra hours for this one" and her mother's reminder, "That should have been you. It would have been you, if you had played your cards right," flooded her sleep, while visions of sinkholes, rollercoasters and beauty pageants taunted and terrorized her.

When she awoke the nightmares only got worse, as she went to work to find walls gone, unfamiliar furnishings, and brightly colored fixtures everywhere.

One morning she went to the supply room to get ink for her printer. She stepped into the space to find the room completely empty. *I must be hallucinating.* She went to check the room number when the wall in front of her crashed down before her eyes.

Oh, my God! Oh my God, her brain screamed. *The world is falling apart.* She stumbled back to her desk. She could barely breathe. *Or is it just me?*

Overnight, it seemed, all vestiges of wood that had seemed so permanent just disappeared. Glass, chrome and brightly colored plastic and vinyl sprang up everywhere: purples, pinks, blues, greens, and oranges were splashed on walls, desks, trim, chairs – everywhere. Pro's senses were on overload with the sights, sounds and even smells of newness – as if her head wasn't already spinning. The hyper-stimulation unsettled her stomach and the third morning, as she rushed to the ladies' room to throw up, for a fleeting moment she feared she might have morning sickness. *Hello*, she jolted herself back to reality. *You do realize that is biologically impossible. You haven't been with ANYONE – for more than four months.*

The world Pro and her coworkers had known crashed down around them and in its place were wide-open spaces. The enclosed environments of the cubicles were gone, replaced by desks grouped in pods. Her new supervisor, Paige, a twenty-four- year-old Vassar valedictorian who actually reminded Pro a little bit of Miss Massachusetts, said it was "to facilitate communication between co-workers."

That was the official line. Pro just thought it made it easier to keep an eye on people to be sure they weren't Facebooking, Instagramming and surfing the web when they should be working. She felt exposed more every day, as the office now seemed flooded with space and light. The bathroom stall became a refuge as each new jolt to her senses and sentiments sent her into another jag of crying. Then the next wave of rumors began.

"They are letting at least half of the old staff go."

"Better put the Unemployment Agency on speed dial."

Pro decided she better get back to therapy as soon as she could. She called Dr. Lamdowski, and he was able to fit her into his schedule. *Whoever had to cancel to open that time for me – bless you and I hope you are okay.*

When she saw him the next day the outpouring of emotion that she hoped would be a release only seemed to emphasize how lost and overwhelmed she felt. She teetered between crying, laughing, and shutting down completely. *Another rollercoaster ride*, she thought dolefully. Dr. Lamdowski listened attentively and suggested that a sedative might help her sleep.

She had told him, "I think the last thing I need in my apartment right now is a bunch of sleeping pills, but thanks."

"I understand. You know, some people find journaling about their dreams helpful."

"You're kidding me, right?"

"No, I'm serious. Even if you just jot down a few words. It might give you a different perspective."

"Ah, you mean I could write something like: Another damn sinkhole dream." She tried to smile.

"Exactly! It's just a thought."

That night Pro put some paper and a pen on her nightstand, then plummeted down into a dark cave with bats flying everywhere. This filled her with a new kind of terror, though she had no idea why. Upon awakening she wrote, "Down a sinkhole into a cave full of bats. What in the world is that about? Too many vampire movies as a kid?" That made her smile.

As visions of vampires danced through her head on the way to work, it struck Pro that it was not hard to imagine Clive and his fleet of advertising associates as vampires looking for new blood.

And find it they would. For the next two weeks it seemed like pink slips were flying everywhere as people were let go and new faces arrived, most of them adorned in bright, vibrant, some would say garish, colors.

"Great," she wrote in her newly minted dream journal, "Last night after being swallowed by the earth into the dark cave, the floor gave way to a world of gaudy colors where people were fighting for their lives in a whirling flurry of dancing pink slips. These dreams were just as alarming, with no place to land or feel safe as she drifted aimlessly in space, dodging the colorful carnage around her in what she came to call her "Sinkhole Battle Series." At Dr. Lamdowski's recommendation, she did try to paint some of the nightmare images – to somehow purge them - but that only seemed to make them more real and more terrifying.

Meanwhile, the office exploded with the seven stages of grief all at once. When Mahmoud was let go, he lost it. "We have twins coming." He laughed hysterically, ironically, "I was actually going to get to take paternal leave. Guess not. How far can severance pay go with two new babies," he raged in tears.

Susan just kept repeating, "We will all be fine. We will all be just fine," like a mantra. Then she sometimes added, when management couldn't hear, "I guess I could always go back to the temp agency." MaryBeth, fighting desperately to ward off despair and depression, chattered incessantly. Alan, in a kind of morose acceptance, seemed a little more detached every day, a little less present in his body.

Anita came back from a meeting to her desk in Pro's pod and burst into tears. It took Pro ten minutes to calm her down. She was grateful that focusing on her co-worker's nerves helped Pro to keep her mind off of her own fears. Finally, Anita told Pro she had just been informed that CBAA was keeping her on. She confessed, "I'm relieved, of course – maybe even a little proud, but I just feel so guilty that I somehow managed to survive when so many people around us are dropping like squashed flies. They haven't called you in yet, have they?"

Pro shook her head. *No, but the day is coming. Meanwhile, I need to keep dogpaddling as fast as I can.*

Do good work, she told herself, *Good work? Oh, God...All right! Get a hold of yourself. Just keep fighting the rising tide of chaos and despair sweeping through the office. Right! Like that will happen.*

With all of the stress she was under, doing commercial art was becoming less and less fulfilling. In the past, she had managed to find some value in the work she was creating. Now it just felt like a fight for survival.

When it was Atkins Advertising, she felt like Mr. Atkins actually cared about her. When she had completed the campaign for the horror movie All the Little Darlings Die last year, Atkins had understood when she finally confessed to him she just couldn't work on any more horror movies. She had felt so guilty telling him, she apologized at least twenty times, but the bloody nightmares had only gotten worse once the campaign was completed. "You identify too much with whatever project you are working on. Don't get lost in your work, Pro," Atkins had told her.

That was when she started seeing Dr. Lamdowski, and he had actually helped the nightmares subside. Now, with everyone's job on the line, Pro didn't dare turn down anything that came to her from Clive, or worse yet, Paige. Her newest project, The Mirror Looks Back, held its own kind of horror for her. She started having dreams of funhouse mirror mazes – each mirror a different image, a different distortion.

I guess I DO tend to lose myself in my work – the way I lost myself in Ash?

Dr. Lamdowski had told her, "The things we define ourselves by determine how we see ourselves – how we know who we are. So, when you look in those funhouse mirrors, who are you without

Ash?" Yesterday when he asked that question, she so wanted to punch him. Instead, she just stared at him.

Looking back at the incident, it almost amused her. *I suppose getting sued by my psychiatrist for assault right now would not be the best thing for me. Too bad. It would almost be worth it.* She smiled at the thought. *I guess I should save my violent thoughts for work where, in the blindingly bright world of the CBAA, I am fighting for my life. Stuff the anger till you get home and resist the temptation to throw glass objects, okay? Just beat up your pillow till you are worn out enough to go to sleep.*

She wasn't sure if sleeping alone – which had taken her months to get used to – made it easier to cope with the shifting landscape of the office. She no longer had to constantly deal with someone else's needs. *My crying won't disturb anyone else's rest,* she had thought with more than a little bit of sarcastic bitterness. Ash hated when she cried. Certainly, she felt lonely and isolated, but the office upheaval provided plenty of distractions and often, at least at work, she was able to push her anxiety down, bury it in her belly and hold on for dear life.

So, on we go! At least it's Thursday and I get to work with the kids at The Gridline. Playing with them and wrapping myself up in their artwork - that makes me feel good. It's my one great escape.

But when she arrived at The Gridline late that afternoon, the kids seemed rattled. *Or is that just me? No, they are definitely a little rowdier than usual.*

She saw Fen rush to the bathroom as soon as he arrived. It caught her eye. He has been doing that for the past few weeks. Today, however, he was gone so long, she asked Carlos to go and see if he was okay. When they came back, Fen seemed sullen, and it looked like he had been crying.

This might be a challenging class. What can I do to help everyone calm down and focus in a way that would be fun? Got it!

"Okay everyone settle down and let's get started," she said. "Today I want to invite you to paint a fantasy world. Those are the only instructions. Use whatever supplies you want – pencil, charcoal, markers, watercolors – whatever would be fun for you. It can be as large or as small as you like and whatever color palette you want. Any questions? Yes, Jessica."

"Do you want it to be something we finish today? I know sometimes we have worked on a drawing or painting for more than one week. Is this one of those?"

"What a great question. For this one, let's just see how far you all get today. If you are having fun with it, we can see about carrying it into next week. Any other questions? All right. Let's jump in. Just let me know if you need any help."

Immediately the room buzzed with excitement for this new project. When they shared their pieces at the end of class there were nature escapes, superhero planets, whimsical creatures – a wide array of fantastical images with lots of vibrant colors. Except for Fen's. While a few of the others had some darker elements, Fen's painting looked like a bombed-out factory with disjointed, broken lines in blacks and grays and a rust color. It wasn't large, but it was very intense. After they all put away the art supplies, he scurried away before she could ask him if he was okay, or if he would like to talk.

As she trundled home, she couldn't stop thinking about him and how disturbing his painting was. Her concern for Fen only intensified her own sense of despair. It was just one more way she felt powerless. She did her best to shake it off when she got home and made dinner.

When her mother called that evening, she let it go straight to voicemail. "Are you okay? We haven't heard from you since Ash's announcement. And today your sister Patricia called and said that Atkins sold the firm and she read there was a lot of turnover. Do you still have a job? It just seems to me like your life is falling apart. Do you need help? Call me."

I know that is your version of concern, Mother, but really it is just one more thing that makes me want to scream.

As she prepared for bed, the message kept ringing through her head.

That night, the dread came raging back with a vengeance. She thought she had gotten used to falling through sinkholes, but this dream was different. She was standing in the lobby of Atkins' Advertising, but the portrait on the wall was of her mother glaring down at her. Then the image morphed to the colorful lobby of the CBAA and she was staring at the big empty space where Grandfather

Atkins used to be. The empty wall opened up this empty space inside of her and she couldn't move. Images from Fen's painting swirled around her with sinkholes and roller coasters as she plunged into a funnel of darkness. She heard and felt the trickling of water. *Oh my God! I'm peeing my pants.*

Suddenly, she was in a fancy restaurant on her fourth birthday, sitting in a puddle, afraid to say anything.

Even after that memory raced through her head, there was no way she could move a muscle to open her eyes, let alone make it to the ladies' room. She felt the puddle underneath her get larger and larger. *Oh my God! Have I really fallen through a sinkhole?*

The darkness got deeper and the water louder – pouring now – not just a steady stream, but a river, a flood. She was drowning – no air, no way to breathe.

The splashing sound overwhelmed her as the tunnel of gushing water took her spiraling down – down – down with no frame of reference, except the distinct feeling she was being swept away – literally going down the drain.

Going Down the Drain

3. SINKHOLE TO SOLABA

She fell and fell forever, until she found herself frozen in the dark. It seemed like she was curled up on the floor, but she wasn't. She was crammed into a horrible plastic chair. The total darkness, cold and damp, engulfed her – the frigid air cutting through her blazer. She held every muscle tight – listening to the nothingness, looking hard into the empty dark.

I've fallen into the existential abyss. That thought might have made her smile – but she suddenly felt like she was five years old playing hide and seek.

She was good at hiding. That Saturday morning, she had found a little space in an old basement closet. She knew it was perfect for hide and seek, especially because the basement was off limits. Playing with Patricia, her 16-year-old sister, Pro prided herself on finding a spot where she would never be found. It was hard for her to pry the door open and even harder to pull it shut behind her, but she had managed.

Sitting in the dark cold was a small price to pay for winning the game. She curled up in a big cloth covered with old paint and fell asleep. Hours later, when she woke up, she realized no one had come to look for her. No one was coming. She thought of yelling and screaming when she couldn't get the door open, but she didn't want to get in trouble for sneaking down to the basement. So, all of five years old, she sat quietly, even when she saw the spiders. Huge, ugly things. As they crawled on her, she froze.

She was afraid to move – afraid to make a scene, as her mother called it. Hours later she was so scared and hungry that she decided if she didn't make a big fuss, no one would ever find her. She screamed and screamed and cried and cried and eventually they found her. She got in a lot of trouble and Patricia got into even more for running off with her friends.

After all of these years, Pro still couldn't decide if the darkness was a safe place to hide or a scary place to get lost in.

Her mind darted back to the present when she heard the slightest rustling off to her left - then behind her a little to the right. As her eyes adjusted to the pitch darkness, she seemed to see the tiniest of eyes peering at her. Rats? Giant spiders?

Get a hold of yourself, Pro. This isn't real. It can't be real. She kept trying to convince herself as she heard more and more rustling – scrambling. More and more eyes appeared, and she felt like a science experiment – trapped. Her hands were not tied. Her feet were not bound, yet she could not move. She appeared to be glued to a chair now. *Death by super-glue*, she thought. *Perfect.*

She tried to pull her thoughts away from the darkness that was engulfing her – the darkness that was no longer empty, but frighteningly full. She cautiously looked around to see thousands of spiders, rats, and scorpions. Her detached brain assessed, *the three things that terrify me the most.*

She heard the quick flutter of wings. *Bats*, she thought. *Oh, NO! Make that the four things that terrify me most.* She remembered being eleven the first night at summer camp and hearing that fluttering sound. That bat had gotten caught in her hair and she wailed until they got it out.

The camp counselor, Melissa, had yelled at her in front of everyone in the cabin for scaring the bat. "If you had just stayed calm, we would have gotten it out a lot easier," she said. "Were you running around like a maniac just to get attention?" Later, when she found out Pro was only 11 and it was her first time at camp, Melissa had apologized – privately. Pro never screamed again after that – not out loud.

The memory flashed through Pro's brain, as the bats swooped down from somewhere above her, sweeping around her. *Will they land in my hair? Claw at my eyes?*

Solaba: the Dark World

She was afraid to close her eyes and just as afraid to open them. Her breathing got more and more frantic and...

It seemed she was arriving home from work and noticed water on the floor. The kitchen sink was overflowing. As she rushed to turn the faucet off, she slipped and fell on the wet kitchen floor.

Opening her eyes, she plummeted back into the nightmare of creepy-crawlers – slithering along the damp floor, scrambling across the walls, clinging to the ceiling. A huge nightmarish dance.

She was too afraid to open her mouth – terrified a spider or a scorpion might crawl in. Darkness crashed against her as the creatures got wilder – more and more frantic. The sound of hundreds of thousands of little wings and legs flapping and skittering through the space made her skin crawl.

Flashes of light from she couldn't tell where kept throwing her off balance, casting huge macabre shadows on the ceiling, then to her left, then over her right shoulder. She found it impossible to get her bearings. She gripped tight to the arms of the chair, frozen in time and space - chilled to the bone.

Then – everything – STILLED. The bats on the walls and the ceiling stared at her. The spiders, the rats, the scorpions surrounded her – all poised for attack. Pro felt her whole body screaming, but nothing came out.

This can't be real, this can't be real, she thought, fighting to gain some kind of composure before her wildly beating heart exploded. The stillness was maddening. She felt her heartbeat in every cell of her body.

And then the entire brigade of creatures slowly crept toward her – stalking – threatening – seeing how close they could come before she shattered into a million pieces. Closer. Teeth bared. Then the tiniest bit closer – taunting, mocking, chuckling – with sinister grins, they came closer and closer still.

One thought coursed through every molecule, every atom of her being. The dam of terror inside her erupted in one long battle cry, "Sssttaaaaaaaaaaahhhhhhhp!" Her scream bounced off the bat-filled walls. All sound, all movement – everything STOPPED.

The whole battalion of creatures froze in their tracks. Was it her imagination, or did they cock their little heads at her? They looked at her askance, as if seeing her for the very first time.

The Dark Creatures of Solaba Creep Closer

What happened next puzzled her even more than the sinister world that surrounded her. She had the vision of a wizard, well, of a very wise old man, or was it a woman, in front of her? Behind her? Everywhere? She couldn't tell. *Great*, she thought, *I'm surrounded by death and who comes to visit? Gandalf played by Cate Blanchett.* While she knew it wasn't Ms. Blanchett, or anyone's Gandalf, the apparition did bring a strange calm that washed over her.

Her heart settled down a bit with this new presence. Pro noticed that she was holding her breath. How could she scream while holding her breath? She had no idea, but she seemed to have managed it. She heard a voice – her own? The apparition's? It reverberated through her.

"Breathe," it said. "You have fallen into Solaba, the Dark World. Just b r e a t h e."

Slowly, tentatively, Pro began to do just that. And as she began to breathe, the tension in the room – space – world – subsided – a little. Suddenly, the creatures moved in a flurry – just one more step. As Pro felt her arms and legs beginning to clench, she reminded herself, *Breathe. Just b r e a t h e.* She shivered and kept breathing.

She heard a voice saying softly, "You have to find the Agency."

What Agency? Pro questioned silently. *A new ad agency? An employment agency?*

"You have to find the Agency," it reiterated.

It was then that she heard the singing - one single transcendent voice ringing through the darkness, calling out to her.

The creatures stirred. They rearranged themselves and a path opened in front of Pro, then it immediately curved around behind her.

As the surface tension fell away, she found her arms and legs worked. She was no longer glued to the seat. Gradually, guardedly, she stood. She took two steps forward. The creatures remained still – watchful.

The voice shimmered through her – calling to her – beckoning her to turn. Then the wizard's voice stirred in her head.

"Think of me," it said, "as a Miraculous Magician. You may call me M2. It is safe to move. Ignore the creatures. You can navigate through them, or you can remain where you are and be overwhelmed by them. They are just your fears."

And they are EVERYWHERE, Pro thought.

Hyper-aware of the dark crawly creatures surrounding her, she stepped out – slowly – cautiously – drawn by the glorious voice she heard calling her. The shimmering singing had no words yet was filled with emotions and meanings she could not discern.

She moved forward carefully, then saw a huge mural materialize in the distance. As she walked cautiously toward the purples and blues and magentas of the floating canvas, images from her past swirled through the landscape of the mural. It wasn't so much that she saw them as much as she had a sense of them – those old, buried memories.

Pro bolted upright when her alarm went off. She was dripping with sweat. It took her half an hour to stop shaking. *Maybe I should call in sick? Oh, yeah, that would help! Then I could just sit and stew here all day. NOT a good idea. Okay, Pro. Get yourself together. Thank heaven the renovation is finally complete, and the dance of the flying pink slips seems to be settling down.*

4. UNSETTLING IN

It was Friday, the end of the second week of the firings. As Pro came into the office lobby with her chai latte – early, as usual - something on the wall caught her eye – something that had not been there when she left last night. There, where Grandfather Atkins had been watching over the family business for years, where there had been an empty space through the month of renovation, was now a huge painting, every bit as imposing as the boss who had ordered it hung there – and just as compelling. When she recognized it as the painting from her dream, she almost fainted.

That's impossible! I know this wasn't here yesterday. I'm sure I've never seen it before – until last night. 🦋

She wanted to rush past it, but she couldn't. The whirls of purples and oranges and magentas stopped her in her tracks. She stood, staring at it, transfixed. It was unsettling, certainly, but the intricate textures of the interweaving colors were almost frighteningly captivating - mesmerizing.

To the casual observer simply passing through the lobby, she supposed it might be pleasant enough. But staring at it intently, Pro found it too intrusive, too personal to feel safe. And the fact that she had seen it in her nightmare was beyond unsettling. She forced herself to pull her eyes away from it and shook off the creepy feeling it gave her, hurrying to her pod.

Elaine popped by her desk at 9:30 as she had every morning since

The CBAA Mural: Worlds

the "CBAA takeover," as she affectionately called it. She seemed to be the one stable point in Pro's topsy-turvy world lately and the fact that she checked in on her meant the world to Pro. Today, however, she did more than just check in.

"Are you booked for lunch?" Elaine asked.

"Are you kidding?" replied Pro. "I will probably just work straight through."

"Nope, we are lunching together – my treat."

"I don't think I should. I really have to--"

"Now, Pro," Elaine interrupted, "You know better than to argue with me. I always win." She grinned. "Meet me in the lobby at 11:30."

In spite of herself, Pro smiled back. "Okay, boss."

"Better not let Paige hear you call me that," Elaine shot back.

"Oh! I didn't think--"

"I'm kidding, I'm kidding!" Elaine laughed. "Later, Sweet Pea." And she was off.

Elaine took her to Lotus Dreams for lunch – the service was quick, and the food was yummy. Once their food arrived, Elaine launched in.

"You're probably wondering why I called this meeting," Elaine began playfully.

"Well," Pro replied, "I'm deathly afraid you're going to tell me you are leaving."

"Well, I am."

The news hit Pro like a bolt of lightning. *Oh my God! How can I possibly survive this,* she thought. Pro had to force herself to keep listening. *If I don't stay focused on Elaine right now, I will fall apart.*

"But hey, I was Atkins' girl Friday. I figured once they knew the lay of the land there was no way CBAA was keeping me around. I've been looking. Life is full of change – my ex-husband taught me that – and I am good at landing on my feet. Clive has been picking my brain this whole time and even asking my opinion more often, which I have to say really surprised me. So, yesterday he told me he wanted to see me in his office bright and early this morning. I figured 'Okay, here it comes. Time to join the dance of the pink slips.'"

"And after all the years you have given to that firm," Pro said.

"To Atkins' firm, you mean," Elaine said, "but it has been pretty obvious that Clive is a different breed altogether. You've probably noticed?"

"Now that you mention it, I have noticed a couple of small changes lately." Pro forced herself to smile, holding her fear at bay. Just the thought of Clive made her shiver.

"So," Elaine continued, "it didn't surprise me that he called me into his office. He thanked me for all the help I'd provided, and he was very complimentary."

"And then he dropped the ax?" Pro asked.

"Hold on, Sweet Pea. This is my story," Elaine said with a grin. "Then he dropped the bombshell. 'I am letting you go,' he said –"

"I was so afraid of that. Elaine, I am so sorry."

"'I am letting you go', he said," Elaine repeated, "'on a vacation. I want you to take two weeks paid vacation and come back and work for me as an office manager. You are one hell of a worker, you are brutally honest, and I would be crazy to let you go.' Can you believe it? That man in his brightly colored suits is full of surprises. I was actually speechless, and you know me, I always have a pithy comeback, or some would say – a pissy comeback."

Elaine burst out laughing and Pro couldn't help but join in, shocked though she was by the news. Her head was reeling with a swirling mix of reactions. *So, she wasn't fired, thank heaven,* Pro thought.

"I wanted to tell you in person before the gossip-mongers got a hold of the news," Elaine told her.

Relief at Elaine's news flooded through her, but then it dawned on Pro that Elaine was indeed still going away, just not for nearly as long. "So, you ARE leaving me," Pro forced herself to lighten up and tease her friend.

"Absolutely! For two whole weeks, but it will be at least a month before I take off. I need time to figure out what spot in the world to grace with my presence." Elaine said with a queenly wave.

"All hail Queen Elaine," Pro shot back, smiling.

She frowned again as fear swept over her. "You do know that two weeks is a lifetime in the office, don't you? It's like dog years – so two weeks is like, what - three and a half months?" Pro smiled ruefully. "What if I'm not here when you get back?" Even as she said it the reality of the possibility hit Pro like a lead weight. *That really could happen*, Pro thought to herself.

"Now, don't look like your puppy just died," Elaine said.

"I don't have a puppy," Pro pouted back.

"You know what I mean. You will be fine. You really will – whatever happens. Pro, life is a journey; it is not any single event. I have been thinking about that a lot since CBAA took over. I don't think you have any idea how strong you really are. And, as you can tell by his latest hire – me – Clive is not afraid of strong women."

Sure. But where does that leave me? If I wasn't strong enough to keep Ash, how am I going to be strong enough for Clive? Pro sulked.

"Don't give me that look. You don't fool me," Elaine admonished her, playfully. "I have seen how bull-headed you can be – when you want to be. You only think of yourself as a pushover. That is just old programming."

"What are you talking about?" Pro said. "Now I'm an old television show?"

"Yes! In a way," Elaine proclaimed. When Pro scoffed, Elaine continued, "Our habits and the ways we're used to being treated program us. They establish how we train ourselves to act automatically. When Clive first burst on the scene it was all I could do not to explode in his face and tell him off. I knew that wouldn't do me any good, but one day, when he really pissed me off, I almost did it anyway.

"I took that afternoon off, went to a nice restaurant and cooled off. I figured if I was all ready to prejudge him, then I was setting him up to prejudge me. Then there could be no hope of understanding where he was coming from... or for him to see what I had to offer. What a waste of time, energy, and an opportunity to get beyond 'business as usual.' I decided my old programming – feeling like I had to defend Atkins, like I have for years, wasn't going to be useful to anyone. So, I made a concerted effort to reprogram myself – to change the channel, so to speak, of my thinking. I got over myself and my outrage and set out to help Clive understand why Atkins had run things the way he had. I guess without even trying to I gained Clive's respect and learned a lot in the process."

"You know that's a LOT to take in, right?" Pro said.

"Yeah, I know it is." Elaine took her by the shoulders and looked in her eyes. "You really are a Pro. You just don't know it yet. Don't let anyone tell you otherwise. Just take the journey – one step at a time. You'll be fine. I will send you a postcard from Cancun, or wherever the hell I end up going."

Elaine's news hit Pro so many ways. As they walked back to the office, Pro thought, *I am so happy for her, and so glad she is staying. And I'm scared. I hope I am here when Elaine gets back.*

Pro also kept thinking about other things Elaine had said. *Life is a journey. Really? I'm not so sure about that. It feels more like some fun-house mirror maze.*

In the lobby, as Elaine went to her office, Pro couldn't stop staring at the new painting.

How could I have dreamed about it before I even saw it?

The mesmerizing images swirling in the magenta sea pulled her in. Vague memories of childhood, adolescence, even college kept emerging – swimming in the mélange of colors, as though they were just on the edge of her brain.

Before any of the memories could coalesce, a doorway appeared in the middle of the mural. It started small and kept growing and growing beyond human scale. The door was formidable, its knob barely within her reach.

Oh, Lord! I am back in the dark dream.

The nightmare came flooding back. Pro looked behind to see all of the creatures – the spiders, the scorpions, the rats, the bats – watching, waiting to see what she would do. There was no place else to go – except through the door.

"You can do this," a voice reassured her.

Whose voice is that? It's familiar. Oh! It's that magician. What's the name?

"I believe we had settled on M2," the voice interjected.

"Oh, right," Pro said aloud, "we had."

"You can do this, Pro," M2 reiterated. "It is yours to do."

Then the thrilling singing voice she had heard before floated through the air, beckoning her onward, and Pro reminded herself, *just breathe*, as she reached up, turned the knob, and opened the door.

❦

🦋 *The Magical Portal*

5. THE SPACE BETWEEN

Pro couldn't see what was on the other side of the door – even after she opened it. She stepped forward into nothingness, but the ground supported her. When the door closed behind her, Pro was aware that this "nothingness" felt entirely different from the threatening world she had just left.

This place feels neutral – kind of an in-between space, she thought. *What does that even mean?* The beautiful beckoning voice – the Beckoner she decided to call it – was fading away. Though she sensed that M2 was close by, watching her, she knew she was alone. And for the moment that was okay, even strangely comforting.

Where do I go from here? Pro thought out into the darkness. As if in response to her thought, the ground shivered – not physically, like an earthquake – but visually she saw the ground before her rearrange itself into four paths that appeared before her. They were four different colors that went in four different directions.

Oh, no! It's a test. I hate tests, thought Pro. *It's a multiple-choice test – one way to "get it right" and three ways to confirm your stupidity. Great odds!*

"And what if it isn't a test?" Pro heard M2 say. "What if it is just a chance to choose."

"To choose what?" Pro challenged.

"A path," M2 responded.

"A path to what? A life path?"

"A path forward. A path that feels right for you."

"But how can I know if it's the right choice?"

"You can't."

"AND what do I do with the paths not chosen?"

"You can't do anything with them because you can never know where they might have led you. You have to let them go, or they will haunt you."

"Oh great!" Pro asked, "So, where does that leave me?"

"Right here, in this moment. Right where you are."

"Pro... Pro?" Whose voice was that? It was faint at first, but quickly got louder.

"Pro!" The voice catapulted Pro out of the test of four paths. "Are you all right?"

For a moment she stared at the figure who had jolted her. Then she recognized the face.

Oh, Lord! It's Paige, my new supervisor. Did I pass out? No. I seem to be upright and all right.

"Are you all right?" Paige asked again.

"Oh, yeah. I'm okay," Pro managed to mutter. "Just a little light-headed. I'll be fine. I'm just going to splash some water on my face in the ladies' room." She darted away from Paige and from the painting.

For heaven sakes, get a hold of yourself, Pro thought as she gazed at herself in the mirror. *What was all that about?* She remembered there were four different "launching pads." *What else? I remember they were different colors and each one lit up a different kind of pathway. It reminded me of a "Choose Your Own Adventure" book.* She smiled at that thought.

I am surprised I remember as much as I do. I guess jotting down my dreams the past week or so has made a difference. So, is this what Elaine meant by "Life is a journey"? But how can I know what path to take? What if I get it wrong?

She shuddered and shook her face dry in the air from the blow dryer, then raced back to her desk. The rest of the afternoon she was aware that Paige kept an eye on her. She stopped by Pro's cubicle.

"Are you doing okay?" When Pro nodded with a shrug, Paige said, "if you need to go home a little early, just let me know." Pro smiled and nodded.

Any chance to write me up and say I am slacking. Well, Miss Ivy League, I am not going to give you the satisfaction. To her surprise, Pro chuckled.

What had Elaine said about my strength? Pro tried to remember. *I know I can be stubborn sometimes, but usually not until I am pushed to the wall. I have certainly never thought of that as strength. It just felt like desperation. Oh! And what did she say about programming? Re-programming? I can't even think of going there.*

Then some voice inside her said, *Hello? Shall we get back to work?* With that Pro put her head down and charged back into the artwork for <u>The Mirror Looks Back</u>, losing herself in mirrors within mirrors within mirrors.

Late that afternoon Mr. CBAA himself, appeared at the end of the hallway like an apparition. He was sleek, with a strikingly handsome face and a bearing that commanded attention. He might have been sexy if he wasn't so freaking intimidating. His piercing green eyes, with a gaze that cut through space, saw everything. From a mile away it was evident that he was a force to be reckoned with – like a cross between Tony Robbins and some kind of shadow warlord. And he looked right at Pro from far down the open hall.

As he charged toward her, his presence engulfed her field of vision. Her blood ran cold. He was both frightening and compelling, with his impeccable posture and his perfect hair. His boldness asserted that he knew who he was.

To her surprise he strode right past her. "Miles. Would you come to my office please?"

Pro buried herself in her work so she wouldn't have to look at either of the men and get wrapped up in what was transpiring between them. For the rest of the afternoon, she immersed herself in a multitude of mirrors.

The evening was uneventful, until she laid down to sleep. Immediately, the four paths from her afternoon hallucination appeared before her.

Terrific! Pro thought. *I have to choose a path, huh?*

She felt M2 smile, "Do you see any other options?"

Good point, she thought back. *All right, I'll play your silly little game. Hmmmmmmm. I am certainly not ready to jump right in and charge down any old path. What if I try them out and see how they feel after a few steps before I commit myself? Let's do that. Which color do I want to try first?*

She gingerly stepped onto the red path only to be startled by huge orchestral music that swelled up and seemed to propel her forward. She ran back before she was caught up in the huge sweep of its majestic sound. When she stepped back, the music was gone.

This makes no sense at all, her brain reasoned, but she decided to try another path – cautiously.

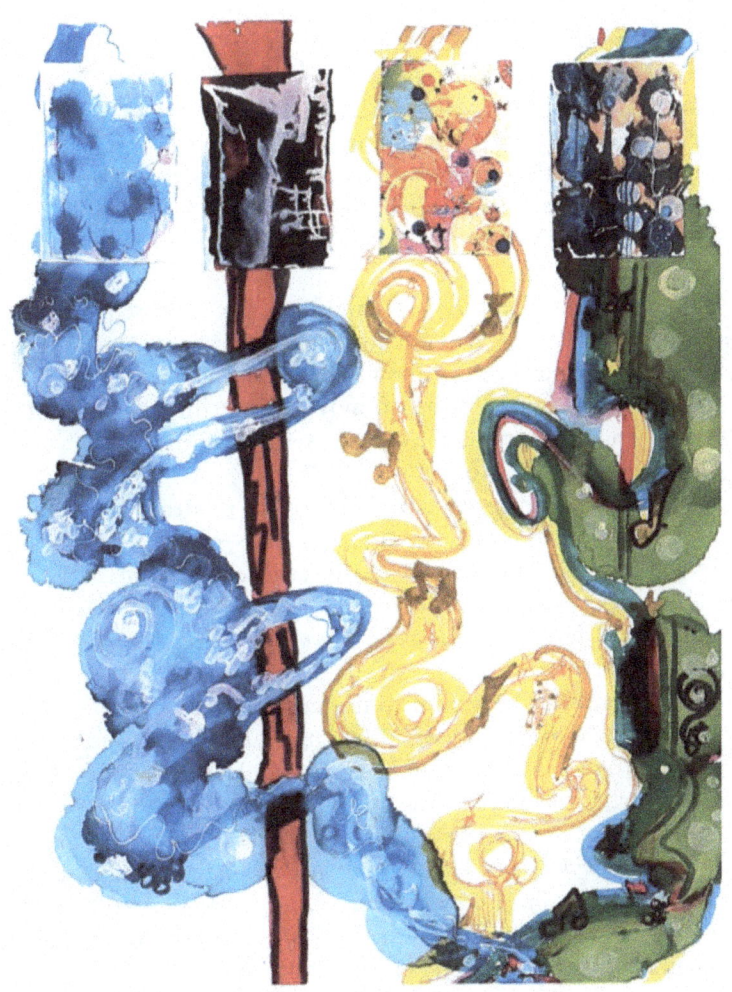

Four Paths

As she took a few steps down the blue path, music meandered with haunting flutes and harps. After the traumas of the dark world, it was soothing, reassuring her she could take her time. Pulling herself away from the temptation to stay there and take a nap, Pro stepped back.

The playfulness of the yellow path with its odd sounds and erratic rhythms made her giggle, which surprised her. Pro was definitely not a giggler. However, the effervescence of the music caught her off guard with its whimsical flow

When she stepped up to the green path, she was filled with a sense of adventure. The rousing trumpet call reminded her of stories of King Arthur and Robin Hood. The excitement in this music enchanted her.

How could she possibly choose? She considered traveling down each path and then backtracking, yet even as the thought passed through her, she somehow knew that would never work. For a little while it was fun for her to move from path to path – always at the beginning, enjoying the contrast between them.

Then, it was time to choose.

With no prodding from her mother and no deadlines to meet, she just knew it was time to face the four paths, make a decision, and move. Even as she considered choosing, she felt her stomach tighten and her throat close a bit.

It's okay, Pro. You can do this. It is not "life or death." It just feels like it.

"Just breathe," reverberated through her head.

Oh, yeah! Good idea. Thanks, M2. Breathe. Remember to breathe.

As Pro took a deep breath, she yawned. Her throat relaxed and her stomach unclenched.

Well, what happens if I look at this as an artistic decision? I just need to choose a color, with its own musical accompaniment. Jumping from launch pad to launch pad was playful. It really was, once I jumped in. So – let's PLAY!

Immediately, she knew the path she needed to take. And though her choice surprised her – it just felt right.

The path Pro chose was perfect for her. It was just what she needed at that moment.

So, where am I now?

Up ahead she saw a neon sign reading "Your Dreams." As she approached it, she saw a dashing figure underneath it. He was a swashbuckler, like a musketeer – rakishly handsome – with warm brown eyes and flowing shoulder-length chestnut hair.

"Dar, guardian to Thanton," he proclaimed. Doffing his hat and brandishing his sword, he made a deep bow to her.

He so surprised her that she curtsied in return, awkwardly, "Pro – Pro Proscher."

Dar nodded his understanding. "Your papers please."

"Papers?" she replied.

"Exactly," he said with a commanding gaze.

"Uh! I . . ." She suddenly realized that she was carrying her shoulder bag. *Did I grab it from somewhere? Or did it just appear?*

She didn't know and it didn't matter. What was important was that her driver's license should be in there.

Digging in the bag, Pro pulled out her pocketbook then offered Dar her driver's license, which he looked at, then promptly rejected. She wasn't sure what he wanted, refusing credit cards, money, even the rose quartz heart she secretly kept tucked away in there.

Dar looked at her like she was an obstinate child who knew the right answer but stubbornly refused to give it.

"I don't carry my passport every day," she said.

He simply looked at her like she had two heads. Pro considered just going back but when she turned to face it, the path was gone. The realization rippled through her.

The only way is forward, she thought.

Then Pro got an idea. Perhaps if she entertained him, she could gain entry. She did a little jig. She even sang a bit of "Does Your Chewing Gum Lose Its Flavor on the Bedpost Overnight" from her Girl Scout days. It was an act of desperation – her voice was not the best.

Dar was amused, but not about to allow her to pass. He cocked his head at her as if to say, *are you going to keep playing silly games? Or are you going to give me what I need to allow you to enter? Why are you pretending you don't know?* Though he just thought it, she heard every word.

Ugh! Stubborn ass, she thought to herself, flopping to the ground. I'm so tired of dealing with people who think they are always right! AND who treat me like I am supposed to know what they're thinking and what they want. Ash, Clive, and now this 'Guardian at the Gate.'

Sitting there pondering her next course of action, she considered staging a sit-in, but thought, *He wouldn't even notice it as an act of protest.*

Okay, she thought to anyone inside her head who was listening, *I give up. Wait – I don't even know what that means right now. I can't go back – the damn path is gone and anyway, what would I want to go back for? I can't move forward because this frickin' fellow won't let me through without my papers. But I don't even know what that means! What am I supposed to do NOW?*

Pro wasn't sure then if M2 actually appeared to her again, or if she simply sensed his – her – THEIR presence. That presence, while it was more than slightly intimidating, reminded Pro once again to breathe. It was easier this time – she was just frustrated, not terrified.

As the breath filled and calmed her, Pro could hear the beautiful voice of the Beckoner once more. The shimmering sound poured through her and somehow gave her the confidence to stand up, charge forward defiantly to Dar and stand her ground, thinking, *I have a right to be here, and you are going to let me enter.*

With a flourish of his feathered hat, Dar bowed deeply to this assertion. He touched Pro's sternum and magically pulled out a paper that contained all of her necessary information. It's title? "A License to Follow Your Dreams." And it looked very much like this...

A License to Follow Your Dreams

I,_____,
Print your name here

do hereby grant permission

to MYSELF
to Follow My Dreams
Whatever it takes and wherever they take me,

On this, the
_____ day of _____ in the year_____.

Signed with Love, Hope, and Inspiration,

_____
Your Signature

She woke up early, her mind racing, yet she was strangely calm. *This is one Saturday I will not be going into the office.* Sitting up in bed, she mused. *Permission to follow my dreams? Really? Why would I even want to do that, considering the bouts of nightmares I've been going through? But last night was different. Why?*

She thought of the four paths and her faced brightened as a smile spread across her face and her eyes widened. She found she remembered them quite clearly as she wrote about them in what was now her Dream Journal.

That's funny. I remember when I was first faced with having to choose one of them, I felt this tremendous pressure to 'get it right,' to 'make the right choice.' I have always been afraid of 'getting it wrong.' Afraid of letting people down or disappointing them. And here these four very different paths were before me – daring me to choose. And as I tried them out, it became more of a game - like a wacked-out version of musical chairs. Ha!

As she made breakfast, then settled in on her balcony to enjoy her morning chai latte, it struck her. *In my encounter with the sexy swashbuckler, I ran a pattern similar to the four paths – well, in a way. Certainly, I felt pressure to 'get it right' as I desperately tried to figure out what I needed to do so he would allow me to pass. The harder I worked to figure it out the more frustrated I became. Okay, then what changed?*

Pro stewed on that question for days, at night dreaming of colors and pathways and musketeers. When she dreamt again of Dar, the dashing Guardian of the Gate, she wrote in her journal the next morning.

I know what I did. I dared to face Dar. I let go of trying to please him and confronted him with the assurance that I deserved to be there, and I demanded entry. With that realization, Pro burst out laughing. *Wow! Maybe Elaine was right. Maybe I am stronger than I give myself credit for – at least in my dreams. Well, at least in one dream. Hey, it's a start.*

That afternoon at The Gridline, she felt excitement bubble up inside her when she instructed her kids. "Today I would like you to imagine having permission to follow your dreams. Imagine a great future for yourself - whatever that means to you - and paint or draw that. You can paint a vision of that imagined future, if that is what you are drawn to. Or maybe it's abstract art - putting a bunch of colors on the page that express the feelings that come up." The classroom burst with excitement. Fen wasn't there. It was the first class he ever missed.

That night, Dar greeted her once more.

6. THANTON, THE ADVENTURE WORLD

Flashing a dazzling smile with a grand flourish of his great hat, Dar bowed to Pro. "Welcome to Thanton, the Adventure World," he said. Grabbing his deep burnt-orange cape and throwing his right arm open, he ushered Pro into a brand-new world.

Striding through the threshold, Pro felt the air charged with energy. *Is it the air itself that's so exhilarating, or is this aftershock? Ha! I did it! I stood up to that dashing guard and made it through the gate.*

The rocky, vegetation-laden path ahead of her seemed a bit daunting, but she was flush with the sense of her newfound confidence. Pro assessed the landscape, noting the walled city on a promontory up ahead in the distance. With sunlight beating down, the chills she had earlier were completely gone. The breeze on her face felt refreshing as she charged forward with a focus and determination that surprised her.

It's an exciting place, but what am I doing here? Rounding a bend in the path, she came into a small clearing. Before she could take another step, three men sprang out before her. Like Dar, they were dashing figures with flowing black capes and boots to their knees. No feathered hats, however. Though their heads were partially hooded, she could see they were smiling— especially the tallest one, who appeared to be the leader. There was something menacing about the way he leered at her.

The leader spoke first, "Greetings, fair lady." He was almost charming – almost.

"Hello," Pro said with as much bravado as she could muster.

"Traveling alone?"

"That can't be safe for a beautiful woman such as yourself," the stouter of his two companions chimed in.

"Oh – uh – no!" Pro lied. "My friends are just a little way behind me."

Unfortunately, Pro had never been a very good liar. As a child, when she told even the smallest fib, her face flushed crimson – as it was doing now, she felt sure.

"Quite a ways back, I reckon," said the third.

The ringleader spoke again, "I'm afraid I will have to relieve you of your purse, milady. And your jacket."

"Well, I would hate for you to be afraid," Pro replied with more confidence than she felt.

His laugh was almost a snort, "Cheeky – but you better hand them over. Who knows, if you make it to the port, you might win them back." The three men guffawed.

It was the leader who spoke again, "You stay right there."

He needn't have bothered giving the command. Pro, for the hundredth time in the past month it seemed, was immobilized – frozen in her tracks.

The men relieved her of her bag and jacket, then pulled a few yards away from her. They were about to rummage through her bag, when a slender, multicolored ragamuffin appeared like a lightning bolt out of nowhere. He dashed by the three rogues, grabbed Pro's bag and jacket, and darted away.

"Stribjus," the ringleader bellowed after him. "Why you…" As his comrades ran after the darting figure, the leader turned to Pro, bowing deeply, "Pleasant journey, milady," then adding with a rakish grin, "Do be careful. There is treachery everywhere." And he was gone.

When she was sure he was not coming back, Pro thawed quickly, then flooded with emotions. She heaved a sigh of relief. *Thank heavens nothing worse happened.* She beat the air with her fists in frustration and shook her head, flummoxed – *Really?* she thought, *Flummoxed? YES! Could this day – week – whatever THIS is – get any more bizarre?*

And I just STOOD there. Why did I just let them take my purse? It's not like there was much money in it – as if that would be of any use here – wherever here is. But my driver's license and credit cards. And the flash drive with the Littlekins and The Mirror Looks Back accounts! And my jacket! They took my jacket.

Wasn't there anything I could have done? I didn't even try to talk them out of it. I just clammed up, waiting for the storm to pass – just like always.

When the storm inside her subsided, even as she considered her options, Pro knew she would forge on to this Thanton place. As she started the trek, she thought, *who knows? Maybe I WILL win back my purse and my jacket.* And she realized she had no idea what that meant.

As the crow flies, the Port of Thanton was not far away.

It was the craggy terrain that took time – and caution. Encircled by a wall, the port city was a stronghold. In what Pro imagined was less than two hours' time, she arrived at the entrance.

Immediately, the cacophony of sounds hit her. Merchants vended their wares at the top of their lungs, customers haggled over prices, and people of many colors bickered in a multitude of languages.

It's a trading port, Pro thought.

The myriad styles of clothing – long flowing robes, doublets, frock coats, tunics, and even sarongs – made it impossible for Pro to have any kind of geographic orientation, or even a sense of what century she might have fallen into.

She carefully made her way through the eclectic crowd, all the while pretending she fit in, acting like she knew what she was doing and where she was going. In truth, she had no clue.

The entryway into the port city was obviously a major thoroughfare. She pressed her way forward into what appeared to be a huge square. It reminded her of the Piazza della Signoria, where she had spent so much time during her summer in Florence. This Piazza was just as crowded, but ten times wilder. People were fighting everywhere.

An argument broke into a screaming, wrestling match at the outdoor café to her right. At a table in the café, two men were arm-wrestling as if their lives depended on it – while swilling beer from huge tankards. She pressed against a wall to avoid the tumble of five more people thrashing into a brawl. She was pretty sure two of them were women.

Spectators circled around two men brandishing broadswords. Beyond that, swordsmen lunged and parried for all they were worth.

Thanton: The Adventure World

All of the violence was intimidating and overwhelming, but what was fascinating was the lack of any bloodshed in spite of this tornado of aggressive exchanges.

Pro took refuge at the corner of a café that seemed for the moment to be relatively safe. She tried to lean against the wall nonchalantly, to be inconspicuous.

A group of boys was brawling not so far away, when one of them got thrown out of the pile and landed on his back close by. When she leaned down to see if he was all right, he looked up at her and broke into a big grin. "Oh! Hi, Miss Proscher."

Then it struck her. "Fen?" *Really? Here? In Thanton?*

"Yep. It's me. I'm learning to stand up for myself." He jumped to his feet.

"Okay. Good for you?" Pro said tentatively as the boy charged gleefully back into the brawl.

She was trying to make sense of that encounter when an imposing woman with long purple-black hair sitting nearby challenged her. "You're new here, aren't you?"

Guess I'm not going unnoticed, am I?

Pro managed to nod, unsure what kind of action might prompt a violent response in this place of boisterous confrontation.

"You get used to it," the woman reassured her, nodding at the maelstrom of brutality around them, "or you leave as fast as you can."

Just then, Pro noticed a raised platform in the distance with – was it really stocks – where a man in rags of many bright colors had his head and arms secured. She gazed at him and, even at a great distance, Pro got the distinct feeling that she caught his eye. Miraculously, he seemed to disappear, and she looked hard at the stocks, which now sat empty. Then Pro got the sense of a flash of colors, rather than actually seeing anything she could describe. The colors seemed to whirl around her and then vanished. When she blinked hard again the ragamuffin was indeed in the stocks, as she had previously observed. And, somehow, he felt familiar.

"Who is the young man in the stocks? He's in some kind of trouble?" Pro said.

The striking raven-haired woman replied, "Him? That's Stribjus. He's an imp and a thief, but really harmless. Don't worry about him. For him this is all a game – even being in the stocks. If you look closely, he actually flows out of the stocks and into them again quite easily. He is a jester of sorts – an acrobat, a trickster. Oh, and he loves to entertain." She smiled slyly, "That way he gets to be the center of attention without getting beaten down."

As Pro turned her attention back to him, the wiry jokester suddenly appeared next to the stocks he had just been in. He was juggling colorful balls quite adeptly and people on the square who were not preoccupied with fighting were pointing and laughing. The colorful balls somehow became a dust cloud of green and orange and yellow. When the colorful smoke cleared, the imp was once again in the stocks grinning widely! Members of the crowd applauded.

It was only then that Pro noticed that in her clinched right hand was the rose quartz heart from her pocketbook. She gazed at it, *Have I actually been clutching it since I passed Dar and journeyed toward Thanton? No, I'm sure – I'm sure it was in my purse. I'm positive… but then, how is it here now?*

Pro held the heart securely in her hand and tried to shake off the confusion that came with the stone's mysterious reappearance. Forcing herself to refocus on – what was that odd young man's name? Stribjus? She asked, "Why is he in the stocks?"

The woman's deep-throated guffaw took Pro by surprise with its hearty outburst, as she mused, "Gareth and his henchmen accused him of stealing from them – some kind of pocketbook they, no doubt, had stolen themselves."

"It was probably mine," Pro blurted out. "Three men confronted me and took my shoulder bag and my jacket a little way out of the city."

"Were they all in black capes with hoods?"

Pro nodded.

"Was the leader tall and handsome with a kind of rugged semi-charm and a cocky wit?" the dark-haired woman asked.

"Yes, exactly," Pro said, "That describes him perfectly."

"That would be Gareth. He fancies himself some kind of legend here in Thanton, especially with the ladies, though he finds himself much more charming than I have ever found him to be." The forthright woman smirked.

It was only then that Pro noticed that her new acquaintance was wearing a sword. With her left hand on its hilt, she extended her right hand to Pro.

Her powerful handshake spoke louder than her voice as she introduced herself, "I'm Zor."

"Kathryn Proscher," Pro said, taken aback by the woman's straightforward strength, "People call me Pro."

"Well, Pro. Welcome to Thanton. And if you have hopes of retrieving your purse – be careful," Zor warned her.

Another flash of colors around her startled Pro for a moment. She steadied herself against a chair with her right hand and looked back at the stocks where Stribjus the trickster was grinning straight at her.

Then she realized she was now actually wearing her jacket. She was sure that somehow this joker Stribjus had returned the jacket and the rose quartz heart to her, though she hadn't the foggiest idea how.

She shoved the rose quartz deep in the pocket of her jacket as a burly drunkard grabbed her by the waist, whirled her around and planted a big kiss on her surprised open mouth. Once the kiss was done, she expected he would let go of her – which he did not. He flung her out and spun her in and whirled her around in what she supposed he thought was dancing. To Pro it was manhandling, but when she raised her arm to slap him, he grabbed it and spun her around into a big bear hug.

Pro looked to Zor for help, but the female warrior shrugged as if to say, *It's your problem. How are you going to deal with it?*

Pro pushed him off and reeled away as he grabbed her waist, taking her around him like a carousel. He lost his grip, and she went flying into the chest of another man, who grinned at her. Swirling away from him spun her back into the arms of her original dance partner.

Panicking, Pro grabbed the sword from his belt and pulled away from him. She pointed the sword toward him, feeling like a trapped rat. She made a broad circle with the long sword, attempting to appear threatening. The rogue only smiled at her and laughed. He thought this was all a great game.

As she took a tentative lunge toward him, he immediately moved in on her, wrapping his arm around the thin blade, disarming her. Pro broke away once more and ran to take refuge behind a café table, praying Zor would come to her rescue. But Zor's gaze challenged her, detached and amused. *This is not my battle,* her eyes seemed to say. *If you have a problem with him – deal with it yourself.*

Pro had no idea how she could sense those thoughts, but she had no time to ponder as the rogue played cat and mouse around the table, now toying with his sword. She felt him thinking, *Oh, so you want to play, do you? This will be fun!*

Pro stood up and shouted back to his thoughts, "No, I DON'T want to PLAY." As the rogue was taken aback at her direct response to his thoughts, another flurry of color flashed around Pro and suddenly she was holding another epee. It surprised her to remember the name of the long thin sword. Its sudden appearance in her hand so startled her she almost panicked. *Now what?* she thought.

She looked at Zor, who cocked her head to one side. Then Zor simply demonstrated fencing formation.

Yes, Pro thought, *Lord, it was years ago, but I took that fencing class in college – got an A, too. That's why I remembered what the sword is called. How could Zor know that?*

With her memory jolted, Pro fell into fencing form, ready to spar with this drunken fool. She was amazed at how much she remembered from class, and how easily she fell into reading the rogue's moves, which allowed her to deftly parry any of his advances. She even got in a turn with a flourish, her sword hissing through the air as she smacked his forearm with it.

That was enough to convince him that she was perhaps not the easy mark he had taken her for and, rubbing his arm, he went in search of another dancing partner. Pro saluted Zor with her sword. Zor smiled and nodded her approval.

Glancing once again at the stocks, Pro caught Stribjus's eye and saluted him as well, quite aware that it was he who provided her with a sword just when she needed it.

As she completed her salute, high above them on the battlements of the city, Pro was sure she saw M2 watching, waiting. Judging? Was the apparition keeping score? *Is this really just all a game to the wizard, too?*

It was then that she noticed Gareth in front of the stocks mocking Stribjus with her shoulder bag flung over his own shoulder. Pro looked once more at Zor and nodded toward the stocks.

Zor considered the invitation and, deciding this stranger had earned some support, rose, literally, to the occasion. Pro grabbed a tankard of beer from the table, and they strode toward the stocks – and Gareth. Zor faced off with him. He wasn't sure if it was a confrontation or a tease.

Standing behind Gareth, Pro confirmed what she knew from a distance – the bag was, indeed, hers. With a quick flash of bright colors, the bag disappeared from Gareth's body and found its home around Pro's own shoulder. Trusting now that this was simply the magic of Stribjus in action, Pro didn't bat an eye. Stribjus was out of the stocks, yet back on the platform once again juggling colorful balls.

She tapped Gareth on the shoulder, and he turned around surprised. As a smug smile crawled across his cheeks, Pro pitched the beer in his face. "That's for stealing my jacket."

She slapped his face. "That's for taking my purse."

Then she belted him in the stomach with the tankard. "And THAT'S for thinking it's okay to accost a lady."

As he doubled over, the gathering crowd laughed while Zor raised her sword in tribute.

Gareth rose, incensed and embarrassed, glaring at Pro. She wagged the weapon toward him, keeping it just out of reach, like a mosquito taunting him. His two henchmen took a hesitant step towards her, but Zor extended her weapon – daring the stouter one of them to intervene. The other was suddenly blasted by flying balls of paint thrown by the impish juggler, who then once more miraculously appeared in the stocks.

As Gareth charged toward Pro, she side-stepped his advance, pushing him into the crowd. Then all hell broke loose. Zor flung one of the henchmen into the other and they went crashing into spectators.

Pro soon discovered that in Thanton there was no such thing as a spectator. Once contact was made, retaliation was, apparently, imminent. Soon there was a brawl of epic proportions. Zor brandished her sword against three attackers at once. Stribjus appeared on Gareth's back, then on his hands and knees behind the bully. With a wink to Stribjus, Pro pushed Gareth over. It was a free-for-all, and to her amazement, Pro was exhilarated.

Her fencing skills came back rapidly, and she was lunging, parrying, and reposting with the best of them. Zor grinned, whacking one brawler's butt with her sword. Her yawp filled the air.

Leaping over heads and darting between legs, Stribjus threw clouds of color at the crowd. He and Zor pulled Pro out of the melee for a moment and Zor told her, "This is not going to let up until everyone is either blind drunk, knocked out, or too exhausted to move. You might want to get out of here."

Pro agreed, "But how? Isn't the main gate the only way out of this fortress? Or do you have a boat?"

"I know a way," volunteered Stribjus as he threw a moss green cape over Pro. "Zor, take this young lady—"

"My name's Kathr – Pro," she offered.

"Stribjus here. Utter pleasure to meet you, Pro," the trickster said. "Zor, please take Pro behind the chapel. I will distract them and meet you there."

As Zor took Pro darting in a zigzag through the streets and alleyways of Thanton, Pro heard Stribjus shout out from atop a high battlement, "We're up here."

A few minutes and a few narrow misses later, they were all behind the chapel.

"I can't believe I actually enjoyed that," Pro said. "But what do we do now? Just hide out?"

"I know a secret tunnel," Stribjus bragged.

"Of course, you do!" responded Zor with her full-bodied laugh. "Go ahead and lead our guest to safety."

Stribjus teased her, "Don't you want to come with us? We would have fun. And Gareth and his gang will need a few days to cool off, don't you think?"

"You have a point," Zor admitted. "Besides, you two might need some protection."

"I don't know," said Stribjus, "Did you see our girl brandish that sword?" Zor punched his arm. "What? What did I do?" Stribjus asked.

"Our girl?" said Zor. "She's a woman, you fool!"

"Well, I am a fool," Stribjus retorted. "Thanks for noticing." Then he ceremoniously jumped up on a bench, made lavish circles with his hands from his heart up to the sky, and with the deepest bow Pro had ever seen, proclaimed, "My humblest apologies, oh, great womanly presence."

Pro giggled with glee as he popped up his head and winked at her. Then she composed herself as she regally said, "Apology accepted. You may join us."

They all roared with laughter, then Stribjus said to Zor, "but you do agree she is ours."

He smiled mischievously and then cackled, "In fact, Zor, I don't think I've ever seen you leap to someone's aid quite like that before."

Zor smiled as she replied, "Well, she earned it."

They wound their way through the underground passageway and once safely away from the city, they sprawled on a stretch of purple grass.

"If only we had thought to bring some wine," Zor mused, whereupon Stribjus opened his ragtag coat to reveal layers of pockets. The interior of the coat was easily five times the volume of its exterior.

Pro marveled at the complex of colors, materials, and layers he seemed to wear so lightly.

He pulled wineskins, bread, and cheese out. "I never travel without food."

As they sat down to eat, Pro said, "Thank you for getting me out of there. It actually felt good to be in the thick of things, but if I had stayed, I'm sure I would have ended up in jail or joining you in the stocks, Stribjus. I really appreciate all that you both did, but why did you help me?"

Zor spoke up first, "As I watched you stand up for yourself and not just wait to be rescued, I thought you had earned my assistance and support. You put up a good fight back there."

"Really?" Pro said, taken a back. "I have never thought of myself as a fighter at all,"

"Well, think again."

"When I saw you outside the city," Stribjus chimed in, "at first, I moved in just to taunt Gareth and his men. I grew up with Gareth bullying people and sometimes I just don't want him to get away with it. When you actually showed up in Thanton, I thought returning some things to you would be a great trick to play on the bullies. But then, when you and Zor confronted Gareth, well, I couldn't be left out of that fun."

They sat in the grass and laughed and ate and shared stories. Stribjus spoke of his six older brothers – warriors all, who flourished in Thanton, while he, as the runt of the litter, had always fended for himself and made fending itself an art, but his childlike whimsy had always been considered frivolous, distracting, and useless. He had ventured out of Thanton before, but only on his own. He never attached to anyone; never thought he could really depend on anyone to be there for him. But Pro and Zor, in their own way, had come to his rescue.

Zor shared a little about the adopted world of Astara where she was raised: a placid, soothing world of healers. Yet, she confessed, "I could never quell the wanderlust and thirst for adventure that drove me. I suppose I inherited that from the violent world where I was born, a world that killed both of my parents."

For Pro, it felt good to share some of what she felt of the tumult going on for her in the land she came from. While memories with Ash resurfaced, as well as her new warlord boss, it somehow felt less overwhelming to be able to talk about those challenges from a distance. It seemed that all three of them never felt they quite fit in to the places where they were planted. With that realization, their coming together made great sense to Pro, in a way. Having been branded as misfits, they were forging a camaraderie.

Pro realized she was really enjoying herself. *Okay,* she thought, *I was just in a huge brawl, and while I certainly don't want to adopt combat as my new lifestyle, that was fun! Nobody really got hurt and I can't remember the last time I felt so excited and full of life. Also let's face it, having two new friends in this crazy world-that-makes-no-sense makes a big difference.*

With that, she dozed off.

7. CHALLENGING REALITY

Pro woke up exhilarated. For two whole weeks she felt energized and hopeful. At The Gridline, she invited her eager students to, "think of someone who has stood up for you – a family member, friend, or maybe a teacher. Or maybe it's a made-up friend. Now imagine them as a superhero. What is their superpower? Remember this can look however you want it to look. Maybe you paint them in a superhero costume exercising their superpower. Or maybe you just paint the energy that pours or shimmers or flies off of them or through them. Whatever comes out of you is perfect." Their imaginations were wonderful.

Beth titled hers *mmmmmmmmMOM*. Little Lily painted a fiery creature she called Fierce Friend. Fen was back and he poured himself into the project. He painted a woman with long brown hair and hazel eyes who danced colors across the page. He titled it *The Protector*.

Friday, Pro completed her work on The Mirror Looks Back as the day ended. She was pleased. *Wow, I hadn't realized it was so late. Everyone's gone.* She was putting her things away when a flash of orange caught her eye. It was Clive, sauntering straight toward her. She had to admit he was strikingly handsome in a burnt orange suit that would probably have looked foolish on most men. But Clive had the flair to pull it off.

Though she felt like spiders were crawling on her skin, Pro rose to face him. Moving away from her desk, she drew forward to the edge of an abyss – another sinkhole.

Time to face the firing squad, she thought with some resolve and more than a little irony.

"Have a seat," he oozed with charm.

Surprising herself, Pro ignored the command – the invitation. *If you're going to fire me, dammit – do it face to face,* she thought. She couldn't speak. It took all of her concentration just to keep from shaking.

She stared at Clive's mouth as she heard him say, "I have looked over your portfolio. There is some good work there. You certainly have some talent, though I am not quite sure whether you are CBAA material. Clive Bennett Advertising Associates has a reputation for cutting-edge designs and..." He reached into the pocket of his burnt orange suit and pulled out a pink slip. He looked as if he were about to anoint her with it, as if it was some kind of blessing he was bestowing on her with his great wisdom.

Her heart was pounding so hard she thought she was going to pass out, but Pro forced herself to look directly at Clive Bennett's sculpted features. *He is undoubtedly handsome, in an aristocratic sort of way – like Ash.* Her eyes blazed.

Dark Shadow Lord or not, he is not going to make me feel like a peasant begging for a scrap of bread, even if I am getting lightheaded.

A dark cavern opened in the pit of her stomach, like a part of her was on the verge of hitting the panic button. *But I'll be damned before I let Mr. Shadow Lord Clive Bennett see tha*t. She stared at him.

He began to extend his hand with the pink slip. As her heart sank, she forced herself to stand just a bit taller than her 5'7" frame and glared directly into his steely green eyes, waiting for the axe to fall. But then he suspended the gesture in midair. He gazed at Pro, examining her face, looking deep into the defiance in her eyes and cocked his head. As a smile spread across his face, he folded the pink slip in half and then in half again. He turned it sideways and lightly beat the air with it.

Is he toying with me? The thought raced through her head.

Pro could feel him sizing her up, as if to say, *I'm going to keep an eye on you. Don't get too comfortable. I'll be watching you.* He almost seemed to chuckle as he turned away. That half chuckle sent a chill up her spine. As he started to walk away, he turned back and gazed at her once more. "Six months," he said. Then he strolled away.

Pro didn't dare move as she watched him fade into the distance. And he was gone.

What was that? she thought, fighting to hold herself together. *What does that even mean? Is he giving me six months' notice to find a new job? Is this some kind of stupid game men play? Ash – Clive – wanting something, but never saying what? What can I do?*

Before the tears could well up, she threw on her blazer, grabbed her bag, and bolted. She got as far as the office lobby when her legs gave way. As she held on to a chair, she looked up at the big mural with its mélange of images swirling, which made her sick to her stomach.

She had to sit down. She hadn't realized it, but she was shaken to the core. *And that painting,* she thought, *That painting! Oh, my God!* The world around her was changing so fast it was impossible to keep up. She wanted it to stop. She needed it to stop. *Just stop,* she thought. *STOP LOOKING!* She screamed inside.

She forced herself to look away from the painting and charged outside. Crossing the street, she plopped down on a bench, closed her eyes and caught her breath.

When she opened her eyes, she was lying in purple grass. Though she wasn't sure why, Pro felt a little calmer. *Remember to breathe,* she reminded herself. She saw two figures close by, but it took her a moment to realize who they were.

I remember. It's Zor and Stribjus. They drifted off, too. And M2… they're still watching. I can feel it. I have no idea why the wizard keeps hovering there at the edge of my mind, but I refuse to let this so-called Miraculous Magician rattle me even more than I am already rattled.

Focusing on these strangers who had just fought by her side made Pro wonder, *who has really stood up for me in my life? My parents? Hmmmmm. I think the jury might be out on that. They have certainly, at times, stood up for the FAMILY, but that is not quite the same thing as standing up for ME.*

Elaine has proven herself to be a staunch ally at the very least. Yeah – she went to bat for me on more than one occasion. Now she is God-knows-where for the next two weeks, but I know she has my back.

Ash? Well, Ash I have to admit, is very good at taking care of Ash. And, hey, maybe I am learning to do some of that myself. I did back there in Thanton – I really did. I stood up for myself, Pro acknowledged.

8. NAVLYS, THE AIR WORLD

Pro couldn't believe how she felt. *I am actually enjoying myself,* she thought, *for the first time since... since... since I can't remember when. Even if my job, my life, my everything is up for grabs...*

Then it happened – as though it wouldn't do for her to feel content for more than a few moments. Pro heard the call of the Beckoner that had roused so many emotions in her. Then M2's words rang in her head, "You are here for a reason."

Pro squinted her eyes and cocked her head to one side as if her piercing gaze could probe the wizard for clarification. None came, but the strains of beautiful music swelled. The soothing musical runs seemed to wash away emotional debris, while the mesmerizing trills that sounded like 100 strings ignited a spark deep within her. She looked to see how her new friends reacted to the glorious voice, but apparently, only she could hear the haunting melody that compelled her to action.

"Okay. Let's go!" Pro said as she bolted up.

"What are you talking about?" Stribjus asked, but before he even finished the question, Pro was off.

Zor shouted out, "Do you have any idea where you are going? This can be dangerous terrain, you know."

"I have to find the Agency," Pro shouted back. While she was often, but certainly not always, careful to assess a situation before she plunged in, Pro didn't hear Zor's warning. She was listening to the melody that called her so intently it hit a space deep inside her that had felt empty for a long time. The music spoke to her of a yearning – a yearning so deep she could never have imagined it. She knew it was a call she had to follow.

"All right, I'm onboard!" Stribjus said, forward somersaulting into action. His excitement helped quell the warning voice in her head.

Are you sure you know what you're doing? The question sent a flare up from her stomach that blasted through her brain. Pro thought back, *Sure? Not at all. I just know I need to do it.*

Pro turned around to flash Stribjus a thankful grin then opened her arms in invitation to Zor. Zor furrowed her eyebrows. Stribjus threw his arms open to Zor as well, almost bowing as he skipped backwards. "She needs us," he yelled at Zor, who then burst out laughing and said, "Count me in."

They traveled for what must have been miles over the craggy terrain. Usually much more cautious, Pro was amazed to find herself filled with determination and what she would have described in someone else as fearlessness. And while the beautiful voice of the Beckoner seemed to be coming from everywhere at once, Pro followed her instincts as if she had just found the inspiration for a new painting – throwing herself into the process with abandon and not fretting about the outcome. She knew - she KNEW she was on the right path.

Ha! Pro thought, *the right path? Really? Yeah! It just feels right – for me. Wow! What a revolutionary thought. I made a choice – and it was – is – easy.* Pro was delighted.

The trio crossed a stream and passed into a canyon with large standing stones.

Beyond them, huge walls of bronze inscribed a curved path. Pro kept forging ahead, more invigorated than she could remember being since her first art class in college.

When they were deeper in the canyon, the corridor widened into what seemed to be a massive bronze cauldron. Pro stopped just for a moment then charged headlong into the cauldron. Even though her head was telling her, *this is a bad idea. You shouldn't be so rash.* She KNEW she had to follow the Beckoner's voice, though she didn't know why. She noticed that unpredictable whirling winds were picking up as her hair blew every which way.

Stribjus whooped, enjoying the gusts that caught his feet, lifting him slightly off the ground. Zor glided effortlessly through the shifting currents of air. Pro lurched forward, almost losing her balance. *How are they walking,* she wondered. She had no idea how to find her footing.

Then it happened. Without any warning at all, the three adventurers shot skyward, as if a magnet of air drew them up – up – up, higher and higher. Catapulted upward, they lost all sense of time and space – scattered across the sky. Pro could no longer hear the Beckoner. She was sure she had led them all to certain death, when their upward momentum just stopped – simply, easily, gently. It was as if they had landed on clouds and suddenly, they were in a world of AIR.

Pro gasped. Billowing clouds morphed before her eyes. She saw buildings of all sizes, shapes, and colors suspended in the air. Two huge, feathered ostrich-like beings sailed past. Shimmering blues and greens and creams, they wafted on invisible currents.

Six-armed maroon monkeys flung themselves through space from ropes to silks to ledges with abandon. Birds with many wings soared, flew, and floated through vast expanses of silver-flecked silks, while flower-like creatures wafted on air currents through nets and spiraled down ropes and poles. None of them seemed at all disturbed by the sudden appearance of three strangers.

"This is Navlys, the Air World," Stribjus shouted across the expanse, "It is a kind of meditation resort. I've heard about it, but I have never been here before. It's like a giant playground!" Immediately, he leapt from mushrooming cloud to net to rooftop in total glee.

"C'mon" he yelled, somersaulting, flying, and cavorting as though born to this airy place.

Not to be outdone, Zor, having assessed the situation, focused on a floating railing that caught her eye. She leapt from the cloud to a swinging rope, then bounced off an umbrella and onto a small series of steps that anchored one end of the decorative balustrade that stretched across an expanse to a floating Highrise.

Using her sword for balance, Zor boldly stepped out onto the narrow rail, prudently testing her footing. Pro watched the confident warrior conquer this newfound skill. Zor progressed a few feet, then backed up a step, then took eight more steps before a sudden gust sent her crouching, balancing the sword on the balustrade itself. For a moment her eyebrows raised, and her eyes widened. When Zor rose from the crouched position Pro noticed it was with more caution.

Navlys, The Air World

Pro watched these feats with wonder, marveling at the courage of her companions, until she slipped off of the placid safety of the cloud she was on and fell into space. She bounced onto an awning far below then found herself launched skyward. She catapulted into a solid blue and gold tower that instantly transformed into a silk curtain. Pro grabbed hold of the shimmering silk and held on for dear life as it swung wildly.

She flipped left, then right, then around, fighting desperately to get her bearings. As she struggled, the silks gathered tighter around. *I have no idea which way to go,* she thought, *or even what is up and what is down. I have always hated roller coasters, being tossed around and upside down and this is – what? – ten times worse?*

Enmeshed in the billowing mass of silk, she felt abandoned. *Where IS everyone?*

Finally, she saw Zor in the distance step off of the railing onto a floating stair that was rising in Pro's direction, only to find it gone. Zor looked surprised to find herself back on the narrow balustrade once more.

Hovering a few feet away from Zor, Pro noticed a blonde-haired figure. Young or old, she couldn't tell, but she decided it was probably male. He appeared to be meditating, oblivious to the tidepool of chaos around him.

Zor now looked annoyed with the tightrope game she was playing on the rail, as buildings morphed into cloth and clouds and back again, a grand cacophony of spatial shifting. She grimaced as she lunged toward a passing pole, slipped, and recovered on the railing, dangling from one armpit, then slipping off the balustrade as it tilted vertically.

Pro saw Zor fall into the arms of the ageless, meditating man. Floating effortlessly, he lifted Zor up and brought her to a carpeted expanse that looked completely still.

Zor huffed and glared at the man and for a moment, Pro thought Zor was going to punch him. The floating man resumed his lotus position, smiled, and bowed his head, which spun him slowly in a kind of forward roll. He completed one easy revolution then was perfectly still – suspended in space. His chest glowed deep purple. He grabbed a passing rope and suddenly soared into the air, caught a silk, and grabbed a net.

Turning her gaze away from the man and Zor, Pro saw Stribjus was only a few feet away from her, floating upside down.

"I don't know what to do – how – how to be here," Pro whispered.

"Use that thing – whatever it is you are holding onto," Stribjus reassured her. "Have fun!"

Oh, yeah – right! Fun! Pro thought. *This is as far from fun as it can be – AND it's ridiculous!*

Out loud she said, "How am I even able to breathe up here? I'm all tangled up – way up – high up in the air for heaven sakes."

"Exactly," Stribjus responded, "Just allow that. Allow yourself to be where you are, then roll yourself down." He extended his palms, passing the encouragement on to her. Then he somersaulted down and away. His movements were buoyant as he swam through the space.

Allow myself to be where I am? What does that even mean, Pro thought.

Pro clutched the cloth in terror as she watched the receding figure of Stribjus float away – down, down, down – off into the distance. Her heart raced. She froze – abandoned – suspended in time and space in a world where there was nothing but weightlessness. *I can't feel my legs, my arms. Oh, no. Oh, no, oh, NO! My whole body is just floating away… I'm disappearing!*

Then something caught her eye – silvery and shimmering blue and just off to her right. She forced herself to focus on it as a point of reference. It was the blond man who had rescued Zor. He was floating placidly in space, his chest now glowing pale blue. He was at her level – calm and assured some distance away. Was he judging her with his smooth demeanor?

Suddenly, Pro had the oddest feeling that M2 was hovering far in the distance beyond the blond man's left shoulder. It wasn't so much that she saw a figure. She just felt a presence there. M2 was watching – always watching – and she felt sure, judging her every move – certainly not offering any assistance. The magician's presence did, however, make Pro aware of her breathing once more.

Tears welled up in her eyes as she took a deep breath. Then she took another and shook off the tears.

Okay that feels a little better.

Pro started to soften her grip on the mass of cloth she was wrapped up in. It seemed soft and rich as velvet, yet light as air.

Pro took another deep breath and decided she would roll down the cloth. Resolutely, she opened her grip on the silk. She dropped several feet.

Whoa! Pro clutched the material again, her heart pounding. She felt the calm steadiness of the blonde man floating a few yards away and the piercing gaze of M2. Pro exhaled long and hard, then allowed air to pour into her lungs.

I can do this. Well, I think I can do this. Lord, I am not even sure what THIS is. A wave of doubt and fear welled up in her once more.

Then she heard a voice reverberate through her head. Was it her own thoughts? M2's?

I can't even tell whose voice it is, she thought.

"It will be all right. My name is Loahn. I feel your fear and I came to help."

I can't do this.

"You ARE doing it, Pro," Loahn said. "You don't have to figure out what it is. Just take one step at a time."

Step? Pro thought back, *Step? Onto what?*

"Don't think so hard… okay? One breath at a time," Loahn said.

As she focused on her own breathing, Pro felt her heart slow down. She eased her grip gradually this time, which allowed her to descend more slowly – lurching, rolling, sliding, unwinding.

A gentle gust of wind startled her, and she grasped the cloth ferociously, closing her eyes tight. When she opened them once more, she noticed that the floating blonde man was at her same level, only closer now. She found herself staring at his chiseled features.

That is the most beautiful man I have ever seen. The thought embarrassed her when she heard his voice in her head say, "Thank you."

Then she realized that what struck her as beautiful wasn't just his outward appearance. His easy confidence radiated calm. In an odd way, the impact of his presence had very little to do with his physical features at all. His chest seemed to be glowing blue – a soft, soothing sky-blue. The peace he exuded momentarily distracted her from her dilemma. With that distraction, the rhythm of her breath calmed even more.

Pro took a few more deep breaths. She had the oddest feeling that the beautiful blonde man was breathing at exactly the same rate, in sync with her, even as her breathing slowed once more. Somehow, she found it reassuring that she was not breathing through this alone.

"It's true," she heard the young man's thoughts, "You are not alone. You have much support."

"Down here," Stribjus called, some twenty feet below. "You're doing great!"

"Are you kidding me?" Pro yelled back. "Define great." She found herself smiling in spite of her predicament.

"You're almost down." That was from Zor, who was now next to Stribjus on what appeared to be stable ground. "You're doing just fine."

Stribjus was rolling around, laughing like a four-year-old. "It's all cushiony down here – like downy feathers or something. Come on down. Let the silk slip through your fingers."

"At your own pace," added Zor.

Breathing deeply, Pro cleared her head. *Okay*, she thought, *I just have to figure out how much to hold on and how much to let go.*

Then she had a random thought of her first driving lessons with a stick shift. After weeks of prodding, she had convinced Ash to take her to a huge empty parking lot and teach her how to drive his sports car. "You talk about how exciting and freeing it is and I want to understand that," she had told him. At first, they had lurched and stalled as she applied either too much pressure or not enough to the clutch. Ash was not the most patient of teachers, and eventually, after so many lessons, she thought Ash would never speak to her again (though she remembered it being only three lessons). Pro adjusted and learned to find the balance between applying steady pressure and steady release. The thought that she had actually experienced that kind of balance before settled her down a bit.

Pro carefully but firmly eased her grip and, gradually, let the cloth slip through her hands as she glided the rest of the way down, focused only on the cloth, her body, her breathing and how they were connected.

At last, she stood next to Stribjus shivering with fear – or was it relief – as her breath came up short once more. Just when she felt about to expire, she felt a hand on her shoulder, and she calmed.

As an oasis of peace filled her, she noticed that the hand on her shoulder belonged to the beautiful blond man she had stared at. Loahn, he had said his name was? He emanated such peace; his age was impossible to determine. He was a blend of wisdom and innocence – or perhaps it was just vulnerability.

She took another deep breath. It was only then that she noticed the clapping and saw that Stribjus, Zor and a crowd of watchers were applauding her. Somehow Stribjus even managed to applaud and do a backflip at the same time.

Pro smiled and curtsied to the crowd. Then it hit her. *I did it*, she thought, *I made it down. I had a lot of support, but I DID IT!* That realization and the sense of accomplishment swelled through her in waves.

She took another deep breath to steady herself and heard the beautiful strains of the Beckoner once more. She looked up, as if she might be able to see where it was coming from.

"What's wrong, Pro," Stribjus asked. "Are you okay?"

"Don't you hear it?" Pro cried, "That amazing voice? It's the most exquisite singing I have ever heard."

Zor said, "I don't hear any singing." Stribjus shook his head as well. "Maybe your ears are ringing from your descent," Zor continued, "Or you are imagining it?"

"No," Pro insisted, "This is not my imagination."

Loahn smiled at her. "It calls you," he said. Only then did she realize that the blond man's hand was once again on her shoulder.

"You – you can hear it?" Pro said.

He nodded, "Yes, I listen. I hear it through you."

"But how…?" she didn't even know how to phrase the question.

"I am an empath," he said. "I sense things, Pro." His crystal-clear eyes, like prisms refracting light blue and green, were shining. There was something odd about them. They glistened. They seemed to radiate light rather than absorb it. She felt him taking everything in with great awareness, but it was as if he was absorbing the experience through his skin.

"I am Loahn." When he moved gracefully to introduce himself to Zor and Stribjus, Pro realized, *something feels strange here. When he moved away from me, he didn't turn his head. It was his body that led him to Zor and Stribjus– not his eyes. Loahn is blind,* she thought with a start.

"I am," Loahn responded to her thoughts. "I have been blind since birth," he said to the three.

It was Zor who spoke next, "but you move with such confidence."

"I sense energy, "Loahn explained, "sound waves, light waves, energy waves from people and things." He turned his focus to Pro, "The haunting voice calls you with some urgency. It also has some fear for you. There is danger ahead."

Pro's eyes grew wide with a fear that almost made her knees buckle. *After all I have been through already? Haven't I taken enough risks?* Her heart sank.

Zor and Stribjus looked at each other. "If there is danger, then it is a good thing you are not alone," Zor said.

"Absolutely," agreed Stribjus cartwheeling into a flip and landing in his best karate pose.

"If I may be so bold," Loahn said, "The voice you hear is quite compelling. I feel how powerfully it draws you. I would like to join you as well."

Zor replied, "Why? We don't know y-"

"I think that would be great," Stribjus interrupted with aplomb. "What do you think, Pro?"

"Uh... well... I suppose," Pro stammered, "the more the merrier?"

"Thank you for being so gracious. I sense this is an important journey, and I feel I have a part to play in it." Loahn said.

"Oh, brother," Zor scoffed.

That word again, Pro thought. *I guess I am on a journey.* "Wait a second," she said aloud, "I can't ask all of you to put yourselves in danger..."

"I don't remember you asking at all." Zor grinned and let out her deep-throated laugh. "Let's go."

"I have no idea where we're going," Pro said. "I don't even know where I am."

"Don't worry," said Zor, "I can guide us. We just need to go this direction." She pointed to an archway that suddenly lifted ten feet in the air.

Loahn spoke then, "With all due respect, Zor, I think I am best suited to serve as guide."

Zor protested, "I hardly think that is a good idea. You are . . ."

"Blind?" Loahn said. Smiling, he went on, "Trust me, my familiarity with the workings of Navlys as a blind empath and my inner guidance will serve much better than eyes that are not sure what they are seeing. I mean no offense."

"Right," Zor said, bristling. Stribjus and Pro shot each other a warning glance. They wisely decided not to say a word.

Loahn went on, "I can lead us out of Navlys. And with my hand on your shoulder, Pro, I can guide us to the voice that calls you. Clear your minds and set the intention to leave this land of wind and air and return to the Bronze Canyon."

As they concentrated on saying goodbye to this world, Navlys simply faded away and magically they were once again in the Bronze Canyon. Returning there, Pro was amazed to find that she felt not only rested, but energized, with no sense of how long they had been in Navlys. Her companions appeared refreshed as well.

Pro thought to herself, *there is no way to make sense of everything I am going through. I have to keep pressing forward. I don't know what else to do.* With no idea whatsoever where the Magical Magician was, Pro felt M2 smile. *Oh, yeah,* she chided them with her own thoughts, *fine for you to smile. I have no idea where I'm going – or even where I AM.*

"Just keep going forward," the wizard invited her.

Like I have a choice? As I leave each world it's obvious there's no going back – there is no WAY to go back, she admitted. *So, on we go,* she thought, *on we go.* She closed her eyes and took a deep breath.

As she opened her eyes, Pro found herself on the bench in Mercy Park. *Whew! I must have dozed off – probably not the smartest thing to do in a public park in a big city. But I feel perfectly safe and calm and actually I have a lot of energy. That was some nap – meditation – dream. How long was I out?* Checking her phone, she was surprised to find it had only been about ten minutes since she had bounded out of the office after the encounter with Clive.

Oh, my God – Clive? Did that really happen? Yeah! I'm pretty sure it did. I stood up to Clive – Mr. Shadow Warrior? I did! No wonder my head was reeling. In some ways things are still up in the air, but Clive had said, "Six months." Next week I better find out what that means. She couldn't help but chuckle at herself. *Yesterday, that dubious response would've thrown me into a tailspin, and now it just amuses me.*

I think I need to treat myself to dinner at a really nice restaurant. I'm going to The Desperado. Wait! Are you kidding me? Are you really going to a five-star restaurant, sit there by yourself and spend all that money? Pro hesitated.

Maybe I should just head home. There's plenty of food there. Nope! You are doing this! All by yourself.

The Tex-Mex restaurant had gotten rave reviews since it opened a few months ago. How a restaurant specializing in Tex-Mex cuisine could achieve a five-star rating was unfathomable to Pro until she tasted her lobster enchilada and shrimp tacos. She even indulged in one of their specialty drinks for dessert as she wrote and sketched in her dream journal. The week before she had stuffed it in her bag and now, she took it with her everywhere.

"Asleep or awake – there's a lot going on," was the first thing she wrote. *I can't believe how comfortable I feel sitting in this fancy restaurant by myself writing.* She smiled as she sipped her Mexicali Mocha Surprise.

Her waiter, Luis, assured her he was in no rush to get rid of her and she made a point of tipping him generously when she left. As she signed the bill, the irony of the restaurant's title was not lost on her, nor was the appropriateness of its tagline, "Escape into a World of Culinary Delight."

The weekend sailed by as she cleaned the apartment, rearranged some of the furniture, took a couple of long walks, and threw herself into painting with abandon. She painted whatever came to her and didn't question it – so different from the measured focused approach she used to take.

Wow! She thought as she prepared for bed Sunday night, *this weekend I've felt so free. I haven't enjoyed myself this much in a long time. Now how do I keep this going tomorrow when I re-enter the battlefield of the CBAA?*

She did her best to push the thought aside as she climbed into bed and drifted off to sleep.

9. VERGON, HOME TO FELAGOR

The Bronze Canyon gave way to desert sand as far as Pro could see, accompanied by the haunting song that propelled her. With his hand on her shoulder to tune into the guidance from The Beckoner, Loahn, the blind empath led them across the empty expanse with confident assurance. Three times as they trekked across the desert Pro saw M2 like a mirage in the distance – still watching.

Breaking over the crest of a sand dune, they descended onto a stretch of flat sand. Before them lay a huge ridge that reached toward the orange sky.

"We're here," Loahn proclaimed.

Pro, Zor, and Stribjus looked around in all directions, seeing nothing but mountains of sand everywhere. Their eyes searched for an oasis, a landmark, anything to support Loahn's boisterous claim. They gazed at the empath, and he smiled. They thought for a moment that they had been led by a blind madman into the desert to die.

"Listen carefully," Loahn said, "I strongly suggest you take a good deep breath and hold it – Ready? NOW!" All at once the ground gave way beneath them. The sand swallowed them up and they plummeted down, deep into the earth. As they tumbled through sandy space, Pro had the fleeting thought, *ANOTHER sinkhole? Really?* Finally, they landed.

They took a quick inventory to make sure everyone was unharmed. The sand had actually delivered them intact, cushioning their arrival in what Pro could only imagine was yet another new world.

"Where are we?" Pro asked, catching her breath.

"This is Vergon," Loahn replied. "I have had visions of this volcanic, underground world. It is a dangerous place."

They appeared to be at a juncture of subterranean paths, offering three directions they might go.

Zor's instincts were on high alert. "This is some kind of trap," she cautioned them.

"That's true," Loahn concurred as Zor glared at his assurance.

Using his lightning speed, Stribjus checked out all three pathways. "They go deep," he reported. "This one on the right gets narrower as it progresses. The path on the left is volcanic – slimy and fiery at the same time, and the one in the middle keeps opening cavern, upon cavern, upon cavern. They're all creepy. I want out. Shall we see which one is the way out? We can separate and…"

Like they do in horror movies, Pro thought. "No! No, we definitely don't want to split up," she said aloud. "We have to stay together."

Loahn separated himself from Pro, sat in the lotus position and focused on his breath rhythm. Stribjus tried to joke, "I don't think this is the time or place for a nap." Centering himself, Loahn focused on the paths and how each felt. Finally, he spoke, "We need to go left."

As Zor started to object, he explained what he sensed. "The other two paths have no life force. They are places to get lost in – paths that eventually lead nowhere."

"So, you have been here before?" Zor asked.

"No, I don't need to have been," he said. "I trust what I sense."

"And what if your senses are wrong?" Zor said. "What if you are leading us into a trap – a path to get lost in."

Loahn flashed an engaging smile. "I guess you will just have to trust me and my senses."

"And why should we do that," Zor challenged. Loahn simply continued to grin. Pro and Stribjus waited for the smoke to clear. "Fine," Zor barked, "To the left it is."

As they forged forward, the travelers discovered the subterranean path was volcanic – fiery and slimy, as Stribjus had reported. Fires, embers, sparks flared up around them. Blowholes of steam erupted intermittently, spewing yellow slime. As one belched steam into the air nearby, it startled Pro with, "You - us – it's just not working for me. You – you – just not working for me, justnotworkingjustnotworkingjustnotworking..." raced through her head.

Ash, Pro thought. From behind her left shoulder, another hole belched steam and slime. Pro heard a child crying in lonely desperation.

Every eruption brought forth another voice. Pro heard her mother in the distance calling her, "Kathryn Marie Proscher! You come here this instant. You cannot just run away every time something upsets you." She sounded exasperated, as usual. "I don't know what to do with that child," her mother's voice continued, "She is just one unbridled emotion after another. You've got to learn to control yourself, young lady."

How old was I then, Pro wondered, *Four? Seven?* She couldn't remember when that familiar refrain had begun.

"I don't know how she's going to survive," her father's words burst from another belching hole. His booming voice always carried. "She can't make a living doing art." Her mother's voice responded, "Well, she better find someone who can take care of her – who can deal with all of her emotional upheaval."

Every step she took was another spark, another voice from the past.

"Watch your step, young lady. I have my eye on you." Was that her second-grade teacher?

Then she heard Ash's laugh. Pro's eyes welled with tears, and she covered her ears. "No, no, no, no, NO!" she cried out loud.

Zor and Stribjus stared at her, bewildered. "What's the matter, Pro?" Stribjus asked.

"I can't take it. I can't take the voices." With years of therapy, Pro thought she had buried those voices long ago. But here they were, more alive than ever.

"Voices?" Zor questioned.

"What voices?" Stribjus added.

Then Pro heard other voices – voices she didn't recognize as they kept pressing forward.

She grabbed Stribjus' arm as she heard a mocking male voice say, "Be a man, Stribjus – be a man." From another steam hole she heard, "Oh, now he's going to cry. Poor little baby." *Don't listen, Stribjus*, Pro thought. Her heart sank as she saw tears streaming down his face.

Even Zor looked distressed. Pro met Zor's eyes and then in the steam from another blowhole she saw a gaggle of girls giggling and pointing at a tomboy with raven hair. She had no idea where that image came from, but she felt the derision of the giggling sear her skin.

Then Pro saw the image of a muscular man with dark red hair and broad shoulders talking with Zor. Pro heard Zor's voice say, "Seorge, what are you trying to say?"

Then the man spoke, "How could we possibly be together, Zor? You're not only a better warrior than I am – you're a goddess. I will always love you." Pro saw Zor's image grit her teeth as he rode away.

How can I be seeing and hearing things from lives I know almost nothing about? Pro thought. *I must really be losing it.* Her palms were sweating, and she clenched her teeth.

"For heaven sakes, pull yourself together! Crying never helped anything," resounded through Pro's head. She wasn't even sure if those were her own thoughts or voices from her past.

Her gaze shifted to Loahn. She saw the fierce concentration in his furrowed brow, with tension around his unseeing eyes and his mouth drawn, lips pressed together.

"This is difficult for you," Pro said. Loahn nodded as his energy merged with Pro's.

His hand steadied on her shoulder. "I hear them, too. You aren't losing your mind, Pro. Breathe deeply. The voices are not your truth. Keep focusing on the Beckoner." With Loahn's assistance, Pro forced herself to concentrate on the music she was hearing.

As they wound their way toward the Beckoner through the steaming blowholes of feelings, the voices they heard got louder and louder as images kept appearing in the billows of steam. Zor took the lead with Stribjus just behind. When they were a few yards ahead of Pro and Loahn, Zor took a step, and the ground suddenly gave way. Stribjus' lightning speed kept her from being swallowed alive.

Pro gasped. *A sinkhole! Lord!* "Be careful," she called out.

"I'm all right," Zor replied, "thanks to Stribjus."

Only Loahn's hand on her shoulder kept Pro from leaping out of her skin. As they carefully skirted the sinkhole, he reminded them all to breathe and focus on the ground beneath them, on the texture of the cavernous walls around them – anything that made them totally present. They shouted encouragement to each other to shut out the voices and images from the past and to keep moving forward one step at a time.

Pro saw it first – and Loahn through her – a beautiful, suspended jewel radiating light – pulsing and shining. Then Zor and Stribjus saw it as well. Despite the great distance, Pro knew this light source was coming from the same direction as the Beckoner, calling to them. The summons filled her with confidence as its voice shimmered. The tremulous tones vibrating through her heart sent her soaring.

Suddenly, she crash-landed as a hulking shadow blocked out the vision of the jewel and The Beckoner's call. Her heart plummeted. Darkness emanated from the creature, if it could be called one. It was a formless mass oozing and engulfing everything in its path. It smelled like sulfur. The four travelers choked on the pungent odor – coughing and wheezing. Pro whirled her arms trying to drive the odor away. As she did, she saw Zor confronted by a shadow being. *Clive? Was Clive here, too? No! Ash?*

As the thing oozed toward them several forms emerged from the black abyss. The creature wasn't Protean and changeable, rather it was many things at the same time – prismatic. Steely and calculated, the dark warrior visage anticipated and thwarted Zor's every blow. Then, the monster launched its own attack. Zor parried a fierce strike to her right shoulder, then reversed her sword to protect her left flank.

The aspect toying with Stribjus kept multiplying limbs and heads, cutting off his masterful avoidance maneuvers at every turn. The gaping mouths spit at him – mocking.

Yellow slime dripped from razor teeth. Rasping voices sent shivers down Pro's spine. Stribjus jerked back as Pro noticed that the limbs were stealthily pilfering his pockets – no matter where he moved.

"Stribjus," Pro shouted, "your pockets."

As Stribjus realized what was happening he doubled his pace and darted place to place arbitrarily to escape the thing's grasping hand. Pro could no longer watch. She stared, transfixed into a silver mirror-like surface. Its mercurial depths gaped back at her every disappointment she had ever had or ever been – to anyone.

Felagor, the monster of Vergon

"You're impossible," she heard her mother say as she saw the disapproval in the mirror. Suddenly, a spike poked out from the mirror toward Pro's face. She flinched, stepping back. Loahn instinctively brought her low to the ground, barely avoiding the spike's razor edges.

"You're just too much for your mother to handle," her father admitted, his face weary. "You're no Miss Massachusetts," Ash's judgmental gaze seemed to shout at her as another spike shot out from the mirrored surface low toward the crouched figures. Loahn leapt with Pro out of its path.

Voices from her past ripped into Pro – a jab to her gut, a stab in her side, a slice across her face. It felt like her soul was bleeding. Pro wanted to scream, to run, but she was rendered mute, welded to the spot. Hypnotized by the cacophony of voices and images that bombarded her, she felt beaten down—lost in mirrors within mirrors—worthless.

Loahn helped Pro dodge the silvery spikes that jutted out as the mirror tried to pull her in close so it could strike.

Meanwhile, Stribjus slid and jumped to avoid the grasping appendages that flew at him. He quickly took inventory of what was left in his pockets. "Hang on," he shouted, racing around filling the hands of his traveling companions, "Wait for my signal." As soon as all of their hands were full, he screamed at the top of his lungs, "NOW!"

Without thinking, each of them threw what he had placed in their hands at the hulking mass of darkness. Blue, orange, and green paint dripped down the mirror that Pro and Loahn faced, breaking its spell.

Sticky goo held the spikes at bay, giving Loahn the chance to pull Pro away.

The red and purple smoke bombs Zor tossed at the ninja disoriented it.

The barrage that Stribjus threw confounded the heads. Colorful goop gunked up groping claws that lashed out at empty air.

The hulking creature's roar rumbled through the ground, reaching a crescendo that threatened to bring the cavern walls down.

The travelers ran for their lives. For Pro, there was no way to determine which way they were headed. She had no way to orient herself, and so she was swept along by her companions. After charging around steam holes bursting with accusations and derisive laughter, and narrowly escaping another sinkhole, Stribjus found a path that led to a narrow ledge that they followed upward. They inched their way along the ledge in single file. After a long while the ledge gave way to an open space where they could at least for a moment catch their breath.

Before they could all charge into chatter, Loahn asked, "Is everyone okay? Is anyone hurt? Take a moment and calm down so you can notice your body and what it wants to tell you."

Zor spoke first, "I'm okay."

"I'm tired," Stribjus said. "Moving super-fast for a prolonged period is tough, but I'm all right."

Pro said, "I'm shaken up, but not hurt."

"Good, good. We were lucky." Loahn quieted and listened. Pro saw Zor watch Loahn intently and noticed that she, too, got calmer. She scoped out the terrain.

Loahn asked Zor, "Do you hear or see any indications that we are being followed or tracked?"

Pro stood quiet and still for a whole minute, listening, and looking attentively.

"Nothing," Zor spoke, "we weren't followed." The four travelers heaved sighs of relief.

"That was terrifying," said Pro, "You all really saved me back there. I could never have survived that alone."

"Stribjus, if it weren't for your quick thinking, we would have been in quite some trouble," Loahn said.

"Good job," Zor said.

Pro watched as Stribjus' face turned a deep maroon in response to the compliments. He was so taken aback, he didn't even respond with a wisecrack.

"What was all of that? My imagination playing tricks on me?" Pro asked.

Zor explained, "That was Felagor. I have heard tales of the terror of Felagor – rumors, gossip, a yarn spun by a lone survivor. But the stories varied so widely they were impossible to believe. Now I understand why."

"So, what do we do now?" Pro asked.

Zor said, "We have to find a way out."

Loahn agreed, "We do, but first we need to–"

"We need to get away from here as far and as fast as we can," Zor said. "Felagor is stealthy. It could come upon us at any moment and engulf us while we sit here chatting." Stribjus and Pro nodded their heads in agreement.

"AND", Loahn continued, "we need to do that from a clear head space. We have all been through a major trauma. Are you exhausted? I know I am."

"But it isn't safe here," Zor insisted. "We must move now – however slowly."

"Perhaps a little further," Loahn acquiesced, but the tension between the blind empath and the female warrior buzzed in the air.

The band of travelers shuffled along for what seemed like forever, until Pro finally said, "I can't keep going. I'm sorry, I am just too worn out."

It was then Pro noticed she was shivering. The caverns of Felagor were hot. Volcanic heat had provided a glow on the cavern walls that had helped them as they wound their way through the tunnels. The adrenaline rush in their escape had charged up Pro's body. Now that she had let some of the panic subside, she realized the air had grown chilly. She pulled her jacket around her.

Before Pro even mentioned the chill she felt, Stribjus said, "It's cold here. I have a cloak in my coat that will help us stay warm. If we huddle together, it will cover us all."

Zor proclaimed, "I will stand watch. You sleep."

"You need to get some rest as well," Loahn said. "Let me know when you need some relief, and I will take over."

Zor scowled.

"I feel you scowling," Loahn said. "Just because I am blind doesn't mean I can't stand watch." He used the word pointedly. "And besides, even you need help sometimes."

Pro saw Zor start to rev up a response, then decide against launching into an argument. Relieved, Pro leaned against the trickster and the empath and fell asleep, while Zor stood guard.

As Pro fell off to sleep, the dreams came. Priscilla, the cocker spaniel she had inherited from her sister Patricia, had run away and she was searching for the old dog in the dark. Out of the darkness all kinds of strange images appeared and swirled around her, spiders and bats, cavaliers and sword fights and people and pink slips flying through the air.

When a bell started clanging a kind of terror swept through her and she awoke with a start. She was soaking wet. It took a moment to get her bearings.

It's just my alarm clock. For a moment she regretted that soothing music had never seemed to rouse her from her sleep. *Nightmares again. Really?* She grabbed her journal to jot images and ideas down while they were still all too fresh in her head.

It did help her to get the ideas out. The familiar surroundings helped her to calm down, but it was hard to get her body going. *I feel like I just ran a marathon. Don't even think about not going to work. That will just make it harder to get there.*

Pro navigated her way through the next couple of days uneventfully. Paige assured her that Clive's cryptic pronouncement meant that her six-month review, four months from now, would determine her fate. Paige also gave Pro her new assignment: <u>Falling Between the Lines</u>. The copy for the book jacket read, "Caliper Ridgeston fights to find meaning in a dystopian world where the rules keep changing." *Oh, this will be a laugh a minute.*

Her sleep, though fitful, was uneventful until a few days later.

As soon as her head hit the pillow, she was disoriented, and her heart was racing. She had no idea where she was. As her eyes opened and fought to find focused, Pro noticed a woman with long raven hair and a sword leaning against what seemed to be a cave wall.

Zor has been standing guard. Which means she probably didn't get any sleep. Thank you, Zor, for watching out for us.

When Stribjus opened one eye at her Pro was only slightly startled. *Stribjus, you even wake up playfully? How is that possible?* She couldn't help but give him a little smile. In reply a huge grin burst across his face, which made Pro chuckle.

As she sat up, Loahn stirred. His chest glowed a soft green as he awoke with an ease and a gentleness that reminded Pro of a flower opening to the sun. *How can a blind person be so incredibly present? He obviously "sees" more than I do.*

Then other realizations came flooding in.

She remembered they were in the recesses of a mountain that housed a terror they had escaped. She had found where the Beckoner was being held but had no idea how to rescue it.

"Is everyone awake?" Zor said. "We ought to get moving."

Pro said, "How can we when we can't see anything beyond right where we are?"

"I can help with that," Loahn said. He focused his attention on his hands. A pulsing azure glow emanated from them. As it intensified, he focused that light out in front of them, he illuminated the area so they could see what he could sense. There were two openings in the rock wall ahead of them.

"How can we know which path to take?" Stribjus asked.

Loahn was the first to answer, "Listen–"

"Why? For what," Zor asked. "What possible good can that do? We need to look for signs of…"

"Please – I know you are used to trusting what you see. But I invite you to listen and allow yourselves to reach out through your skin to sense finding a way through - the way out. Listen for the truth beyond what you see – beyond your expectations. Imagine clearing a path. As you concentrate on that intention, see which of the entrances ahead seems to be more open or to have more light for you."

Pro looked on bewildered. *How could such an important decision be left to mere imagination and conjecture,* she thought.

Loahn replied to her unspoken doubts, "The more you pay attention to what you sense and feel, the more you can learn to trust the answers that arise."

Stribjus grinned.

Of course, Stribjus is having fun, Pro thought, *He's used to taking risks. His whole life is a risk.*

"Right!" Stribjus proclaimed. "I mean, the right opening is the right path – the path we are looking for."

Pro watched Zor's gaze follow her sword. She held it point up, then, as she lowered it, it faced the opening on their right. She said nothing.

"The path to the right draws me as well," Loahn said.

Following the trail of light made by the glow Loahn generated, they set off to the right. They meandered through twists and turns, barely avoiding a huge drop off around one corner, when Loahn stopped. "Listen," he said, "What do you hear?"

It was Pro who spoke first, "It sounds like water." The others agreed. They followed the sound to a ground spring that became a stream. Though Zor shouted out a warning, Stribjus splashed water on his face and took a deep gulp. "Come on, it's fine," he said.

Pro was parched and drank big mouthfuls. Loahn joined them in drinking, while Zor held back. When they had their fill, they followed the stream until, at last, they saw light pouring in up ahead.

Cautiously making their way along the widening stream as it rushed through the caves, they heard a roaring, rumbling sound. For a moment, Pro feared that it was Felagor pursuing them.

As the travelers ventured forward, they came to the mouth of the cavern that opened onto a vast landscape. *Oh,* Pro realized with a huge sigh of relief. *It's a waterfall! That's the sound I heard.* Her gaze tracked the stream they were following as it joined other tributaries, creating a multileveled waterfall that glistened in the blinding light that fed into a river. With no idea of where they were headed, the four traced their way along the banks of the ambling water, striving to get as far from the caves of Felagor as they could.

10. THE KERMUFFLES

The landscape that stretched out before them was the strangest combination of elements. Pro saw some trees that made mushroom-like canopies. Others had branches that were swept up, so that leaves only appeared across the top. The exposed branches were gnarled and rough as if roots had grown out from the trunk skyward.

As they made their way away from the mountain, Pro noticed what she could only describe as large sack-like pods with oddly shaped, smooth trunks and small branches, like little arms peeking out – reaching out? From the top. Some of these clung to the side of the mountain while others were in clumps.

Loahn said, "I passed through here long ago. You can be sure the Kermuffles are watching us."

"I have been here before, but have never seen any signs of life, beyond the odd vegetation," Zor said.

"I'm not surprised," Loahn said. "The Kermuffles keep their distance."

Pro said, "I think if I lived so close to what we just encountered, I would keep my distance, too."

"Not me," Stribjus bragged. "I thought I handled that terror pretty effectively."

"You did, Stribjus, and we are very grateful," Pro agreed.

"But don't think for a second that it can always be that easy," Loahn said.

Pro noticed that Zor seemed strangely quiet.

"I'm just saying," Stribjus went on, "that I did a pretty great job back there." With that, he leaned against one of the huge pods. Pro heard whispering and high-pitched squeals as the pod moved a few feet away from him. The movement took him so by surprise he would have fallen over, if he hadn't been so nimble. He looked at the pod quizzically. Then he strode to another pod and placed his hand on it. No response. So, he leaned against it. No response. He touched another pod, then another – no response. The next pod lurched as he approached it.

He cautiously re-approached the first pod he had leaned on – the one that had moved. He reached out with one finger, but before he could make contact it moved three feet away.

Pro observed, "I've seen plants that recoiled their leaves when they were touched, but never one that literally moved away."

Loahn said, "That particular pod is not a plant, Pro. They are Kermuffles. Stribjus, the game you are playing is not very nice."

"But it is SO much fun," Stribjus cried. He jumped in the air, landed in a wide stance, spread his arms, and yelled, "Blllllaaauuuuugh." The two pods leapt in the air and scrambled away. Stribjus, full of his own bravado, grabbed Zor's sword as she stood there amused and the imp raced away after the pod people.

"Stribjus!" Zor yelled after him. She pursued him, and Pro felt they had no choice but to follow.

"It's just a game," Stribjus yelled back.

Pro was grateful that Loahn stayed close. Getting separated in this strange land did not seem like a good idea.

They ran over the rough terrain in pursuit of Stribjus as he terrorized the pod people. *What had Loahn called them,* Pro thought, *"Kermuffles?"*

Quite fleet of foot, Pro saw the Kermuffles run as a tightknit unit, fracture into several individuals, then regroup as one. They raced adeptly across the uneven terrain.

But if he wants to catch the Kermuffles, why isn't Stribjus traveling at lightning speed? Pro wondered. *Oh! I get it. He doesn't want to catch them. He's toying with them – playing cat and mouse.*

One more thought scrambled out before she could shut it down: *Is that what Ash was doing with me? Playing cat and mouse? Just giving me the run around? For five years.*

She stumbled on a huge root, barely managing to stay upright, and brought her mind back to the task at hand. Better focus, or you will hurt yourself.

Coming to a vine bridge over the river, the Kermuffles continued

The Kermuffles

to run as fast as they could, followed by Stribjus, then Zor, who bellowed, "Stribjus! You are in so much trouble."

As she came to the vine bridge and looked at the river surging far below, Pro hesitated. *I'm not sure this is such a great idea.*

Fearing she would fall behind and lose her friends and watching Loahn deftly crossing she took a deep breath and gingerly worked her way to the other side.

There the vegetation thickened. In addition to the canopy trees and those with root-like branches soaring skyward, there were trees with multiple roots and multitudes of vines. They reminded Pro of banyan trees she had seen when she and Ash had gone to Hawaii to celebrate their second year together. *Ash, again! Ugh!* She tucked the thought away as she ran after her friends.

Odd, she thought, *I do think of them as friends, even after such a short time. At least, I think it has been a short time.*

Indeed, time and space seemed strange to her in the worlds she had recently encountered. In fact, as she thought about it, she had no idea how much time had elapsed. *And I can't think about that now,* she thought. *I'm already lagging behind.*

Even Loahn was up ahead now. *How is this even possible? How can a blind empath wind his way so adroitly through the overgrown jungle? Some kind of sonar? Come on, Pro, catch up!*

Finally, Stribjus followed the retreating Kermuffles out of the thick vegetation into a clearing. He was having a grand time playing the ferocious warrior. Watching from a distance Pro figured it was just another game he was playing. She thought he could never harm anyone. *But remember, you've only known him for a short while.*

Zor strode up to him and grabbed her sword back. Loahn caught up with them right away. As Pro approached the clearing, she saw her friends almost completely surrounded by the pod people. Only the path Pro was on remained open. Pro held back, reticent to charge into the circle of the Kermuffles when a rush of anxiety slammed into her – a raw stark terror greater than she had felt facing Felagor.

Oh, my God! she thought. *These pod people are huddled together because they are scared out of their minds.*

Automatically taking a defensive stance, Zor brandished her sword as if to say, "Don't worry about this fool. If you want to attack us, you will have to deal with me."

Loahn stretched out an arm to calm Zor down and encouraged her to lower her sword. Almost simultaneously he reached out with his other arm to the Kermuffles to reassure the pod people they meant no harm. But the Kermuffles recoiled, trembling and frantic.

Loahn's chest blazed orange throwing the Kermuffles into a frenzy. They stamped their little feet. It sounded to Pro like a stampede as they focused all their attention and energy on the intruders. Pro stood transfixed. A piercing buzz arose from the Kermuffles, shaking the ground like deafening thunder.

Then Stribjus, Zor, and Loahn vanished.

Pro gasped, horrified that they had literally been obliterated. Her heart pounded with the realization that their disappearance left her all alone.

Pro's gasp alerted the Kermuffles to her presence. Slowly, they turned their attention to her, and Pro froze in her tracks. She gazed around her at the hordes of Kermuffles. *They look so innocuous*, she thought, *how could they have made that happen?*

She had no idea what to do, but every Kermuffle eye – each of them had three - was focused on her. *Wait a minute. I'm holding my breath.* She wasn't sure how she had the wherewithal to have that realization, but she did. *That can't be helpful. Just breathe – slow down – and breathe.* She took a long deep breath. It seemed to help clear her head.

So, she took another.

As Pro focused on her breathing, she noticed M2 suddenly hovering in the air over the middle of the circle. Having no clue where the thought came from, Pro wondered, *Am I connected somehow to that magician? Did I cause M2 to appear? How? Just by slowing down my breathing? How is that possible?*

The Kermuffles scurried together for protection, waiting to see what this new—obviously powerful—being would do.

"I need your help," Pro said. "My friends disappeared, and I don't know what to do."

M2 replied, "Your friends are safe. You don't need to depend on me for help, Pro. There is help all around you. You have only to find the Agency."

Pro looked all around her but saw only a huge huddle of frightened Kermuffles. "I don't know what you mean," she said.

"Follow your breath," the wizard said. "See where it takes you – what you notice."

As she continued to breathe, she felt her awareness expand. *What was it Lohan had said in the cave? Something like, "Listen beyond your expectations – for the truth."*

Pro reached out with all of her senses. Suddenly she had a sense of people huddled over books or staring at computer screens in various locations. They all seemed connected to her somehow – watching her. Her immediate reaction was to recoil defensively, to shrink back, self-conscious and confused, sure they were only observing her to pass judgment. Then she had the oddest feeling that they were not judging her. They were peeking in on her, witnessing her experience with curiosity and an odd kind of detached support.

"Are you the Agency?" Pro asked tentatively. She listened but heard no response.

M2 encouraged her, "You have to ask them for help."

I couldn't possibly do that, she thought to herself. "Why would they bother to help ME?" she said aloud.

The thought that she was unworthy made her shudder. She tightened up. For a moment she felt isolated – again. M2 waited patiently, without pressuring or demanding anything from her. Pro remembered to breathe once more – all by herself. As she remembered, she took long deep breaths, felt her shoulders relax and her chest release, literally giving herself breathing space.

With another deep breath, Pro felt a shift in her brain. It was as if she was taking a step into another dimension. She had a vision of those watchers that she sensed in various locations and dimensions. Pro sent her thoughts out.

Okay, I don't know exactly who is out there, but ... I hope, er... if it is not too much trouble ... could I ask, um... would you help me? Please?

Not really sure who she was asking, Pro was surprised that she was actually reaching out. As she opened to connect with support, to breathe it in, she relaxed even more. She smiled, her eyes welling up with tears, *there's so much help around me I've never been aware of before.*

Thank you. Thank you! she thought. Then, as she stepped back into her own altered reality, she said it aloud, "Thank you! Thank you for your support. Just knowing that you're there – that there is something bigger than me – someone watching, witnessing, caring what I do gives me hope. It really makes a difference."

No wonder so many of us believe in God. The thought of something greater puts things in a whole new light – a more expansive perspective. I'm really not alone.

With that, M2 vanished.

The Kermuffles seemed dumbfounded. They stared at Pro. She hoped that they realized she was gaining confidence, but not in any way that was combative or threatening. She smiled at the Kermuffles and watched as they communicated amongst themselves – shifting, even moving apart a bit. She couldn't be sure, since she was unfamiliar with Kermuffle body language, but she got the impression that they were relaxing just a little.

Pro drew in the air. She pointed to herself. Next, she gestured gently at the Kermuffles and inscribed a circle with her arms to include them. Then, with her palms open and inviting, she gestured out to the space around them where she had asked for help.

The Kermuffles looked around suspiciously to see if there was some kind of threat around them. They looked at each other and shook their heads, then they looked back at Pro.

Finally, she brought her hands to her heart one on top of the other and, with her elbows close to her body, let them fall open, palms up, with just the slightest nod of her head.

The Kermuffles leaned toward her. They seemed curious about what she was doing and some of them cocked their heads. She made the gesture again and nodded once in encouragement. *Here, let me give you some courage*, she thought opening her arms once more.

That thought amused Pro and she smiled, then waved for the Kermuffles to try the heart opening gesture. Very tentatively a couple of them did, with their little branch-like arms.

Gradually more and more Kermuffles joined in as Pro kept repeating the gesture.

As she did, her fingers tingled, so Pro began to move them – just barely, the very lightest of movements. The fluttering of her fingers made her feel even lighter and more playful, so she shared that light playful movement with the Kermuffles as well. Some of the Kermuffles began to shake their little tree branch hands. As they mimicked that small light movement it translated to a shivering of their limbs.

So, Pro very lightly shook her hands as well. It made her smile. Pro and the Kermuffles fluttered their hands back and forth at each other and then all around them. She wasn't sure why she was holding up her hands and moving her fingers, it just felt fun.

Then it dawned on her, *this is the American Sign Language gesture for applause. The Kermuffles and I are applauding each other!* She squealed with delight. Though she had never thought of herself as a dancer, her handshaking soon infused her entire body. As she shook playfully, a favorite memory surfaced out of nowhere.

When she was little – what was she – six? Seven? Her sister Patricia's cocker spaniel, Priscilla, had jumped into a fountain to cool off on a walk one hot summer day. Pro, against the protestations of her nanny Carlene, jumped in after the rebellious dog. When Pris was finally coaxed out of the fountain, she shook the water off – and Pro, copying her, did the same. Though Carlene was very upset with both of them, shaking off the water had sent Pro, well, little Kathryn (as she was known then), into gales of laughter.

She hadn't thought of that incident for so long. For the first time, it struck Pro that both shaking off the water and her laughter had actually helped her shake off the fear of being judged by onlookers, or even fears of Carlene's and, by proxy, her mother's anger and frustration with her. She had somehow, she realized now, allowed herself to actually play, regardless of Carlene's threats of her parents' impending wrath. And here she was, dry this time, shaking off the fear.

And apparently, so were the Kermuffles. Although some of them appeared hesitant, eventually they, too, found themselves drawn into the dance. As more and more Kermuffles joined in, they seemed to be shaking off their fears, too. At least, that was Pro's hope.

As their movements got freer, they made all manner of weird and interesting sounds. Their hums, buzzes, squeals, and sighs surprised and delighted Pro so much that she started making them, too.

"Mmmmmmmmmmpaaaaaaaa! Sqeeeeeeeeeechchchchc! Ploooooooooooo-mbumbumbumbum," she voiced, joining in the cacophony. She had no idea how much fun it could be to make weird noises, though making the crazy sounds did spark some vague recollection of when she was three or four. Then, of course, she had to grow up.

While the Kermuffles danced out their fears, Pro fluttered her fingers.

This is for all of you out there – watching.
Thank you! Thank you. . . For what?
For witnessing—supporting—caring enough to keep watching.
Hey, what if you flutter along with us?
Is it too silly, or could you join the celebration?
Pro took a deep breath. *Wow! I am so proud of myself for having the courage to ask for help.*

From their reticence, Pro surmised that for some of the Kermuffles, this was perhaps the first time they had ever allowed themselves to play. *Do they even know HOW? They're so cautious and withdrawn – like they're hyperaware that danger might be lurking around every bend. Of course,* she reminded herself, *that dazzling analysis is based on observing them for how many minutes now?*

As she continued to dance, Pro felt the mysterious M2 smiling. She still was not sure she could completely trust this enigmatic stranger who kept appearing and disappearing, but she had to admit the magician had been a great help here.

She made the heart opening gesture once more. *Thank you, M2.*

Suddenly, one Kermuffle started a high keening as it flapped its little branch hands and shook out the fear. Soon, all of the Kermuffles were making the same sound. Pro tensed up again until she realized that this sound was not at all threatening. It seemed playful and filled with gratitude. It made her laugh – not the giddy, light, ladylike laughter she was used to - but a rich combination of giggles, gasps, shrieks, and a deep-throated gut laugh.

The Kermuffles scrambled toward Pro – ALL of them – then abruptly stopped both the movement and the sound. They looked at her quizzically and she felt their appreciation. But she also felt something else. Was it a sense of expectation, or was it a challenge, as if they were saying, "This is so FUN! What now?" And then all the Kermuffles cocked their heads.

Pro froze.

With hundreds of Kermuffles focused on her, Pro felt like she was in first grade again – her first day of school. Miss Garfield was nice and friendly, but little Kathryn Proscher felt some enormous expectation placed on her. There was something she was supposed to do, but no one told her what it was. One more potential explosion in the minefield of her childhood.

Pro thought of Clive. *Oh, God, Clive! I went too far, didn't I? There and now here. Too far. Now they're going to make ME disappear.*

Oh, man, Pro gasped, *I'm holding my breath again, aren't I? Why do I do that?*

One of the Kermuffles carefully stepped forward. This jolted her back to the present and then Pro remembered to breathe. As she felt the intake of air calm her, she noticed that the being was in no way threatening. On the contrary, this Kermuffle was apparently facing fears of its own to step out from the pack.

Pro sensed that the brave creature was a kind of leader. She decided to think of it as the King, uh, Queen, hmm, she settled on Kquing of the Kermuffles as a good compromise.

The Kquing of the Kermuffles gave her what she imagined must be a Kermuffle bow – leaning way over from what on a human body would be ankles. It looked like it was about to topple over, but no, the creature was perfectly in balance. Pro received the gesture as a sign of gratitude and an honoring of her and what she had just brought to all of them. Pro curtsied back, grateful that they seemed to have connected somehow.

Then the Kquing spoke, which to Pro sounded like, "Brixtum quimp ttttrittle basken whalff. Kreet shtunten brak klast bresken?"

"Excuse me?" Pro replied.

With the help of much body/pod language the Kquing and Pro managed, at least so she believed, to have the following conversation:

"We thank you for the great lightening. What would you ask of us?" the Kquing prompted.

"I need my friends who disappeared to be brought back."

"Oh, you want those violent creatures who disappeared to be brought back?"

"Yes!"

"Oh! I understand. Brought back, yes?"

"Yes," Pro reiterated.

"Yes, I understand!"

"That's great!"

"Yes," chirped the Kquing. "There is no way that is ever going to happen."

"Why not?"

"Because they are DANGEROUS – violent, out of control. You saw them – waving that sword around! Who knows how many of us might be harmed? There is no way they are coming back. They are in a safe place."

No matter what she did to persuade, the Kquing stayed strong in their resolve. They would do anything else for her – but bringing her dangerous friends back was too much to ask.

Frustrated, Pro shut down. *Okay, wait. Breathe. Good. Again.* Then she looked around. *M2? Where are you? I know you aren't far away. Well, I don't know how I know that, but I do. I could use some help here.*

Getting no response, Pro focused on her next breath. Just breathing more deeply released her shoulders and her lower back. She took one more deep breath and sent out a call for help. Even as she sent out the call, Pro was aware it was not a call of desperation. It was simply sending out the thought, *Can anyone out there help me? Is anyone willing?*

She heard a thought in response that said, "You can do this. When reasoning isn't working, try a whole new approach."

Pro looked around, wondering where the thought had come from. Then it dawned on her that it really didn't matter. She needed to listen – to be open to trying something else. Now, if she could only figure out what that should be.

Wait a minute, she thought, *figuring out what to do is exactly what I needed not to do.* The Kquing was right, Stribus had waved the sword around in a threatening manner. She couldn't deny that. And the way the Kermuffles opened to her was due to her own openness, giving life to gratitude with her voice and her body. *But where do I start now?* she thought. *Well, let's clear the slate and start over. Think fast, Pro.*

Flying by the seat of her pants, she said the first thing that popped into her head, "Schprong, baby." *I haven't thought of that phrase in ages. Can't take credit for it either*, she reminded herself. *That was all Martin. Martin, my loveable mechanic-slash-artist-slash-lover. That one time, when I got stuck in a painting I called 'Time to Forget,' he was determined to find a way to make me laugh. He swiveled his hips and shoulders and said,* "Schprong, baby." 🦋

I love how it became a 'thing' we did to remind each other to lighten up. I haven't thought of that in years and years. Ash was not much of a "schpronger." Thanks, Marty! What have I got to lose? I'll try it.

So, she did just that. She swiveled her hips and shoulders, moved her arms like she was shaking maracas and finished off with splayed hands by her shoulder, palms up. "Schprong, baby!"

The Kquing looked confused, so she did it again. "Schprong, baby." The Kermuffle Kquing tried the movement, but with no hips

Schprong, Baby!

per se, the effect was more like a leaf trembling in the wind. The Kquing tried the movement once more, then looked at Pro, exasperated. This was not going well. But she had to figure out something and soon. She had to find a way to get her friends back from wherever they had been banished to.

Okay, now what do I do, Pro thought. *To get the Kquing thinking a different way, I have to think a different way. But what does that even mean?*

From out of nowhere the thought popped into her head: *Think pink bubbles.*

Pro didn't know what to do with that bizarre instruction. Yes, she loved playing with bubbles and even bubble baths as a young girl, but what could that have to do with her current crisis? She didn't know what else to do, so she passed the information along.

She held her hands as if she was holding a basketball in front of her, then waved her fingers gently – for pink – and finally with an impulse through her fingers she opened her arms up and out. "Think pink bubbles," she said aloud as she made the gesture.

The Kquing looked at her, intrigued, Pro hoped. Pro made the gesture again with, "Think pink bubbles." This made the Kquing laugh as they tried the gesture. As they repeated the words with the gesture several times together, the Kquing nodded approval, becoming more and more playful.

The Kquing skedaddled over to other Kermuffles and showed it to them, encouraging them to try it as well. They seemed to be impressed by her wisdom, as they gave it due consideration, then tried it themselves. It made them squeal as they played along. Soon, another dozen Kermuffles had joined them.

"Think pink bubbles."

"Think pink bubbles," dozens more joined in, jumping up and down. "Think PINK bubbles! THINK PINK BUBBLES." 🦋

Then following their leader, the Kermuffles scrambled toward Pro eagerly. They leaned toward her in anticipation of her next bit of priceless wisdom.

Ack! What do I do NOW? As Pro groped for the next thing to say and do, she started to wave her hands and rock her body in a circle. *Okay, this buys me a little bit of time. Oh, Lord! Please don't let me screw this up. We are making this up as we go. Think pink bubbles, Pro! You can do this.*

Pro spiraled her arms in the air above her head, then at shoulder level and said "Coooooommmmme." As she opened her arms out,

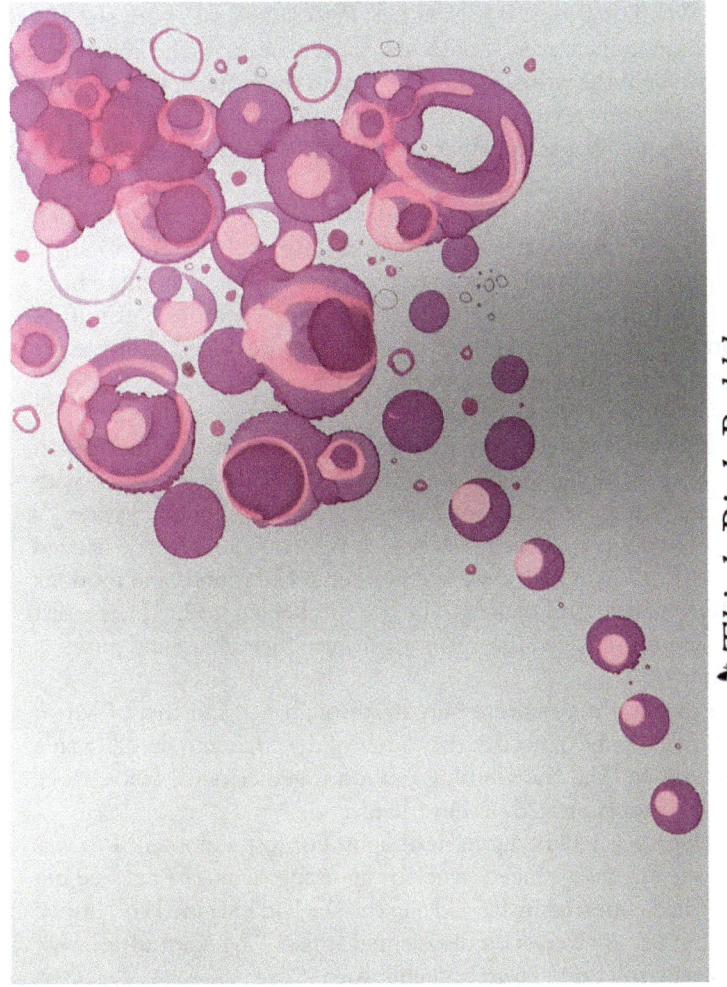

Think Pink Bubbles

she said, "Together!" Then jumping in the air (because Kermuffles seemed to like to jump) with a big "Ah!" she wrapped her arms around her torso in a big hug, shook her body, and, bending her knees, finished with a yummy, "Mmmmm."

The Kermuffles looked at her in amazement, then looked at each other. When they looked back at her, Pro could have sworn she saw admiration in their eyes, though she wasn't sure how she knew that.

She taught the words and movement to the Kquing, who seemed to learn them reverently. This was obviously very important information. "Come together, Ah-mmm... Come together, Ah-mmm."

Going out from the Kquing, the other Kermuffles were learning it rapidly. "Come together, Ah-mmm!" They were careful to share the mantra and it swiftly spread to the entire horde. It became a huge dance of joy, celebrating this new wisdom. As more Kermuffles began to gyrate and spin the whole clearing was filled with the joy of, "Come together, Ah-mmm!"

Then Pro got the attention of the Kquing once more and coaxed them to synchronize the movement with her. As they began to align their movement, more and more Kermuffles aligned with them. This huge dance of joy inspired her as she thought, *what might happen if all of this joyful energy was focused?* With no idea why she needed to do it, Pro began to orchestrate the wonderful sounds and motions the Kermuffles were making. She got the Kquing to help her enlist more and more Kermuffles to synchronize their chant and jump all together.

Pro felt a momentum surging through her and the crowd of Kermuffles as she danced at the center of the circle and they all made the sound and did the whirling motion together once, twice, three times. Pro concentrated on her friends.

There was a blinding flash of light. For just a moment Pro was afraid she might have been struck by lightning. Then she realized her friends had appeared by her side just as she had imagined and hoped they might. They were a bit disoriented at first. The Kermuffles were completely still now – watchful and wary.

Before any of her companions had a chance to respond, Pro danced the movement she had taught with, 'Come together, Ah-mmm!' Zor, Stribjus, and Loahn looked at her as if to say, "Who ARE you?" Pro smiled and repeated the dance, reassuring them that they were all safe and among friends.

"Boy, I'm so glad to see all of you," Pro said. "Everything is fine. Just follow my lead – and please no moves that might seem aggressive. I don't want to lose you again."

Zor had her sword sheathed at her side when the trio reappeared and in the calm, playful joy of Pro's dance she had not drawn it. The trio gazed at the Kermuffles, who were no longer huddled and cowering in fear. They had spread out more, appendages extended – watching and waiting to see what the trio would do. Loahn's chest glowed a soft pink, which sent a buzz through the Kermuffle crowd.

Stribjus looked around at the Kermuffles sheepishly. He slowly copied the movement that Pro had just shown them. "Come together – Ah-mmm!" The Kermuffles whispered to each other.

Carefully, Stribjus approached Zor and placed his hands out with the palms up.

It was clear he was asking that she place her sword in his hands. Pro scanned the Kermuffles to see how they were reacting. They looked alert, but because he did not reach for the hilt, as far as Pro could tell, they remained calm and attentive. Solemnly, Zor placed her sword in Stribjus' hands.

Stribjus slowly showed the sword to the crowd of Kermuffles raising it above his head, then he kneeled down. Pro heard him say, "I'm so sorry I tormented you. I was just having fun. I had no idea I was being cruel, because that's the way it is in my world."

There was no way to know if the odd little creatures understood him, but Pro sensed it was important for him to say. He placed the sword on the ground, bowing his head, "My humblest and deepest apologies." As he raised up, Pro saw a tear rolling down his cheek.

The Kquing came forward. The leader seemed to be giving several instructions, as some Kermuffles ran off and then several came forward to remove the sword and place it off to the side where everyone could keep an eye on it. Then the Kquing opened their arms to the pleasantly bewildered travelers, danced the movement phrase and invited everyone to "Come together – Ah-mmm!"

Pro hugged Stribjus and Loahn and even Zor. She had never been so happy to see anyone. Pro felt M2 smiling and heard, "Excellent work, Pro. Most excellent work."

What followed was a celebration of joyful camaraderie the likes of which Pro had never seen before. Food seemed to appear from nowhere, laid out on flat rocks. The bright colors of the foods added to the festivities and suddenly Pro realized she was very hungry. Pro thought she recognized tropical fruits and an array of vegetables. Although she was not normally a very adventurous eater, Pro's hunger encouraged her to sample some of everything that was laid out before her. The blue fruit with seeds that effervesced on her tongue surprised her and made her laugh out loud. The orange and yellow leafy food reminded Pro of lettuce, but somehow it seemed crunchier and more playful. *Can food be playful?* Pro wondered. The idea intrigued her, as some Kermuffles dance-tumbled by, delighting her with their antics.

The Kermuffles led the adventurers in a call and response that reminded Pro of a square dance. Stribjus looked like he was having the time of his life, dancing up a storm and making weird sounds. Pro also noticed that he went out of his way to be kind and thankful to as many of the Kermuffles as he could.

The four travelers danced with abandon, enjoying the Kermuffles and each other. Pro was surprised at how easily Loahn picked up the dance movements without being able to see them. He had an astounding ability to track the energies around him.

A hugging dance started with small playful body contact that grew into tiny snuggles and finally into full-blown group hugs. The travelers hugged as if they were long lost friends, which in a way, Pro thought, they really were. She was so relieved they were back.

Stribjus was having the time of his life, dancing up a Kermuffle-storm. When he grinned at Pro and pointed to Zor, Pro's mouth dropped open as she saw the princess-warrior not only surrounded by affectionate Kermuffles, but hugging them back! *I never would have imagined that underneath all of the fear I saw not so long ago was so much Kermuffle affection. Guess maybe I shouldn't jump to conclusions when I first meet someone, remembering I am only getting part of the whole story.*

They all danced together, made sounds Pro had never heard before and ate and drank their fill. It was clear to Pro that she was the guest of honor of this celebration. *Well, at least one of them*, she thought, *and for once, I'm actually enjoying the attention!*

In the past, she had shied away from being in the spotlight. When she received the Penelope Pearson Award for her senior art show in college, she was proud of the accomplishment. But as she was presented with the plaque and cash prize at the Gallery Awards Ceremony, she had almost been apologetic, as if she was hearing her father say, "We're proud of you, of course. Just remember you have to be practical. Careful you don't let this art nonsense go to your head."

Even as that memory flashed before her, it had no power here, in the onslaught of playfulness and joy that she was sharing with a whole new group of friends. She knew in part she was able to enjoy the attention she was being given because it was being shared with her friends, with the Kquing and, in fact, with all of the Kermuffles.

The revelry culminated with the Kermuffles returning the sword to Zor and waving the travelers on their way.

11. RIDING KERMUFFLE WAVES

When her alarm went off Pro felt rested, even energized and playful. *Playful? How can anyone wake up playful? Well, that's what it feels like. Now I understand how Stribjus did it. Thank you, Kermuffles.*

She quickly jotted down as many details as she could remember. She sailed through weeks buoyed up by the Kermuffle celebration. She even started painting again, as ideas materialized in vivid colors on canvases. When she started to overthink or go into worry mode, she would remind herself to "Think pink bubbles" or "Schprong, Baby." Immediately she would smile or laugh and charge into whatever was facing her feeling refreshed. With a series she called "The Kermuffle Paintings" she honored the fear and affection and joy she found in Kermuffleland.

This is so much fun. When is the last time I had this much fun painting? Maybe never? Even in college going with the flow was never one of the things I did best — well, I did, but in dribs and drabs. This feels different. Painting playfully is my new mission. And on we go.

Pro found her teaching at The Gridline was really changing, too. One day she brought in bubbles. "Today we will be blowing bubbles, then painting them." The atmosphere in that class was ebullient as they all ran around blowing bubbles of various sizes.

"But how can we paint them, when they pop so fast I barely have time to pick up my brush?" Luisa had asked, with more than a hint of frustration.

"That is a terrific question, Luisa," Pro responded. "You're right. So, you have a few options. What some artists do is take a photo of what they want to paint and work from that. And while some of you might try to do that from a small image on your phones, for this project I think that might set you up to try and 'get it right' or 'do it perfectly.' What I would rather you try is either painting it from memory or just paint the feelings it gives you, whether that ends up looking like bubbles or not. In fact, if feelings come up that you don't want to have, you could put them in bubbles and let them float away." The energy in the room was sky-high as their paintings exploded with color and delight. Fen was the most enthusiastic she had seen him in weeks.

In another class the main focus was "Just paint however you are feeling and if you get stuck at all, shake it off and say something silly, like, "Schpring." Then on the same piece of paper, if you like, add something new - start at a different point on the paper or grab a new color and see where it leads you."

Playing with her young students that way encouraged Pro to approach her own painting with a newfound sense of ease and exuberance.

Wait a minute! What was it Elaine had talked about the day she got her CBAA promotion? What was the word? Ah! It was reprogramming! Is that what I'm doing? My childhood certainly programmed me to worry, think too hard and not trust myself. And I defied some of that with my art, but the old pattern still rears its ugly head.

Hmmm. Reprogramming. "We interrupt our regularly scheduled worry session for a special bulletin of pink bubble thinking, schpronging, and schpringing," she said out loud. She burst with glee, surprising herself with a deep, rich, full-throated belly laugh. She threw her hands up, thanking the universe and the Kermuffles as she fluttered her fingers. *These are sparkle fingers. I totally get why this is American Sign Language for 'applause.' It feels so celebratory.*

When she told him about her dreams Dr. Lamdowski reinforced the changes he saw in her. "Our dreams can be a powerful force. Sometimes we're able to work things out in our dreams in ways we would never have imagined. Good work, Pro!"

She didn't even try to explain her dreams to her mother and sister. They were sure the transformation they were witnessing had to be due to a new man in her life. "Come on," her mother insisted, "Tell us about him."

"There isn't anyone to tell you about," Pro replied. "Yes, I have started dating again – and before you say anything, yes, I'm being careful because there are a lot of jerks out there. I've met a couple of nice guys. In fact, Thom and I are getting ready for our third date. He's a sweetheart."

"I knew it," her sister Patricia chimed in.

"I said he's A sweetheart, not MY sweetheart. The last thing I need to do is pin my hopes on some man – no matter how great he is."

At last the spell of the nightmares had been broken. Even things at work were going better. Pro was navigating her way through the dystopian world of <u>Falling Between the Lines</u> without getting caught up in it.

When Elaine returned from her two-week spa vacation in St. Thomas, she insisted on taking Pro to lunch again. They had just gotten settled at their favorite table at Lotus Dreams when Elaine launched in.

"So, spill the beans. What's going on with you?" Elaine asked. "I saw you were shifting even before I left for my trip, but now you have all of this energy. In fact you have a bounce in your step I've never seen before. What's up? Is there a new man in your life?"

"Elaine, really? You, too? That's what my mother and sister said. OK, I have started dating again, but there is no one special. I'm not looking for anything serious. And I am certainly not looking to find my happiness in someone else. That's a big shift. Talk about reprogramming."

"See, like I told you, you DO live up to your nickname. Congratulations, Pro! I'm proud of you."

That evening Pro received a call out of the blue. It was Doria Fleming, an old friend from art school. "Doria! How in the world are you?"

"I'm doing great, Pro. I have an exhibition coming up," she said.

"That's wonderful, Doria. I'm not surprised. I always found your work dynamic."

"Thanks, Pro. I appreciate that. The exhibition is actually why I'm calling. One of the artists had to cancel at the last minute and the launch is next week. There are three of us carrying the bulk of the exhibit – Dana Barton, Karl Swift and myself. We just need a few more pieces to flesh out the gallery showing – otherwise one wall will be empty. What do you think? Do you have some art you'd like to show? The installation is next Wednesday for a Friday opening at ImagineArts Gallery. There will be a little champagne and cheese event for the initial reception, then our work will be shown for six weeks."

"Wow! I love that gallery. But that is SOON."

"I know. I'm sorry for the short notice. To be honest, the artist you are replacing… well, do you remember Jake Bonnevitch?"

"Little Jakey? Of course, I do. I always thought his work was brilliant."

"I don't know if you knew – he battled a lot with depression."

"I remember he always seemed to be down on himself – no matter how positively the class or Professor Tilson responded."

"Yep, that's our Jakey. Well, he OD'd yesterday. His family is dealing with far too much to even consider his work being included now.

"Oh, my god! I'm so sorry to hear that. I remember he kept to himself a lot, but I had no idea. He was a really sweet guy. That's awful."

"It is. Incredibly sad. We're dedicating the exhibition to honor him. So, I really need you. What do you say?"

"Is there a cost involved? Is there a theme? What would you need from me?"

"Because you're saving my butt, I will cover the cost. And I have a truck if you have any larger pieces that need transporting. It's a collection of artists, so we are calling it Artistic Visions. Unfortunately, the press release has gone out and the posters are made and distributed, so your artist's statement and bio will only appear at the gallery showing itself. Is that cool?"

"Sure. I'm happy to help out. Actually, it sounds like a terrific opportunity. I've been so wrapped up in making a living the thought of exhibiting my own art never even crossed my mind. I appreciate you thinking of me, Doria."

"Are you kidding me? You're a lifesaver. Thanks, Pro. Let's talk in the next couple of days and work out details."

Only when the conversation was through did the impact of what she just committed herself to really land. *What have I just done? Am I out of my mind? What do I even have that I can show? Pieces from school? I guess I could pull some of the work from my senior show out of storage. But those were painted years ago, and they don't really represent me anymore. My work since then has felt so piecemeal.*

Could I really show some of the Kermuffle paintings? Is it crazy that the thought gives me goosebumps, makes me giggle and terrifies me all at once? Totally! They're not even matted or framed yet.

Pro took a deep breath. *Then I guess there is work to do!*

The next few days were a whirlwind in which Pro laid out her artwork, chose four Kermuffle pieces to display, framed and matted them, wrote her artist's statement and before she knew it, she was ready for the installation.

When she saw her four pieces on the wall in the gallery, she heaved a sigh of relief.

I can't believe I did all of that in eight days. It came up so fast there was no time to get stuck in my head second-guessing myself. Otherwise, I don't think I would have decided to "ride the Kermuffle wave." I certainly wouldn't have found the courage to exhibit versions of my Kermuffleland adventures; they're so different from the rest of my work. Maybe this was a crazy idea. Well, no turning back now. There they are – and whatever happens, happens.

Only after her art was installed did the impact of how this all came about sink in. Thursday after she got home from The Gridline she cried a lot.

I have been so busy between work and getting my pieces prepared, I haven't had time to think about you, Jakey. Little Jakey. I remember laughing when we first met and you introduced yourself that way – all 6'4" and 160 pounds of you. You loved that contrast – that irony. I remember we never knew how you would show up – what color your hair would be or how you would be dressed. It was like you kept trying on all of these personalities. And I remember your kindness.

Jakey, I am so sorry that you're gone. It should have been you installing your brilliant artwork yesterday. I do appreciate the opportunity. I'm just sorry it came this way. I hope you are at peace.

Friday was a blur. Only as she was dressing up for the evening launch did it strike her: *I have been so busy getting this together I haven't told anyone about it, not even the kids at The Gridline. I didn't even think to invite anyone to the opening reception tonight.*

Hmmmm. Who would I have invited if I had actually had time to think about it? My parents? No, I don't need to be faced with their judgment, especially not tonight. My students? I don't think inviting a bunch of eight-to-twelve-year-olds to a champagne event on a Friday night is exactly appropriate. Elaine? For sure! But let me just get through tonight and I have a few weeks to let people know. Here we go.

It was a festive event. While the primary focus was on the three artists who were exhibiting much more work, Pro's paintings got their share of attention. She was grabbing some champagne when she saw Professor Tilson, her favorite art teacher, perusing her work. Her heart raced.

Of course, she would be here. We were all her students. I want to say hi, but… Get over yourself, Pro.

"Professor Tilson. How kind of you to come."

"Of course. I wouldn't have missed it."

"So, what do you think?"

"It's a very interesting exhibit."

"You know what I mean." *Dammit, I promised myself I wasn't going to put her on the spot. Too late for that now.*

"You've been doing a lot of commercial art for a while, haven't you? I remember you emailing me that you were working for an advertising agency?"

"Yes. I worked for Atkins Advertising for four years and recently Clive Bennett Advertising Associates took over the firm."

"I'm guessing you haven't had a lot of time to devote to your own artwork?"

"That is certainly true.," Pro replied.

"That can be a challenge – absolutely. Do you really want to know what I think?"

Nope. Not at all. Big mistake. I take it back. But what she said aloud was, "Yes, of course."

"Well, I can see how your work has gotten refined."

"Thank you."

"But that is not always necessarily a good thing. These four pieces are part of a larger series you are working on called Dreamscapes, correct?

Pro nodded.

"Perhaps these pieces have more coherence in that larger context."

So basically, they make no sense now? I get it.

"There is a lot of exuberance and energy in your work here and that is compelling, yet that sometimes seems to be at odds with the slickness of the lines. There is also a lack of cohesion, as if you are trying to cram too many ideas into a single painting. That is especially evident here in 'Kermuffle Revelry,' particularly with four specific figures that don't look like they belong in this world you have created."

I would say that pretty well captures how I feel right now. No idea where I belong. And here I thought things were going so well.

"I'm sure you are just finding your own style and that can be tough when commercial work places specific demands on you. I will be interested in seeing how your work evolves. It is really nice to see you again, Pro. Best of luck."

Pro was numb. The blood drained out of her face and she couldn't move.

So, basically, I don't know what the hell I'm doing – besides cramming too many ideas together. Guess I'm not the artist I thought I was. Sorry to disappoint you, Professor. I guess I let you down, too, Jakey. I really wanted this to be a tribute to you that would have made you proud. I'm so sorry.

"Pro? What a surprise."

The voice jolted her out of her reverie like a barrel of ice water slammed in her face. Ash.

Pro forced herself to breath and compose herself as she slowly turned to face her ex-boyfriend.

"Hello, Ash." She didn't even try to muster a smile.

"I had no idea you were part of this showing."

Pro shrugged. *You look better than ever. Damn you!*

Then Pro noticed his stunning companion, who looked at Ash expectantly. "Oh! This is Madeline Styverling... my fiancé. Madeline, Kathryn Proscher, ah - Pro."

So, this is Miss Massachusetts – in the flesh. Beautiful long naturally blonde hair, perfect dazzlingly white teeth. The two of them are, without a doubt, a power couple.

"It's a pleasure to meet you, Kathryn."

Pro nodded with a slight smile. *Is this really happening? Unbelievable.*

Pro stared at Ash, who was flustered. "I didn't realize you were part of this exhibition. You weren't mentioned on the flyer we saw."

"I was a last minute replacement," Pro said, her gaze drilling through him.

Oh, yeah! Thanks for reminding me. I wasn't even originally invited. Jakey had to die for me to be here.

"So, this is your work?" Madeline asked.

Just keep your focus on Miss Massachusetts and pretend that you don't need to scream at Ash and rip his face off for showing up like this. This is not a dream.

"These four pieces, yes," Pro replied.

"They caught my eye from across the room," the beauty queen lawyer continued. "They're so colorful and fun. They remind me of something my kid sister would do."

"Oh! Your sister is an artist?" Pro struggled to stay focused.

"Burgeoning", Miss Massachusetts said with a radiant smile. "She's twelve."

"Ah," was all Pro could say, refusing to look at Ash. "Would you excuse me?" Pro forced herself to stay composed as she walked slowly out the door of the gallery and past its big glass windows. Only then did she brace herself against a building and force herself to stifle the mix of emotions that threatened to come rumbling up. *Just get home. You can fall apart there.*

When she slammed her apartment door and locked it behind her, she collapsed against it and crumpled to the floor. She cried and wailed for what felt like hours before she mustered the energy to climb into bed.

Great! I'm an artist who lacks cohesion and paints like a twelve year old. Please God, let me drift off into Kermuffleland.

Instead, she plunged into a sinkhole of visions and voices, where her paintings, and Ash and Miss Massachusetts and Clive and Little Jakey and Professor Tilson, even her mother and father whirled around knocking her off balance as she fell and fell into the earth that swallowed her with no silk clothes to grab onto – no safety net – falling through steam holes bursting with ridicule and judgement.

To her surprise, she landed, finally, on her feet. She was waving and smiling and, as she had requested, there were the Kermuffles. They were jumping up and down and waving goodbye with their little branchlike arms. Pro felt Zor and Stribjus and Loahn around her and she smiled at them gratefully. She was safe. She took a deep breath.

I'm okay.

12. THE CLEARING

They had barely left their new Kermuffle friends when Pro stopped in her tracks.

"What is it, Pro?" Zor asked.

"You're hearing it again, aren't you?" Loahn said.

"Yes. The Beckoner is calling to me again. And I know I have to answer."

Was the group of listeners I felt in Kermuffleland– was that the Agency? I thought so then. But now, that doesn't feel right somehow. For just a moment back there, I thought I had found what I was looking for. Apparently, I was wrong.

She said to her friends, "The Beckoner holds the key. I know she does."

Zor nodded. "Well, if we want to have any hope of rescuing the Beckoner, we need to regroup and create a game-plan. We have to get out of this jungle to get our bearings."

Loahn said, "We also need to get some rest." Before Zor could protest, he added, "It's been a really full day."

"We'll keep going till we find a clearing," Zor said finally.

Loahn smiled. "Yes, of course."

Pro was amused to see how Zor reacted to Loahn's smiling response. While it wasn't quite clear if Loahn's voice held just the slightest bit of sarcasm, Zor betrayed the hint of a smile. Pro was surprised that Zor looked not smug, but pleased.

They forged ahead through the dense vegetation. The tall trees with many roots made the traveling rough. Pro was amazed that there were no biting bugs to ward off. She heard a low buzzing noise at times, but never saw anything remotely bee-like.

Darkness came upon the travelers quickly. The dense jungle gave way to a clearing. Thanks to supplies in Stribjus' coat, they were able to create a fire there.

As they settled down to sleep, it came out of nowhere. Felagor. Its ferocious heads blew out the fire with an enormous wind that scattered the travelers. They were plunged into darkness so suddenly that Loahn had no time to focus his energy to provide light, or even diminish the red glow of his chest that responded to the attack. 🦋

Stribjus, tripped up by one of the appendages, fell, rolled, then somersaulted to his feet. The shadow lord-part of the creature lashed out at Zor, stabbing her shoulder just above her heart. Even in the pitch blackness, Pro could feel herself pulled toward what she knew was the mirrored surface she had faced before; she could hear the voices of judgment and doubt roaring through her head.

Loahn rebounded fast, radiating light so the travelers could get their bearings. Back on his feet, Stribjus hurled smoke bombs of purple and green, paint bombs of yellow and orange, and balls of sticky goo at the creature. This time, however, Felagor was ready for Stribjus' attacks. The monster's heads gusted the smoke away, blasting the paint and sticky goo back at the travelers.

Stribjus did a forward roll, barely escaping the hand that reached out to grasp him. Loahn managed to pull Pro down before they were covered in paint and immobilized by goo as the voices pounded away at her. She put her hands over her ears, but it felt like the voices were racing inside her head.

"I can't do this anymore – not with you."

"You think you're an ARTIST? Don't be ridiculous!"

"I'm sure, you're just finding your own style."

"Pro? Really? PRO? Hahahahaha!"

"Exactly like my sister... she's twelve."

"YOU CAN'T MAKE A LIVING DOING ART."

She could feel the mirror pulling at her, drawing her in, even as she noticed one of the appendages grabbing Loahn's ankle, which sent him toppling before Stribjus stomped on it and the

Felagor Attacks in the Night

hand released its grip to pursue the trickster. Even wounded, Zor fought the dark warrior-part of Felagor. Then Pro felt in her own gut the kick the creature made to Zor's stomach. Zor went flying, landing with a thud.

Fighting to get through the barrage of voices in her head, Pro heard Loahn calling out, "Pro, we have to get out of here." Rivetted by the mirror, she felt like she was in a trance, seeing all of this occur, but not really connected to it.

"Zor is in trouble. She needs help," Stribjus said.

Frozen, Pro watched Stribjus drag Zor out of reach just as the dark lord lashed out and two of the appendages dove toward the warrior princess. Pro saw Loahn help Stribjus pull Zor into the jungle and out of harm's way. Zor wasn't moving. *Oh my God! Is she dead?* Pro thought. Then she was plunged back into her own dilemma as the creature split the air with its earthshaking roar. Sulfurous smoke curled around Pro's legs.

Just as Felagor's claws appeared before her face to pull her in, Stribjus wrested Pro out of the clutch of the terror's mesmerizing power, leaping over a hand that grabbed for his leg and dodging two heads that hurtled toward them.

Pro still felt like she was in a dream, moving underwater. Felagor's roars followed the travelers as they stumbled through the darkness to the safety of the jungle. They managed to reach another clearing. Pro prayed that Felagor could not move through the undergrowth to find them, as the call of the Beckoner engulfed her. *The music feels different somehow. Why is that? This isn't a cry for help. It's a call to wake up. What? What needs my attention?* she thought, as the Beckoner's music brought her back to conscious awareness.

The light from the torch Stribjus had crafted helped Pro shake off the trance she felt herself in. She saw Loahn cradling Zor with one hand on her stomach and the other by her shoulder. She could see blood oozing between his fingers and spilling across Zor's torso.

Loahn shouted, "Stribjus, we have to stop the flow of blood in her chest."

"Done," Stribjus said. Pulling a scarf from his coat, he applied pressure to the wound.

Thank God she's breathing, Pro thought, as she saw rainbow light emanating from Loahn, surrounding Zor then pouring into her. It felt to Pro like he was willing her to heal, pulling her back from the dark invitation of death.

But the process was taking its toll on Loahn. She knew it somehow in her bones, then heard it. Loahn wailed as his own body became wracked with pain. Pro watched in horror as Zor gained strength, but Loahn writhed like life was being wrung out of him.

When voices called out to Pro she knew what she had to do, though she didn't consciously understand why. "Stribjus, we have to pull them apart."

"Why? He's helping her. She's getting stronger. See?'

Pro was insistent, "Help me. Now!"

Though Loahn's hands seemed almost welded to Zor, Stribjus and Pro managed to disengage them from her body. Then they moved the princess out of Loahn's reach.

Loahn fell back immobilized.

"See how Zor is doing," Pro said to Stribjus as she hovered over Loahn. Heaving huge breaths, Loahn appeared to be hyperventilating.

She placed her hand on his chest. She looked into his deep blue eyes. "I'm sorry, Pro," he whispered. She had no idea what he was talking about, but it broke her heart. All she could think to say was, "Just rest. It will be all right."

Are you crazy? What about this could possibly be all right?

"Zor's breathing better now," Stribjus reported. "It looks like her chest wound is knitting back together. It's stopped bleeding completely."

After several moments, Pro heard Zor ask, "What happened?"

"You were hurt – badly," Stribjus told her. "We had to get out of there. We were afraid we were going to lose you. If it hadn't been for Loahn, I think..."

"Where is he?" Zor asked.

"He's here," Pro replied. "He's really weak. If we hadn't pulled his hands off of you, I was afraid that . . ."

The look on Zor's face stopped Pro cold. Only in photos from war torn countries had Pro ever seen a face truly stricken with grief. But she saw it now.

"We have to get help," Zor said.

"I can run back to Kermuffeland and see if they will help us," Stribjus offered.

"We don't have time. Stribjus, on the inside edge of my left boot is an amulet. I can't move my arm right now, so I need you to hand it to me. Please."

In the blink of an eye, Stribjus had the medallion in Zor's right hand. Zor struggled, but she managed to hold it up. Pro saw that it was silver with a blue stone shining in its center.

Zor stared at the medallion with reverence. Pro wondered if that's what prayer was like for Zor's people.

As Zor summoned what little strength she had to speak, it sounded like an invocation, "Astara, this is your daughter Zor. Hear me now. Aknathoon, Ak jeel. Akthoon kortembi. I need you. I need your help. I need your healing power. Sornlall. Sornla bloon klaster. Please. Please find me. Find us. Aball skool. Aball skoolan." That request took the last bit of strength she could muster. She fell back to the ground, unconscious.

Suddenly, eight beings of light materialized. For a moment Pro thought she had died and that they were angels. They said not a word as they encircled the four weary travelers then Pro, too, lost consciousness.

She woke up in a cold sweat. She could barely breath. What time is it? 10:15? *Oh, God! I'm late for work.* Pro ran to the bathroom and splashed water on her face. She was shaking. *What a mess I am. Should I just call in sick and admit defeat? No. No! Soldier on.* She charged to the closet and was grabbing clothes when she realized, *It's Saturday!*

"It's Saturday, " she reaffirmed out loud. "At least, I'm pretty sure it is Saturday, unless I slept all the way through Monday." She checked her phone to be sure.

Yep, it's Saturday, all right! So many terrible things happened last night, it feels like it's been days.

On her phone she saw that there were three messages from Doria.

I can't go there right now. I can't bear to listen to any voices from the outside world.

Pro texted, "Sorry, Doria. I am exhausted. I need to burrow in for the weekend. I'll let you know when I come out of the tunnel. I hope the exhibit is going well. Thanks for everything."

"Thus ends my responsibilities for the weekend," Pro said aloud, trying to smile, or at least to hold back the tears she felt welling up inside.

Now if I could only stop thinking - about the gallery and last night and Professor Tilson, and Jakey and Zor and Loahn and on and on.

She heaved a sigh that drained the adrenalin, panic-induced energy out of her.

I wish I could run away, but I'm too exhausted to move.

Back to bed! She threw herself down and hugged her pillow tightly. *I think that is the plan for the weekend. Don't think about Ash, or Miss Massachusetts, or Jakey, or...*

13. ASTARA, THE HEALING WORLD

Pro dreamt of an incredible roaring that pulsated through her, then turned into machinery. She found herself on an assembly line painting doll's eyes – but only the left ones – *How do I even know that?* – before they were popped into the heads of dolls. A doll became her older sister, Patricia, that laughed at her as she ran away to hide and seek and hide. She hid in a closet full of furry inquisitive creatures who trembled fearfully at every little sound. When she peeked out, she smelled something crisp and clean like citrus. Then she saw Clive and Ash strutting down a hallway arm in arm. Their path was crisscrossed by men and women dancing by, throwing wide swaths of colorful fabric before the two men so their designer shoes never had to touch the ground.

The fabric turned into neon smoke with a faintly acrid smell and she heard what sounded like sparring martial artists, then felt herself pulled into a funhouse of horrors. A cacophony of sounds warped into schoolmates laughing – her mother's stern voice piercing the darkness. The sound of a child's weeping echoed through the empty dark.

Then a calm settled over her, like a vibration creating a soothing blanket of peace. The nightmares melted away and she drifted on clouds, floating deeper into sleep.

She awoke more calmly than she could ever remember awakening before. There was no sudden start as an alarm went off, just a peaceful drifting into awareness.

She was on a large crystalline bed that shimmered silver and pale blues and greens and the lightest of grays. She would have expected the crystalline bed to be hard and uncomfortable, but she had never felt so protected, comforted, and safe. The bed caressed her. Pro was not exactly sure she was not still dreaming. Everything around her seemed to glow with a soft, soothing light.

Where am I? Am I in a hospital? And what am I wearing? She could only describe it as a loose-fitting shift of the softest material imaginable. It was feathery lavender.

Pro tried to move but felt like she was in a stupor. As her mind became more alert, Pro began to look around her. The room had warm pools of light providing a soothing ambient illumination.

Surveying the room, she realized she was in a sphere. It was a good sized, transparent sphere with no discernable door. While it was transparent, Pro was also aware that her spherical home was awash with color, a rich mauve through which a rainbow of other colors rippled. The soft light show was soothing, as was the faint smell of sandalwood and roses. The silky sound of suspended chords drifted to her from an instrument she could not define.

Pro sensed the sphere was somehow alive, like a companion attuning and attending to her needs. As she became more conscious, she felt a churning in her body. Then, it seemed the rainbow pattern of colors through the crystalline bed, the reassuring smells and vibrations, were helping to release the knot in the pit of her stomach, the catch in her throat, and the pounding in her brain.

Looking out beyond the confines of her healing sphere she saw geometric shapes of various sizes, many of them inhabited. It was like being in a strange geometry land. *Maybe I am still dreaming. Wait! Define dreaming.*

Her eyes came into focus, and she noticed in a spinning diamond nearby an odd young man juggling smaller objects that kept changing colors and shapes, which apparently made him smile and laugh and even backflip – while he juggled. He was wearing a loose-fitting tunic of pale oranges and golds. Stribjus, her mind informed her. Then the memories came flooding back.

When he noticed her, he stopped juggling and leaned her direction. The quizzical look on his face with his eyebrow raised silently asked her, "Would you like some company?"

Astara, The Healing World

Not at all sure what she needed, Pro shrugged. With that tacit permission, Stribjus stepped out of the membrane where he was juggling and simply stepped into Pro's sphere. She felt it expand to accommodate his additional energy.

"Good morning," he said plopping down facing her.

"Is it?" she asked.

"Is it good or is it morning?" he bantered back. "Well, it is good, because we are still alive. As for whether or not it is morning – I have no idea. I have not yet figured out how light works in this world. Or time for that matter. But I know you have been asleep for a very long while."

"Where are the others? Are they all right?" She noticed for the first time that her entire body ached.

"I haven't seen Zor or Loahn since we were brought here."

She gazed at Stribjus as he stood on his head, waving his arms and legs like a semaphore signal, wriggling his fingers and toes at her. Pro just stared at him.

How can he take all of this so lightly? she thought.

He took a multicolored scarf out of his coat and stuffed it in his mouth. Then he began to pull one bright yellow corner of the scarf out of his left ear, then a green end out of his right ear. As he ran the cloth back and forth between his ears the scarf kept changing colors.

"Just clearing my head," he quipped, flashing her his crooked grin.

Pro couldn't bring herself to smile. In fact, she felt sadder than ever as she thought: *Everything is so easy for you, isn't it, Stribjus? Just make it a game, laugh at it and everything is fine.*

Withdrawing the scarf from his head, Stribjus placed it around Pro's neck, then plopped down next to her, his leg snuggled against hers. Neither of them spoke, unsure what to say. Finally, Stribjus sang a little ditty:

"Wrapped in gloom and feeling glum?

"Monsters blotting out the sun?

"When there's nothing to be done –

"You can always turn – and – run."

Pro snapped, "I guess when you move as fast as you do, running away is always the perfect solution."

She regretted the words as soon as they were out of her mouth when she felt his body shudder and saw the pain behind his eyes as he winced.

Stribjus looked into Pro's eyes. "Fair enough, but does wrapping yourself in gloom make you feel better?"

Pro considered that idea as she gazed into his eyes. "I don't know. Maybe sometimes it does. The truth is – it's what I am feeling – and I spent way too many years trying to stuff the feelings people around me didn't want to deal with," she said, tears welling up. "And besides, why isn't it okay to be sad? Life isn't always fun."

"I know, believe me, I know," he said. "I'm sorry, I didn't mean to tell you to stuff your sadness or ignore what you're feeling."

"You just seem to laugh things away. Like it doesn't matter that two of our friends may be close to death, or even dead for all we know."

Stribjus gingerly brushed the tears from Pro's cheeks. "When I was growing up there was so much to feel sad about, with a family that had no idea what to do with me and brothers always fighting to prove they were strongest, I rebelled against it – the sadness. So, I suppose I overcompensate. Sorry."

"There are worse faults to have."

"I guess." He smiled. "And I get that it can be aggravating at times. Honestly, I never really thought about it before, but I think I use humor and magic to remind me that things can change—and they will change, no matter what I do. So, if I can take something that, from one perspective might appear not so nice, or even ugly," with that, he pulled an orange toad-like creature from behind Pro's left ear, "and turn it into something that is perhaps softer – that some might consider more beautiful."

As he passed his left hand over his right, covering the toad, a beautiful bouquet of feather flowers burst up from his hands. The action startled Pro and in spite of the myriad of feelings running through her, she half-smiled and almost chuckled.

Stribjus grinned at her. "If I can help someone smile or laugh, even just for a moment, I think that makes a difference. I hope it does anyway."

Pro marveled at this bit of unexpected wisdom. *I think I need to remember that,* she thought to herself. *It's an option – AND I still can honor feeling sad if that's what I need.*

"If I'm driving you crazy with my positivity, just let me know." He grinned. "If you need to be left alone, or a friendly ear, or someone to hold your hand – I'm here for you."

"That is really sweet of you, Stribjus. Right now, I have no idea what I need. I don't want to deny or avoid the sadness, but I don't want to get wrapped up in it either."

She paused as she considered how she saw him slightly differently now, "You really are wonderful, you know."

When he smiled back, Pro thought he almost seemed shy, shrugging his shoulders as she looked deep into his eyes. She hadn't noticed before how they sparkled brown and amber. And now she saw the pain and sadness behind their sparkle.

Still gazing into his eyes, she asked, "Are you okay? I mean, REALLY, are you okay?"

Stribjus was stunned by the question. Pro could see when his shoulders twitched that the question jolted him. As he opened his mouth, she was sure he was going to come back with some light-hearted retort, but he was speechless.

Pro took his hands as his sparkling eyes stirred with confusion and welled up with gratitude.

"I don't think anyone has ever asked me that before—not quite like that. Not since my mom passed… and that was years ago. Thank you for asking."

"I care."

"Why should you care about me," he asked. "You barely know me."

"Are you kidding? You're my friend. You're right, we have known each other very briefly and already you have saved my life at least twice, when you could just as easily have run away at breakneck speed. How many people would do that for someone they hardly know? So, I am really asking—how are you?"

Stribjus looked in Pro's eyes, then at her mouth, then away, then back at her. She saw a barrage of reactions flash across his face so fast that she couldn't pin any of them down, except to imagine that they mirrored the complex feelings running through her: doubt, fear, hope, caution, relief, even curiosity.

As he turned his head away, almost tucking it into his right shoulder, she could feel it wasn't shyness or timidity she was witnessing. It was much more. Pro put her arm around his shoulder and Stribjus melted into her arms with a sigh and the barest of whimpers.

"I know," she whispered, "I'm afraid, too. I hadn't even realized how much you three mean to me. But the thought of losing any of you right now is devastating. Especially when I am the one who put us all in danger. How can I forgive myself if Loahn dies?"

They held each other for the longest time. The physical contact said so much more than any words could say.

The image of Ash holding her flashed in Pro's head as she thought, *I've never felt this kind of comfort and support when I was with Ash. Why was that? I know he tried, especially after Grandma Molly died, he had held me for what seemed like days and weeks. But it was never like this. Why not? What's different?*

As she and Stribjus cried and sighed in each other's arms, she felt completely present with his emotions – and her own, even as part of her was ferreting for answers, striving to make sense of the images and emotions charging through her.

Pro's thoughts raced on. Handsome, strong, stoic Ash. He was all of that, but that wasn't all. He was a gentle and passionate lover, and he knew how to bring her body to life. In fact, it was in their lovemaking he felt most present to her. *Why does this feel so different? Why does sitting here with our arms wrapped around each other, with no hint of sexual charge, feel like the most intimate moment I have ever had?* Pro wondered.

When the answer came Pro felt like someone had rapped the side of her head and grabbed her shoulders.

Maybe the sexual charge, or the absence of it here is part of the difference. Not always, but more often than not, the comfort of holding each other led Ash and I to sex. And the sex was great, but with that came some level of expectation, maybe a kind of pressure to perform, and a sense of escaping into sex, so I didn't have to face all of the other things I was feeling.

"So, this is a new level," M2 said.

Okay, but a new level of what? Honesty? Openness? Vulnerability? Oh, my God, it is! Ash never really allowed himself to be completely open – well, not this open with me. Never in our five years together did he ever really let his guard down. He had to be the man – to be strong for me, and for his own sense of self.

And I never allowed myself to be completely honest about my feelings with Ash either, she admitted to herself. *Somewhere deep inside my shields were always up, too. And with good reason,* she thought. *How many times have I been ridiculed for being too emotional – too sensitive?*

"You have to be strong to survive in this world, Kathryn," her mother had said. "Otherwise, people will just walk all over you."

The realization sunk into Pro's stomach as she thought, *I learned to equate vulnerability with weakness.*

But wrapped in vulnerability with Stribjus, she didn't feel weak. *So many feelings are raging to the surface as we just hold each other,* she thought, *but it doesn't feel like I am giving my power away – not at all. I'm not giving up or giving in.*

Pro felt M2 close by, smiling paternally – or was it maternally? *Well, parentally.*

Then with a jolt, a question coursed through her. *Do I have the courage to be vulnerable?* She sighed. *M2, do I have –* but she couldn't even finish the question. It was too much to try and wrap her brain around, so Pro just held Stribjus tight and let her feelings flow however they would. In fits and starts they both sighed, laughed, cried and held on to each other for dear life.

Pro had no idea how long she and Stribjus had been wrapped in each other's arms when she felt a gentle hand on her shoulder.

Pro opened her eyes to see a vision of loveliness next to her. A diamond headband held back the woman's long flowing raven hair, while its sapphire stone shone with a powerful energy. The stone itself seemed to emanate peace, but Pro was aware of waves of sadness that swelled through the woman who wore it. That whirl of emotions held her attention so steadfastly that it took Pro a minute to focus on the beautiful face beneath it. The woman was radiant – and strangely familiar.

She looks so much like Zor, Pro thought, *but so different in aspect – humbler, with a kind of sweet grace and a great sorrow. A twin sister?*

The woman smiled the smallest of smiles. "It is me." The sadness in her eyes jolted Pro's solar plexus.

"Zor?" Stribjus jumped in. The beautiful woman nodded.

"In the flesh. Looking a little different, I know. Are the two of you all right?"

Pro felt a thick layer of anxiety lift off of her heart, though the turmoil churning in her solar plexus remained. "We were just trying to figure that out – what all right is, I mean. Seeing you up and about is a big relief. You're alive!" Pro gave Zor a huge hug. She felt Zor brace against the hug, but her friend didn't pull away. "We weren't sure if you made it. We were concerned about you and Loahn."

"So, how are you, really? Where are we? How did we get here?" Stribjus rapid-fired the questions.

"I am recovering rapidly," Zor said. "We are in Astara, my adopted home. The healers here told me Loahn took on most of my pain and injuries. I'm worried about him." Pro felt Zor's shoulders tense up as she fought back tears.

"He is presently in one of our other healing domas." The male voice startled Pro. Her attention had been so wrapped up in Zor, she hadn't even realized there were several people present. It was a veritable entourage. An older couple stood closest to Zor, while two men and two women were in attendance further in the background.

Zor introduced them, "This is my father Helastion and my mother Melara. My friends Pro and Stribjus."

Pro noticed the white billowing robes first, laced with copper trimming. Traveling up with her gaze, Pro couldn't tell if the light that she saw shimmering off of the beautiful iridescent robes was shining from the fabric itself or was actually radiating from Zor's parents.

As she looked into their faces, what she noticed was a potent gentleness. Pro was sure she had never met anyone so radiantly powerful, yet so soothing and reassuring at the same time as the two beings standing before her.

"Thank you for helping us," Pro said.

Helastion inclined his head. "It is what we were made for – to reach out to those in need and assist the healing process."

What you were made for? Pro thought. The phrase took her aback. *I have never thought about my life that way before. What was I made for?*

Melara broke her reverie. "Thank you for bringing Zor back to us. It is the first time she has ever asked us for help since she left home."

"Could we see Loahn?" Pro asked.

Helastion spoke again, "I was about to suggest that."

"He could use your healing support," Melara added.

Stribjus crinkled his eyes. "Healing support? I don't know anything about healing people."

Zor said, "I don't think that's true, Stribjus. Your playfulness makes you a very healing spirit."

Pro could have sworn she saw the jokester blush.

"The healers of our world do very deep work," Melara said, "but when the wounded person is surrounded by the support of those who know them and care about them, the healing process goes deeper and is accelerated."

"What can we do?" Pro asked.

"See him in your imagination as healthy and vibrant," Helastion said. "It is vital now that you help him remember who he is – how strong he is… Take us to Loahn."

"Me?" Pro stared at him bewildered.

"No." Melara smiled. "My husband was making a request of the space. The orientation here is spatial, rather than linear. If you wish to connect with or find someone specific and if they are available to your energetic connection, a pathway will light up to lead you to them." Melara's hand unfolded toward a row of lights that had appeared. "This is the path to Loahn."

Melara and Helastion traveled hand in hand, leading them not so much through hallways, as through open spaces that glowed with various qualities of light. More structures of various shapes and sizes came into view as they left Pro's sphere.

Melara said, "What you are seeing around you as we travel are the domas. These are chambers of mutable configurations. All members of our world occupy such spaces and restructure them to their needs, so they expand and contract as you might have noticed, but they can also completely reconfigure based on what is needed and the intentions set forth by the occupants.

Zor chimed in, "You simply need to request what you need – food, a shower, a larger bed – anything and it materializes for you."

"Just by asking?" Stribjus said in amazement. When Melara nodded, Stribjus continued, "In my world you have to fight – for everything."

Pro saw before them a transparent pyramid where an elderly teal being was humming and beating out a rhythm as something fluttered down from the room's peak. As they drew closer, Pro saw that they looked like purple rose petals.

A little further on their left Pro saw dancers forming patterns for/to/with a young woman in what appeared to be a reclining chair.

The dancers kept changing patterns – sometimes around the girl, sometimes in front of her. It was a magical flowing dance.

As they watched, Pro noticed they were dancing geometric configurations – now in two lines, then a diamond, softening into a

Domas of Astara

circle, then flowing into a spiral.

"It's a beautiful dance," Pro said. "How can it be that it strikes me as provocative and soothing all at once?"

Melara said, "The dancers' configurations are assisting the young woman in repatterning – reprogramming her questela – what you might call her brain/body connection. But it is more than that. The questela takes into account her senses and her landscape of emotions. Questela is an integrated ever-changing process of connection in service to wholeness. You might think of it as consciously firing on all cylinders – aligning the physical, the emotional, the intellectual, the mental, the spiritual, the sensual and the energetic bodies."

Wow! That is a lot to take in, Pro thought. *Wait! Did she say reprogramming?*

"This re-encoding, given form by the physical patterns of the dancers, creates energetic flows that stimulate profound kinetic shifts. These shifts are calibrated to this young girl's particular needs, helping her to realign with the truth of who she really is – beyond what she has been told she was or should be. That is what you are sensing. It is an important aspect of the process questela."

Questela? Pro thought. *I have never thought about the brain/body connection or the notion of a human being firing on all cylinders before, let alone in such expansive terms. I like that there is a word that captures that synergy. Questela. I want to remember that.*

They passed a huge geodesic dome with a monolithic crystal obelisk in the center, surrounded by a large circle of people, well, some of them looked like people, of various hues, ages, and genders.

"What is that?" asked Stribjus.

The group stood by the dome as Helastion explained, "That is the Circle of Light, comprised of 90 of our elders – beings from many worlds. At any given moment, 27 of them are sitting in circle shining light, peace, and love throughout our world and to other worlds as well."

"But some of them look so young," Pro said, her gaze soaking in the array of species that comprised the Circle of Light.

Melara smiled, "We have some old souls as young as four who we consider our elders. Look at the youngest there, the little, purple-skinned girl to our right. What do you see in her face?"

Pro was taken aback. *All right, the innocence I see I expected,* Pro thought, *but there is a depth in her eyes and a serious expression on her face as she sits in perfect stillness. She seems so wise.*

Helastion went on, "In Astara we believe that each being has its own wisdom. It simply takes some longer to find and trust themselves than others. With no prompting whatsoever, that young being – we call her Ora – began meditating and focusing light and peace when she was one."

Melara said, "We are almost at Loahn's doma. He has been in a deep suspension since we brought you here. Sleep is a great restorer."

"So, he is just sleeping?" Pro bit her lip. "He's not in a coma?"

"It is accurate to describe his present state as 'being in a coma'. He is in what we on Astara call suspended life," Helastion clarified. "While he appears quite passive, this is a state of high potential, as he decides whether or not to return to consciousness."

"Wait. So, he gets to choose? Whether he dies or not?"

"What you would call his soul," Melara continued, "does, in a sense get to choose, though he might not be aware that he has a choice. That is, in part, why we brought you to him, though each of you is still in your own process of recovering from the traumas you have undergone."

Helastion explained, "We are able to encourage lucid dreaming to accelerate the healing process through various senses, utilizing the arts. We have been preparing the space here for Loahn's healing circle."

"What does that mean?" asked Pro.

"Healing is a process, which often takes place in stages," Helastion continued. "Accessing the subconscious and bringing hidden patterns into light can help a being transform."

"From what Zor has told us," Melara said, "we believe that the creature Felagor brought all of your subconscious fears to the surface. It is small wonder you are all traumatized. There is a level of recovery each of you needed individually before you could assist each other in healing wounds that are deeper than the physical. Pro, the dreambed you were on used vibrations, colors, and smells to assist your healing dreamstate. Stribjus, the juggling and magic play you were doing served to help you recover from your encounter with Felagor—to begin the processes of clearing and realigning your energies. Here in Astara, we have developed a number of healing protocols."

"Patterns of color, movement, touch, hearing and smell stimulate brain wave activity and cellular regeneration," Helastion said. "We help the cellular and DNA structures remember what it looks like, sounds like, and feels like to be healthy. That is what you have been witnessing on our journey to Loahn."

Melara continued, "You will see it even more profoundly as you sit with Loahn in his doma and participate in his process as a lucid witness."

"Lucid what?" Pro asked.

"Lucid Witness," Melara said, "Your presence as a support and a witness impacts the healing process profoundly."

"So, how do we help?" asked Stribjus.

Melara said, "All you really have to do is sit in the love you have for your friend. That makes a big difference."

With that, they stepped up to a sphere that was translucent. As Helastion waved his hand in front of it, the barrier became transparent. There, in the sphere that swirled with many colors she saw Loahn lying on a bed, his upper body raised slightly. His stillness sent chills up Pro's spine. Waves of sadness fluttered through her. *What if Stribjus and I pulled Loahn away from Zor too late to save him? What if he never wakes up?* Pro forced herself to drive the thought away.

Helastion said, "His body is recovering rapidly but his spirit needs healing. The challenge he has faced was not just physical. It was more than that – a kind of crisis of self-definition. He has designed himself to protect those he cares about. Their well-being is most important."

The visitors stepped into the sphere, and it expanded to accommodate them. Pro noticed the smell. It reminded her of lavender mixed with sandalwood – an earthy sweetness.

Loahn looked so peaceful that Pro couldn't tell if the turmoil raging inside of her was just hers, or if it also was part of the struggle Loahn was undergoing, underneath the layers of what Helastion had called suspended life.

"We will leave you now to be with your friend," Melara said. "Zor will guide you through a process to assist Loahn in his healing. The Circle of Light is shining sacred light to and through this doma to assist each of you in this process of healing."

"We wish you a smooth journey and many blessings. We will check in on you afterward," said Helastion.

And with that, they were gone.

14. SLEENAJE

Pro and Stribjus and Zor looked at Loahn. No one knew what to say.

Pro could feel the tension in the air – the energy it was taking them to hold themselves together.

After a long silence, Zor said, "I suppose we should begin." Pro and Stribjus looked at Zor, uncertain what she meant.

"I have been called to initiate a healing circle for us all." Zor continued. "We all have much sleenaje to do, but only if you are willing. Melara reviewed the protocols with me earlier, assuring that my instigating the sleenaje would be most helpful. I have not led one in over two years, but I do believe she is right. This sleenaje is mine to lead. But only if you all agree."

Pro spoke up, "What is a sleenaje?"

"Sleenaje is what Astarans call 'a shifting of old patterns,'" Zor explained. "It is a term used for any event of great change, however also describes the ongoing action of that transformation. It may take many forms, but ANY shifting out of an old habit and into a new pattern of behavior is a sleenaje."

What does that remind me of? Pro thought. Then she remembered. *Elaine talked about reprogramming. Is that what sleenaje is?*

"What do we need to do for this sleenaje?" Stribjus asked.

"First, we need to open to receive help. Then we focus our energies together to activate the process of this healing circle. In sleenaje, serving as a lucid witness is just as important as being an active participant. We activate this healing with a statement. I will demonstrate."

With a deep breath, Zor slowly opened her arms wide stating, "I open to receive support for this process of transformation." Even as she said it, Pro noticed Zor was trembling. "If you agree, please affirm your willingness to enter this healing process using whatever words reflect your truth."

"Do we have to throw our arms open?" Stribjus asked.

"It is not required," Zor replied. "While the physical connection often strengthens your affirmation of the statement, some people find it too intense, especially in their first experience of sleenaje."

Pro expected Stribjus to burst out laughing, but his face was drawn and intent as he said, "Okay – sure – I open myself to this healing process – whatever that means for me."

"Wait," Pro said. "I thought this was a healing circle for Loahn, not something about our own shifting."

"They are intrinsically connected," Zor said. "To support the transformational process for someone else may very well cause changes in the person or persons who facilitate the process. This affirmation acknowledges that possibility, so that the transformation may reverberate through all participants for the greatest good – and the greatest impact."

Pro was not prepared for the terror that bolted through her. It ripped through her heart and the emptiness in the pit of her stomach jarred loose an old, buried sense that healing for her needed to be private… to be secret, as if letting someone know you needed help was – what? Like giving away your power?

Is this statement dangerous, she thought. *I don't know why, but it terrifies me.*

She heard M2's reassuring voice. "You are not alone, Pro. I am always with you. You are more than ready for this process."

Hearing his voice in her head, something snapped in Pro. *Oh fine, NOW you show up. Where were you when we were all facing death,* she thought back aggressively.

M2 said in Pro's head, "I was there, supporting you, warning you, guiding you. But Felagor so occupied all of your senses that you could not see, hear or sense my presence."

Pro wasn't sure whether to believe the wizard or not. *Fine,* she thought, *there isn't much point in arguing.*

M2 did not pursue the subject. "You see the opportunity that is being offered. You get to choose what you wish to do with it."

Pro decided that stubbornly holding on to her anger would do her no good. So, she remembered to breathe deeply.

As she gazed at her three friends, Pro felt no pressure from them to jump into the proclamation of the affirmation – she felt only great care and concern. She didn't know why that made tears well up in her eyes. Quietly and hesitantly, she said, "I open myself – no, that's not it. I, uh, I open to transformation—and…"

Even as she said it, it didn't ring true. Pro was disgusted with herself. *I don't feel the truth of that statement. In fact, it feels like parts of me are way too scared to open themselves to transformation at all – let alone state it out loud. So, how can I say it if it feels like a lie?*

"However scared, however tentative you might be, making a statement – whatever statement you choose – helps you to set a clear intention. Commit yourself verbally – the other parts of you will catch up in their own time," M2 said.

Pro took more deep breaths to steady herself. *I can't believe it is so hard just to make a statement,* she thought. *Loahn's life hangs in the balance, and I can't even bring myself to say some sentence I am afraid I can't live up to. What kind of friend am I?*

She heard M2's voice again, "A much better friend than you give yourself credit for. You can do this, Pro. And we applaud you for doing it on your own terms in your own way. We believe in you"

Now all I have to do is learn to believe in myself, Pro thought. *Yeah, right! No problem.*

Pro took one more deep, deep breath and set her resolve, saying, "I open… to receive support… for the process… of transformation."

As she spoke, Pro felt a rush of relief pour though her whole body as she sensed a multitude of unseen witnesses lending their support.

Pro became aware of waves of soothing light flowing through her. Then the doma shifted its configuration. It became a geodesic dome. Pro wondered if the others perceived the shift the same way.

Next, the gentlest, most reassuring voice she had ever heard emanated from the doma. It felt to her like the voice was another aspect of M2 that said, "As you follow your breath in and out, allow it to expand your physical awareness, your sense of space – your very consciousness."

The soothing voice quelled her fears as she felt herself sink into a deep awareness.

M2 said, "Focus your attention in your mind's eye to the center of the doma."

As Pro shifted her mind's gaze to the center of the doma, an image materialized. She saw Zor's wounded body and Loahn approaching it. Pro saw Stribjus and herself observing, their own bodies quaking from their encounter with Felagor. The walls pulsated – like a heartbeat, throbbing.

Shimmering silver figures stepped out of the walls and surrounded the apparition that was Zor. They floated to her broken body and pulled out streams of blood red cloth which covered Zor's torso while white cloth streams poured from her head and solar plexus.

As his body lay in the coma, the image of Loahn rushed to Zor's body gathering the red cloth as the silvery figures wrapped him in it. Pro could see he was taking on Zor's pain. Steams of white cloth sprang from Loahn's head and chest to surround Zor. It seemed to Pro that Loahn's life-force was rushing in to protect Zor and stem the flow of blood and life force draining out of her. Then the action s l o w e d   d o w n – stretching time to an agonizing crawl.

"Noooooooooooo!" Pro saw her image scream.

The apparition of Loahn looked at the ghost of Pro as she sensed his voice saying, "I have to, Pro. I have to protect, comfort, and heal those I care about – so they don't have to be afraid – they don't have to suffer."

Pro sensed her own voice. "You can't, Loahn. It's too dangerous."

"It is what I DO, Pro," Loahn said. "I merge with those who touch my heart. I lighten their load and siphon the pain away."

"But you're not siphoning Zor's pain away. You're taking it on." Pro's voice wailed, "and you are drowning in it."

It was true, the red streams of cloth were waves engulfing Loahn, while the white cloth streams poured from him to soothe and energize Zor. Part of Pro noticed that it was actually a beautiful spectacle she was witnessing, this dance of red and white - or it would have been if what it symbolized wasn't so horrific.

Then Pro heard Zor's voice, "It is not your place to die for me, Loahn. I have spent my whole life preparing to do battle – facing death."

As Zor observed the scene, Pro saw her face contract and distort in pain. Loahn's sleeping body stirred.

The silver figures continued to pull out streams of reddish cloth, which the conjured images of Loahn and Zor wrapped around their wrists. They pulled against each other in a kind of tug-of-war – each unwilling to give up their pain to the other. At the same time, they cast the white cloth aside – each unwilling to allow themselves to claim more of the life force that poured between them.

Pro heard her own voice ring out, "Loahn, you HAVE to STOP. You are getting weaker."

Zor's voice raged, "I am the scout – the vanguard. I go first – the first to fall, so I will never be left behind again – the way my parents left me. You will NOT die in my place."

Loahn's voice in reply was just as loud, "I cannot stand by and let you die. That goes against everything I stand for – everything I am. I was raised to protect those I care about."

Then strains of the Beckoner's call reverberated through the room, first faintly, then gaining momentum and volume.

Pro heard M2's voice ringing through her head now. "There is death here, Pro. You must DO something." *The magician was telling the truth*, she thought. *He was there and I guess on some level I did hear his voice but was not conscious of it.*

Loahn's voice said, "I can't let you die. Let me save your life."

Zor asserted, "At the expense of your own? No! No one saves anyone, truly, Loahn. We all have our own journeys. Ultimately, we can only save ourselves. And you can't save someone from themselves. It is not your place to die for me."

Pro heard herself mutter, "I don't know. I don't know what to do. I can't do this. I don't know how…"

M2 interrupted, "It is possible to save them both, but you must get out of your own way and TAKE ACTION – NOW. Or one of them dies."

Pro saw and heard herself move toward Zor and Loahn, calling out, "Stribjus, we have to pull them apart."

As they pulled Zor and Loahn apart the red ties snapped, releasing them both.

Even though she knew this wasn't happening, that it was a memory which called forth thoughts she didn't even remember having, Pro was shaking as she heard M2 say "You did it, Pro. You stopped Loahn before he went too far and lost his life. YOU made that happen."

"With Stribjus' help," Pro said, "and yours."

"Yes," M2 replied, "but you are the one who instigated the action."

The dancers and the cloths vanished into the walls, leaving the friends shaken to their core.

Loahn's body was shivering – quaking. Pro and Zor held his hands, while Stribjus held his ankles so he would not quake off the bed. They looked at each other. They couldn't tell if he was wracked with pain or cold. Then a huge low moan rattled through Loahn's body and filled the room. He shook again and cried uncontrollably – thrashing for what felt to Pro like hours. Then he was still – spent. His breathing evened out. He was calming down. Pro, Zor and Stribjus heaved a collective sigh of relief and then all of them fell into a deep sleep as the doma materialized soft places to land.

15. RECOVERY

Pro awoke in the darkness. It took her while to get her bearings She laid very still.

Where am I? What world am I in now?

She sat up and turned on a light. She was in her bedroom - nighttime. *Ah! Planet Earth. I remember you – vaguely. Yeah! That place full of Clives and Ashes and Miss Massachusettes – Professor Tilsons and Jakeys.*

"You're not an easy place to be, you know," she said out loud as she went to the kitchen and grabbed some pomegranate juice. "Not easy at all."

She perused the juice bottle. Hmm. Pomegranates. In Greek mythology, wasn't it pomegranate seeds that Persephone ate in Hades? And then she had to go back there for months out of every year.

"A few months in hell," she found herself talking aloud again, "I know the feeling." *Hold on, Pro! The last thing we need to do is probe the world of Greek mythology.*

"I have quite enough worlds to deal with right now, thank you very much." *Okay, who was I saying that to? Myself? God? M2?*

Wait – M2? Maybe I really am losing my mind. Thank God Zor is all right. And I think Loahn will be okay, too. But I am not. She shook her head violently to ward off the tears. *You need to eat something, Pro.*

"Not hungry! I can't take this. Maybe I should paint."

Are you crazy? With Professor Tilson looking over my shoulder and Ash and Miss Massachusetts dancing around my head, the last thing I need is more evidence that I'm a failure.

"Too much thinking. It's exhausting. I'm exhausted. I need to go back to bed."

She wrote a little bit in her journal – about questelas and sleenajes, then curled up under the covers and drifted off to sleep.

It was hours later, or so it seemed to Pro, when she awoke. She saw Zor sitting alert, gazing at Stribjus smiling and moving in his sleep. When he popped up wide awake, it startled Pro so much that she almost screamed. The three friends smiled at each other.

Loahn stirred.

Pro took his hand. "Can you hear me, Loahn?"

She felt his fingers move in her hand and sighed with relief.

Eventually Loahn opened his unseeing eyes and smiled at her. "I can Pro. Why did you stop me? I mean… you saved my life…"

"I led us all into danger."

"Well, these things happen," he said with a half-hearted smile.

"I wanted you to live." Pro squeezed his hand.

"You're awake," Zor said.

"I am," replied Loahn. "I guess I must have needed a little rest."

Stribjus started crying and laughing at the same time. For a moment, Pro thought he was hysterical. *I feel exactly the same way.*

Pro asked, "Stribjus, are you all right, my friend?"

Stribjus nodded and shook his head, then seemed to do both at the same time. "I've never seen anyone so concerned for the well-being of another. In Thanton, warriors form alliances, but they would never sacrifice themselves for someone else."

Loahn said, "I wasn't making a sacrifice, Stribjus. I was just merging – that is what we do in my world. But it has never been like that before. In my home, Erinmar, I have merged with dying creatures and helped to light their way to the next world, but I have never experienced such turmoil and struggle for life or death as I did with you, Zor."

Zor leaned down to Loahn and they laid their heads together as Zor confided, "I didn't think I cared about dying, but I guess I do. I had to be armored – the warrior. Always prepared to fight. Willing to protect others and to die if that's what was called for."

Loahn said softly, "And that doesn't feel the same now?"

Zor shook her head. "I don't know, to be honest."

Loahn nodded. "I merge and hopefully bring comfort and ease suffering. In my world, the truth we live is remembering that we are more together than we are alone. But instead of merging and getting stronger when I helped, we fought. And so, I got weaker. That has never happened to me before."

"I'm not used to trusting people or asking for help," Zor bowed her head. "My home planet was all about life or death. Being wounded, my defense mechanisms kicked in. I am so sorry I put your life at risk. That was never my intention. Thank you for letting my adopted people help you."

Loahn replied, "I am grateful we both survived."

The friends smiled at each other for the longest time, no one quite knowing what to say.

"May we enter?" From outside the doma, Melara's voice broke the awkward silence.

Zor looked at her three friends. "You can say, no," she reassured them. "The process we have all just undergone is taken very seriously here." She gave them a few moments to consider how they were feeling before she asked, "Is it alright with you if Melara and Helastion visit us once more? They are my parents, Loahn." He smiled his permission to her, while Stribjus shrugged and Pro slowly, carefully nodded her head.

"It is permitted," Zor said.

Melara and Helastion passed through the walls of the doma, and their gentle light seemed to pervade the space.

Helastion spoke first, "We know you are undergoing much deep healing."

"And we wanted to prepare a feast for you," Melara added, "nourishment for your healing and a proper welcome to Astara." She gestured in the air and shimmering silver figures appeared from the walls with tables of colorful delicacies piled high.

Helastion spoke. "We want to thank you for bringing our daughter Zor home. You are welcome to stay here as long as you like. We also have a particular message for you, Pro."

Melara gazed intently into Pro's eyes. "You have been exploring new worlds and have shown great courage facing so many fears. There is grave danger for you out there. Here you can rest and be safe."

I've never thought of myself as courageous. Oh, there was plenty of foolhardy behavior – when I charged into the unknown. I thought that was just the recklessness of a wild little girl – but courageous? No.

Helastion said, "Please stay with us. Live with us. Heal with us. Stay safe."

Stay safe? What does that even mean?

"Thank you for that lovely invitation," Pro said aloud. "I will have to think about it."

Melara nodded in acknowledgment as Helastion turned his focus to Loahn. "We are so grateful that you saved our daughter's life," she said, "even though we do not support how you put your own life at risk in the process."

Helastion glanced at Melara, and a knowingness passed between them. Then he said, "We speak now of underlying truths we sense..."

"For such truths often go unspoken and opportunities are missed," Melara added.

Helastion nodded in agreement, "We would ask you to consider taking our daughter's hand in marriage. We have never seen her so humbled or concerned for another's life. And we sense the potential for a burgeoning love developing between you."

Zor blushed a deep crimson and glared at her parents, yet they continued.

Her father said, "While you have much to learn about creating clear boundaries, Loahn, those are skills which we can teach you, but your compassion, your insight, and your incredible shining heart would make you a most fit Inspirer for Astara and a wonderful partner for Zor."

Melara added, "We only ask that you consider the possibility. And with that – we will withdraw." She smiled and nodded at her husband.

Helastion said, "If there is anything else you require, simply intend it, imagine it, request it and it will appear."

"And if I want bars of gold?" Stribjus asked.

"They can be manifested. But they will be of little use to you here, and you might find that they only weigh you down," Helastion replied, smiling. "We have no currency, nor a need for it. What is requested is provided."

"We will take our leave," Melara said. "Please eat your fill and get more rest. The processes you are undergoing can be overwhelming. They take some time to integrate."

Helastion smiled in agreement, offered his arm, and they stepped out of the sphere.

After a long silence, Loahn asked, "Inspirer?"

Zor explained, "Those who guide here on Astara are called Inspirers. They do not lead per se, or even rule, but they help to expedite the will of the people and the initiatives set forth by the Circle of Light. While there are ceremonies periodically to determine who the Inspirers will be, for a long, long time the lineages of Helastion and Melara have frequently been chosen. It is a calling they had imagined for me, but one that never felt like mine."

Pro realized she had never seen her warrior friend so nervous as she continued. "I have to apologize. I am beyond mortified. I know parents have a special gift for embarrassing their offspring, but for them to put you in such an awkward position when you're just recovering – unforgiveable."

As Zor took a breath, Loahn said, "Is it true?"

"What?"

"What your parents said."

"Well, they were seriously asking you to consider being an Inspirer of Astara at some point. They don't take such things lightly," Zor replied as she looked away.

Loahn smiled at her evasive response. "That's not what I am asking, oh great warrior princess – and you know that."

Zor's head bolted up at his words, but Pro noticed as she looked in his eyes – those eyes that saw so much beyond his blindness - and he grinned warmly at Zor, there wasn't the slightest hint of sarcasm – only affection.

Loahn went on, "Were they alluding to something more than concern you might be feeling for me? They said something about–"

Zor seemed a bit defensive as she sputtered, "Well, naturally – I am very grateful. After all, you risked your life for me, and–"

"Ah! I've made you even more uncomfortable than your parents did," Loahn interrupted.

There was silence for a long time.

Pro said softly to Stribjus, "We should go."

Zor reacted immediately, "No! Please – stay. I... I want you to hear what I'm going to tell Loahn."

Pro nodded and Stribjus, to her amazement, kept silent and still.

Zor took a deep breath and faced Loahn. She took his hand between hers with gentle strength. "I care for you – all of you – more deeply than I have ever cared for anyone – and it is not just gratitude. Yes, there is that, but it is also admiration and something that I can't explain that scares me because I don't know how to trust it."

Zor stood up and moved away from Loahn. She took another deep breath and continued. "The first nine years of my life were on Triantus. When I was born, civil war had been ravaging my world for more than 50 years. I was raised from the age of three to be a warrior and I killed many of my own people by the time I was seven. At nine I was badly wounded. My mother prayed and prayed over my ravaged body for days. She barely slept or ate, so intent was she that I would heal and live."

"It was the power of her incessant prayers that reached the group of elders called The Circle of Light here on Astara. The Astarans rescued me shortly before my world destroyed itself. Eventually, Helastion and Melara adopted me, but I have never felt completely a part of this peaceful place – and certainly never felt worthy to serve as an Inspirer for it."

Then Zor got very quiet and serious. Turning to Loahn, she said, "Loahn, you deserve an honest answer to your question."

"My question?" Loahn asked.

"I do have strong feelings for you," Zor said. Pro noticed she was trembling as she spoke. "While I have tried to convince myself that it was out of friendship, gratitude, admiration – and it is indeed all of those things – I have to admit that I care about you more than I have ever cared about anyone in my life." Her mouth curled into a wry smile. "I thought I didn't fear anything, but it scares me to admit this."

"I…" Loahn stopped himself and was silent. Pro found his inability to speak sweetly charming as a light pulsed from his chest in pink and blue and yellow.

Zor said, "You don't have to say anything. In fact, I don't want you to – please. You are in the middle of a huge healing process, and I do not want you to respond out of gratitude or because of your gift for merging." She reached into a cloth purse on her hip and pulled out a necklace. It was a beautiful silver setting with a crystal that was a soft greenish blue.

Zor placed it around Loahn's neck. "I had this amulet made for you. The stone is Amazonite. It is a powerful crystal that assists the wearer in having clear boundaries. It will not inhibit your ability to merge to whatever degree you wish, but it will help you be more mindful of that process, so you do not simply merge because that is what you have always done."

Loahn gazed down toward the glowing stone on his chest, then looked again in Zor's direction. Pro thought his unseeing eyes sensed Zor more deeply than any 'seeing eyes' possibly could. "Thank you – for seeing me and for caring. I look forward to getting to know you and your world more." He smiled warmly.

Seeing these two strong-willed people so sweetly shy with each other made Pro's heart race. Why does this seem so much more meaningful than anything I ever had with Ash? In five years, did we ever share with each other so deeply? Did Ash ever really see ME? Did I ever let him? Ash and I proclaimed our love for each other many times, but that pales compared to this sweet sharing between two people who have not even acknowledged their feelings for each other as love.

All four of them fell silent until Stribjus said, "There's food!" and they all burst into laughter. Pro hadn't really paid much attention when the food had materialized. As she did so now, she noticed mounds of what looked like fresh fruits and vegetables, steaming bowls of soups, a tower of desserts. It was an incredible display.

"Food here comes from many worlds," Zor said. "If you have questions about any of it, feel free to ask."

The four friends ate, drank, laughed, and shared stories, then slept for hours and hours.

When Pro awoke to find herself back in her apartment, she was calm. "Astara is working it's magic," she wrote in her journal. "I can feel what a healing place it is – definitely a place to spend more time."

The thought amused her as she took a shower and had some breakfast. Her phone assured her it was Sunday, 11:17 am. She noticed she had more new voice messages: three more from Doria, two from her mother, one from Thom and one from Ash.

Really? Just have to turn that knife – after all these months of silence?

"Nope, not going there," she said aloud. "I'm just going to write and sketch in my journal, thank you very much." She played in her dream journal, capturing as many details as she could.

There are so many things I want to remember. I'm not ready to paint yet – or face the world, either. I know why you left it, Jakey. You were such a sweet, gentle soul. This is not an easy place to be. We have to keep proving ourselves and we get judged at every turn, and you can't trust people to be who they say they are. If I feel safer in my dreams, so be it. I declare Sunday another sleeping/dreaming day. Astara is becoming more and more real for me. And who knows? Maybe I'm not coming back.

The last thing she wrote was 'Astara calls' before she melted into sleep.

16. LIFE IN ASTARA

Pro had no idea if it was days or weeks or months that passed. While Zor, having grown up in Astara, had her own doma, the doma housing Loahn had expanded with extra rooms to accommodate Pro and Stribjus, as well as spaces they all shared.

Zor had regained her own strength, yet somehow seemed softer – not weaker at all – just a bit gentler with herself and others. She taught her friends the traditional Astaran greeting signifying both hello and farewell. Two people begin with their right hands on their hearts. Then they each inscribe a counterclockwise circle with their left hands, finally clasping hands and touching their foreheads to the back of each other's hands either one at a time or simultaneously, depending on the intimacy of the connection.

Why does that greeting feel so powerful to me? Maybe it's because there's such an honoring of each other – like respect and affection rolled into one. No, not affection. Vulnerability? Either way, it's lovely. I hope Stribjus will practice with me.

Loahn was meditating frequently and healing rapidly. Pro saw that he and Zor were growing closer with every passing day. They meditated together, took long walks on the beaches and mountains that were manifested in domas, held hands often and both smiled far more than she had ever seen either of them smile.

I did have times of laughter and sweetness like that with Ash. I guess that was before the lies. Let's not think about that – about him. He is many worlds away – in so many ways. Now here I am in Astara – wherever this is. And for how much longer?

Then she heard M2's voice. "You will know when it is time to leave, Pro. Meanwhile, you get to practice being here."

Here, meaning Astara? Pro asked in her head.

"Here meaning wherever you are," M2 replied. "And you happen to have the perfect teacher for that skill right here with you."

Stribjus?

"Stribjus."

Stribjus was just Stribjus – playful, quicksilver, juggling, inventing new ways to look at the world. He enjoyed darting around Astara, and he shared with Pro how amazed he was at how this world functioned so differently from his own.

To keep himself occupied, Stribjus started teaching people to juggle. Then he began organizing juggling competitions: Who could juggle the most objects? The most varied objects? Who could juggle the fastest? The slowest?

Pro asked him one day, "Why in the world are you setting up competitions in a world where everyone can have everything they want?"

It surprised Pro that Stribjus thought about that for a minute before he answered. She had seen how schooled he was by life to think on his feet and make fast decisions to survive. "Well," he finally said," I guess it reminds me of home – but only in good ways. The difference is, on Thanton the competition was always focused on winning to prove that you were better than someone else, so that the winners were lauded, and the losers derided. The competitions I set up here are all about playfully challenging and appreciating ourselves and each other."

Pro said, "I can see that sense of play as you challenge yourself and those around you, to go further. That is exactly the way I like to teach art."

"So, you understand."

"You are an inspiration – did you know that?"

"Well, of course." He grinned and stuck his tongue out. Then he looked her in the eye. "Have you any idea what an inspiration you are?"

Pro had no idea how to respond. She gave a wry smile and shrugged her shoulders.

Pro had noticed that Stribjus, once he restocked his magical coat, at first had a hard time trusting that he didn't have to hoard things in order to secure his next meal – or feel ready to escape at a moment's notice. Slowly, he was settling into this new- found abundance. Contentment was a new skill he was gradually learning to acquire.

I hope I can learn to master the skill of contentment, Pro thought one day. *I suppose I am – on some level – dealing with my own fears about abundance and having everything I could want.*

With an endless array of art supplies at her disposal, Pro found herself drawing and painting with a fervor she hadn't had since college. As she was recovering from the traumas she faced with Felagor, she found herself dreaming, drawing, and painting with a new kind of freedom. That freedom surfaced in her paintings, often in ways that surprised her.

Pro gazed at the triptych she had been working on. The painting series grew from a dream she had of a female warrior. At first, she thought it was Zor, but as she painted, it evolved as an amalgamation of Zor and herself. The warrior was dressed in full battle regalia – armor, shield, sword – the works. In the dream she was facing, by herself, an army of oppressors who were waiting for her to make the first move before they descended on her. She looked around, considering her plan of attack. Then, she did something unexpected. She took off her armor. In the last painting of that triptych the army appeared to vaporize as she laid down her armor.

Weeks passed filled with the camaraderie of her special friends, exploring the wonders of Astara and lots of painting guided by her dreams.

It's wild! she thought, *I'm trusting my impulses. Yay me! It reminds me of painting at Grandma Molly's as a youngster, but this feels different, too. It feels fuller, deeper – richer.*

But something is missing, she thought one day. *Why am I not content?* As she was witnessing Loahn and Zor get closer, Pro wondered, *is it yearning – for a partner – that feels like an empty space? I don't think so. Stribjus and I have certainly gotten closer, though not in a romantic way at all. He's more like a wonderful combination of a playful younger brother and a cuddle buddy.*

Melara and Helastion have not been shy about introducing me to romantic prospects. I am sure they mean well, and that they are hoping my interest in someone will encourage me to settle in Astara. I admit, of all the "contenders," as Stribjus likes to call them, Xander is easily my favorite. He has shown me some of the wonders of this healing world. Okay, at first his handsome features and confidence reminded me of Ash, but he is warmer, gentler, and certainly more attentive. We have had some lovely walks in all kinds of landscapes – in some huge domas – and had some deep conversations about life and journeys and possibilities. But I don't need my life to be any more complicated right now than it already is. And let's face it – romance is complicated.

Zor came to her one evening after supper looking distraught.

"Zor?" Pro asked, "Are you all right?"

Zor shook her head. "I don't know what's going on," she said. "I'm having all of these sensations. Loahn and I have been spending a lot of time together."

"I've noticed," Pro said.

Zor rushed on, "I've been introducing him to Astaran habits and customs."

"And you've been having fun?" Pro asked.

"We have," Zor replied, "but lately I have noticed a shift in the beating of my heart. It seems to beat a bit faster when I see him – or even when I think about him as I am now. Is that crazy? That's crazy."

"No," Pro reassured her, "It isn't crazy at all. It sounds to me like you're falling in love."

"Oh, no! Really? Is that what you think? Love? That's terrible."

"Why would that be terrible?"

"Because," Zor said without missing a beat, "doesn't love mean losing all control?" Her brow furrowed, "He is so kind and gentle and funny. He makes me blush – blush. I never blush. But it's more than that. All of these feelings confuse me. I don't know what to do."

"Well, I'm certainly no expert," Pro said. *Ha! What an understatement! With Ash, I was always trying to figure out exactly what I should say. Confusion always scared me to death – I was so afraid of doing something wrong.*

Zor stared at her expectantly. "I don't know," Pro finally admitted. "Do you have to do anything? Can you just enjoy the time you have?"

"I'm not sure," Zor said. "Me, the great warrior, and this is what throws me into upheaval? It doesn't make sense."

Pro shrugged, "I don't think love makes any sense at all." To Pro's surprise, Zor initiated a huge hug.

Remembering that conversation unleashed the doubts in her head. *Did loving Ash feel like losing control? Is that what I think love is?*

Pleasing someone's every whim? Fighting like crazy to be what I think they need me to be? Ugh!

Am I missing Ash...? No, that's not it. It isn't Ash.

She did think of him often, however. He appeared in her dreams and somehow surfaced in her paintings. In one he looked like her father disguised as a judge in a courtroom. In another there was an Ash/Clive larger than life and in charge of a kind of Willy Wonka paint factory. That dream gave birth to a painting in which she was a small unruly child. It seemed that each time she dreamed of, thought of, drew, or painted Ash, it was in relation to some part of her that had been buried somewhere - some old version of who she thought she had to be. She wondered if that's what Loahn experienced in his healing-merges, a kind of losing of himself.

Did I lose myself in Ash? I suppose I did – in some ways. Okay, in a lot of ways.

"Ash – get out of my head!" she yelled aloud in response to that thought.

With that, she startled herself awake. She was back in her apartment, sitting up in bed. Her mind was racing, while physically she felt like she had just run a marathon. She looked at the clock, glowing in the darkness. *It's 2 am. What day is this? Sunday? Monday? Does it matter? I guess it really does if I'm supposed to be at work in a few hours. Ugh! Maybe I just won't go in today.*

You never miss work, Pro – ever. Well, of course not! My workaholic parents drilled that into me – a relentless work ethic. And I am grateful for that. I am nothing if not dependable. Hmmmm. I am nothing.

Pro shuddered. *I am not nothing. But what am I? What do I even define myself by? By Ash – not a great idea. That ship has definitely sailed without me. By my work? Lord, I hope not, though it has certainly been a stable element through everything I 've been going through. I just feel bombarded by way too many thoughts of Clive and Paige and Ash and Professor Tilson and my parents and everyone's expectations of me. And Jakey keeps running through my mind. What is it Doria said the day of the installation? She said she wondered if Jakey OD'd accidentally or intentionally. They would never know.*

The thought that little Jakey died alone in his room, maybe deliberately, tore at her heart.

Pro forced herself to get out of bed, grabbed a power bar and some pomegranate juice and wrote and even sketched a bit in her dream journal. As she wrote about Astara, it became more and more real.

Okay, why is it that in Astara I am painting prolifically, but here I can't even bear to go into my studio? Why is that? Maybe because there, I'm not worried about what anyone else thinks. So, how can I bring that freedom to my painting in THIS world?

Melara had talked about safety, but what space feels safe? Certainly not this planet. Not right now. Let's face it, I don't even know what I'm doing here. Am I drifting? Floundering? What do you even want, Pro?

"I DON'T KNOW!" she screamed. "I simply want to sleep."

But isn't that just running away? I don't know. Maybe it is. But I barely have the energy to get out of bed right now.

"And what if you get lost in your dreams and can't get back," a part of her reasoned out loud.

Then I guess I'm just certifiably insane. Should it scare me that the thought of being certifiably insane doesn't scare me? Probably.

"So, your big solution is just running away?"

Well, I can't go to work. Not like this. Great timing, Pro. Of all the times to call in sick, leave it to you to pick the week of your six-month review. Okay – not ideal, but that's where I am.

Pro shot off a quick email to Paige: "Sorry, but I am feeling really ill. I won't be in today. It's not a pattern. I promise. In my four years with Atkins, I never missed a day. Elaine can verify that. I turned in the final proofs for Falling Between the Lines on Friday. Don't have any loose ends to tie up. Right now, I can barely get out of bed. Thanks for understanding."

And what if she doesn't understand? Then I guess I will just have to deal with the fallout. All I know is that I have to take care of myself right now.

"So, you think you can go into your dreams and hide forever?" As she spoke the words out loud, she wasn't sure if the question was hers or Dr. Lamdowski's.

At least in my dreams I have a purpose. There is something there that calls to me, and I have to find out what it is.

I can't think about all of this anymore.

With that thought she drifted off to sleep.

She dreamt of many things, but most prominently of M2, Felagor, and the Beckoner. *How do you paint a voice that sings more beautifully than you have ever thought possible? Right now, all I can do is imagine the Beckoner as a shimmering light that inspires, even as she strives to illuminate the darkness in Felagor's world of Vergon.*

A chill ran up her spine as she thought of Felagor, and she shuddered to shake it off. She knew so many things were stirring inside – yearnings, doubts, questions, new ideas spurred by the worlds she had visited, and much more. She would have to come to terms with her fears and confusion.

But how? Does the painting help? I think it does. It certainly helps me to sort out the myriad thoughts and feelings that are running rampant through me, but to what end? "You have to find the Agency," M2's various voices insisted.

"WHAT Agency? WHO do I need to talk to? WHAT do I need to DO to find it?" Whenever she asked, the wizard went silent. She was left adrift in her own thoughts. *I don't know what the next steps I need to take are, but I know I can't stay here. It's a lovely place and yet, I'm starting to feel trapped.*

Indeed, in one of her recurring dreams she saw a crystalline structure pour from Helastion and Melara's mouths to surround them all – to encompass Astara. She had painted it, obscuring their identities in the painting.

After one more night in which the Beckoner once again called to her in her dreams, Pro decided she had to bring this up to her friends. They gathered together after dinner.

"I need to talk to all of you about something," Pro said.

"And I have something I need to say as well," Loahn chimed in. He was beaming. "May I go first?" he asked.

"Of course," Pro said. "Please."

"Thank you," Loahn replied. "I have been thinking about this for a while now and how it might look. And because of how we have all come together and all that we have been through – Pro, Stribjus – you are a part of this – so…"

"Princess Zor," he said smiling. "With the time we have been spending together, the admiration and affection I have for you has only grown. I do love you, Zor."

Zor looked away, and sputtered, "Uh… I…"

"Would you be interested in considering the idea of marriage?" Loahn asked.

Zor gazed at him and smiled, "Well, I certainly find the idea… hm… interesting."

Stribjus and Pro traded smiles through tight lips to keep from reacting. Then Loahn burst into a huge grin and got down on one knee.

"Zor," Loahn said, "I love you! And I think you love me, too. Would you do me the honor, oh great warrior princess, of accepting this proposal of marriage?"

Zor looked into Loahn's eyes and smiled, but her smile seemed tight. Pro thought she looked like she might burst into tears. Zor pulled back and turned away. Pro watched her breathe deeply, then stand taller, while Loahn waited expectantly. Zor turned back to face him. "Loahn, you are a remarkable person. You have so much to give, and you give it so freely. But I have two major concerns. One is that your propensity for empathy might be reflecting my own love and need for love, rather than what is actually true for you."

Before Loahn could respond, Zor continued, "Please don't say anything. I know you have been using the amulet I gave you to establish clearer boundaries. I have seen you use it. But I think we both still have much growing to do."

"And your other concern?" Loahn asked gently.

"I do love you, Loahn. And I have never said that before, at least not in a romantic sense, to anyone before. I feel the depth of the love you have to give and parts of me yearn and ache to receive it, and parts of me fear that is just an invitation to give up my own strength and sense of self to someone else."

As Zor turned away, Pro could see Loahn's muscles contract as he struggled to reach for Zor and held himself back. Pro felt the same inclination. She wanted to run over and hug Zor and tell her she was loved and loveable and that everything would be all right. But she somehow knew Zor needed her own space right now and would accept no help. So, like Loahn, Pro held herself in check – watching, listening, and holding still. The silence and stillness seemed to go on forever.

Finally, Zor turned back to face Loahn. "Your proposal is – touching, terrifying – wonderful. I can't say no, Loahn, for I do love you."

But before Loahn could leap to his feet and embrace her, Zor added, "But I can't say yes, either. Not right now. Can we please take more time to get to know each other better? There are so many feelings to sort out. I feel like I have prepared my whole life to rush into battle, because I thought that was the legacy from my world. But nothing has prepared me to rush into love. It scares me. And I can't believe I just admitted all of that."

Loahn stood and slowly approached her. Gently taking her hand, he said, "You can take all of the time you need. I am not going anywhere without you. Thank you for your honesty. Your own heart is so much bigger than you imagine." With that he kissed her hands tenderly and they embraced. It was one of the sweetest moments Pro could ever remember seeing.

I know that longing and that fear, Pro thought. *I don't think I ever realized how much courage it takes to love and to let love in. I am amazed at how open, honest, and giving both Zor and Loahn are through this whole crazy process. Process. That word again.*

"It appears that something auspicious is transpiring here." As she recognized Helastion's voice, Pro jolted out of her reverie and felt her heart drop into her stomach. Helastion and Melara had entered unnoticed.

"Congratulations! We are thrilled," Melara said.

Zor responded first, "What?"

"Loahn approached us two days ago and asked for our blessing," Helastion said.

"And, of course, we were overjoyed to give it," Melara added. "We are so happy for you."

"It has been a blessing for us to see you all regaining your health. Now it is time for the ceremony of the proclamation of engagement," Helastion said.

Melara smiled. "It is such a wonderful time. Every comfort will, of course, continue to be provided and there will be months of festivities before the wedding–"

"I didn't say yes," Zor interrupted.

"But we thought…" Melara said.

"We need more time," Zor said. "There are a lot of things to sort through. I didn't say no, but I didn't say yes."

"Then surely it is just a matter of time," Melara said.

The response to Melara's assurance was silence.

"Speaking of timing,' Pro interjected, "I am glad you're here. I've been dreaming about this, pondering it, painting it. I don't quite know what to say. Melara, Helastion, Astara is an incredible place – so welcoming, so full of healing and abundance. I am forever grateful for all that it – and all you have offered us. And – I need to leave."

17. WHAT PRICE SAFETY?

It felt like a bomb had gone off in the room. The stillness was overwhelming.

"I have been dreaming more and more of the Beckoner," Pro explained, "and I can't stay here any longer. The longer I stay, the easier it is to stay – the easier it can be to forget what I need to do."

"Which is what?" Melara asked.

"Find a way to rescue the Beckoner."

"Pro, do you understand the magnitude of the dangers you are facing?" We almost lost our daughter. Loahn almost lost his life. It is not just Felagor – there are worlds out there ready to devour you. We cannot let you put yourself in harm's way," Helastion said warmly, but firmly.

"When you have a chance to think this through – to consider all that you have here weighed against all of the danger that awaits you out there, we know you will understand why we cannot let you leave right now," Melara added. "If you need anything just ask and the doma, as always, will provide."

With that Helastion and Melara walked to the edge of the doma. Helastion pressed his palms and fingers together then, with his palms still touching, twisted his hands three times. Next, he inscribed a column with his hands on either side of his body, and a crystalline structure appeared around the entire space anchored by eight columns of light. And they were gone.

Pro ran to the edge of the doma, but where she could easily pass through its porous membrane before, now there was a barrier.

She could not see it, but it was there. She charged into it with her shoulder several times, getting angrier and running with more force each time. It wasn't what she expected at all. It wasn't like running into a wall. It was more like charging into a mattress – it did not hurt her a bit, yet it was clear that the barrier was not going to give way.

It's as if it is absorbing the energy of my attacks.

"We're trapped," Pro said. "We're not going anywhere."

"But Helastion has said we could leave anytime we choose," said Stribjus. He hopped outside of the doma, then sauntered back in. "See?"

Pro responded, "I know Helastion and Melara have both said that, but it has never felt like the truth to me. It has always felt to me like there was a kind of binding here.

I couldn't put my finger on it, but I know it's there – here. And now it is right here, surrounding us. And I am the one who's not allowed to pass through."

"I will go and talk with them. My parents are not unreasonable – most of the time," Zor said, trying to smile. "I should go now, but I will come back tomorrow. Good night."

Zor moved to one of the pillars, placed her hand on it and moved out of the doma.

Over the next hours, Loahn and Pro talked and kept testing various parts of the boundary around them to see if they might pass through it. Loahn could pass through with ease, but Pro could not. Stribjus occupied himself with food and juggling.

That night, Pro dreamt of invisible barriers that kept appearing and disappearing. In one, she was trapped in a maze where the walls kept shifting and, looming overhead was the huge figure of her mother – or was it Melara?

The next day, Zor returned with new information.

"Why are they holding us – me – here?" Pro demanded. "It is pretty hard not to take this personally."

Zor said, "My parents say that what holds people here is fear."

"Yes," Pro agreed, "I am afraid of the power they wield. They're holding me here. Why is this just happening to ME? All of you can apparently come and go as you wish. I've tried running into the barrier. I even tried to gouge into it with a knife and while it seems like it's giving way, it has an elasticity that I can't cut through. I know they say this is for my own protection, but I can't stay here."

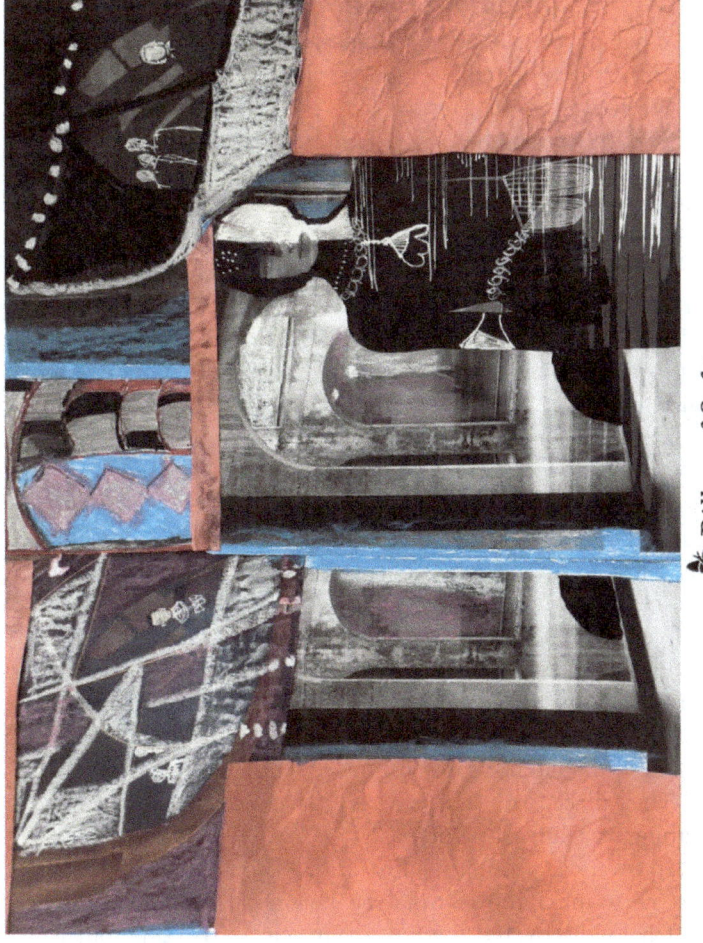

Pillars of Safety

Zor replied, "On one level it is indeed true that they are, in your terms, holding you here. Astara offers a safe haven to all, and that is compelling – safety, when there is so much turmoil and conflict out there, holds a lot of appeal. The force-field that surrounds you is calibrated to your fears, Pro, and it is strengthened by the doubts and fears any of us, including Melara and Helastion, have for your safety."

"What if you all surround me and we try to run through it together?" Pro suggested.

"We could try," Zor responded, "but the reality is attacking the force-field only strengthens it, as that attack engages your energy in combat with the fear. It is a paradox – the more you give in to fear, doubt, and despair, the stronger the walls get. The more you resist and fight against the fears and doubts, or even try to ignore them and push them away, the more your energy feeds the walls in a different way – and the stronger they get."

"All beings must have some sense of safety to be able to go forward," Loahn said. "I believe we have each been working on that in our own ways. We may now be ready to go on." He smiled lovingly at Zor but did not continue.

"They have told me I need to stay here for my own protection," Pro said. "As you just said, Loahn, I do feel like this healing process has given me some sense of safety. I feel braver – encouraged somehow to go on to whatever is next for me. I guess being trapped here also feels like a kind of penance – how dare I be ungrateful after what I've put all of you through."

"Pro, you have not put us through anything," Loahn spoke up. "Every choice we made to accompany you has been of our own free will. You don't owe us anything. And does wanting to leave mean that you are ungrateful? I don't think so."

"This place isn't so bad, is it," asked Stribjus, "Having everything we want – instantly?"

"It isn't bad, Stribjus," Pro said, "But the Beckoner keeps calling out to me. I know I can't stay here and ignore that call."

"I have discovered there is a way out," Zor said, "but it will require three things from us: A clear intent to leave, a clear destination and a willingness to focus our attention on moving forward – no looking back."

"I will do anything," Pro said, "I'm ready to leave – no doubts, no hesitations can stop me. I am determined to leave, but I can't ask all of you to do that."

"Wait a minute. You do not get to choose what decisions we make," Loahn said.

"Absolutely! Who do you think we are?" said Stribjus, flashing his crooked grin.

Pro couldn't help but smile. "Okay, men!" she said, "Lovely, powerful Zor. What are your thoughts about leaving Astara?"

"I think it is decided, Pro," Zor said, "We are not letting you leave here alone. Agreed?"

Pro saluted, grinning. "Yes, oh great warrior princess."

"Good," Zor nodded playfully. "Next, we must have a clear destination. Otherwise, we risk drifting between worlds. So, do we go back to Vergon and face Felagor? I'm strong enough now."

"No," Pro blurted out. Her knee-jerk response made her stumble before asserting, "There's no way I'm putting you in danger again. And it would be fool hardy to face Felagor once more without some kind of plan."

"Great," chimed in Stribjus. "Why don't we stay here until we've made a plan?"

Pro only hesitated for a moment before replying, "No! With the dream I had last night – I need to get out of here to think clearly. But I don't know where that leaves us."

"I know where we need to go," Loahn said. His three friends waited for him. He took Zor's hands and held them firmly.

Zor looked up into Loahn's blue-green eyes. Unseeing though they were, they shone with wisdom. "Erinmar?" she said.

Nodding, he addressed Pro and Stribjus. "Erinmar – my world?"

"Yes," they said in unison.

"For now." Pro added. "I know nothing about your world, Loahn, and in the past charging into the unknown has scared me to death. I would play out so many worst-case scenarios in my head – like the doubts my parents planted in me about making a living as an artist."

"That's understandable. Fears about facing the question marks of the future can be stultifying. And how are you doing now?" asked Loahn.

"Now – a lot of questions come up, like, 'What do I gain by only imagining the worst possible futures?' If that's all I consider, how does that serve me? Okay, I do think it can keep me from being foolhardy and jumping in blindly – sorry, Loahn - no offense."

"None taken," the blind empath smiled back at her. "Metaphor acknowledged, accepted, and appreciated."

"Thank you," Pro replied. "So, what if I open to other possibilities? Erinmar might be the BEST thing that could ever happen to me. I can't know if I don't try. My new policy is, as of this very minute, 'no more catastrophizing.' I'll imagine great possible futures instead. So, let's do it!"

"That's an amazing shift, Pro. We are all agreed, then – we go to Erinmar." Loahn flashed a smile at Zor. "I am excited for my parents to meet all of you."

Zor averted her eyes. "We can get our bearings there and decide the next steps to take. The only thing we need to do then is focus our attention on where we are going – letting go of the past and charging into what is next."

Right! How hard could that be? I'm afraid, but why? I know I want to leave – I have to leave. So, what's holding me back?

Then Pro heard M2. "Is there anything you used to believe about yourself that keeps you from moving forward?"

Well, I used to believe what was most real was my fears.

"Of what?" M2 responded.

Hmmmmm… not being good enough, strong enough, creative enough.

"And what is true for you now?"

Good question. Pro furrowed her brow. *Good question indeed. Maybe I have to let go of who I thought I was, or who I thought I had to be – to please my parents, or my bosses… or Ash. But how do I do that?*

"So, what do we do now," Pro finally said.

The silence hung in the air.

"Let's sit in a circle," Zor said. They arranged themselves so that the women faced each other, and the men did as well. Zor handed out two glowing rings to each of her friends and kept two for herself. "Put these rings on your index fingers, please," she said.

Zor continued, "Allow your breaths to deepen – to replenish you as you inhale and carry away any tension as you exhale. As we align our breaths, we give thanks to Astara. Her artists-healers came to us when we were in dire need, and we give thanks for the love and support that they have given us in the healing process – space to heal."

Loahn added, "Now we breathe even deeper. We breathe into the stillness at our core, allowing, releasing, and then letting go of any fears or doubts about leaving Astara."

As Zor took a deep breath, Pro sensed the depth of feelings and the urge to cry that the warrior princess suppressed.

Why is it that we think the suppression of tears is somehow stronger than their expression? I was certainly raised to believe that, but I'm not so sure it's true. In fact, I remember my mother saying, "Don't cry, Katherine. People will think you're weak."

"All thanks to the Astarans. We are ever grateful." Loahn said.

"Now," Zor said, "position yourself between two of the pillars of light."

As they repositioned themselves, Pro felt as if she was breathing in more openness, more ease, and more clarity. *Thank you, Astara – for the generous gifts of your healing and abundance. No doubts, no regrets, no looking back now.*

Loahn said, "Let us focus our intent on our new destination – Erinmar."

Zor said, "Now point your ringed index fingers at the columns of light on either side of you."

A few moments passed. Pro felt waves of calm washing over her and through her. A peace settled deep within her – a kind of trusting, letting go and opening into what she didn't know. But it was the deepest peace she had ever felt. As she opened her eyes, she saw the pillars of light and the crystalline barrier dissolve.

She heard the urgency in Zor's voice, "Step outside of the doma immediately." As she and her friends stepped out of the doma, Pro saw the crystalline barrier re-form.

When Helastion and Melara appeared before them. Pro fought back the urge to panic.

Taking a deep breath, she thought, *they have no power over me. They are not my parents; I am not five years old. I am a grown woman, dammit, and I get to choose what I want to do.*

"You have no idea what you are doing, Pro" Helastion said. "The dangers you will be facing are vast."

"And they are mine to face," Pro said. "Your fears can't hold me back, no matter how much you say it's all about my safety."

"Don't be unreasonable," said Melara. "We only want what is best for you."

"Why is it that when people disagree with you, they always say you are the one being unreasonable?" Pro challenged. "I am not being foolhardy. This is what feels true for me."

Helastion said, "Loahn, surely you can reason with her. There is no need for any of you to put yourself in danger. Zor, you just came back to us – barely alive. How can you leave us now?"

"Perhaps sometimes the most dangerous thing we can do is play it safe," Loahn said.

Zor said, "I love you so much. I am eternally grateful for your love and all you have given me and my friends. I will be back, but now – I have to go. And I know you would not wish to hold us here against our will."

Pro stood her ground and stared the Astaran couple down. Helastion and Melara heaved a sigh of what Pro took as resignation.

"We will miss you all – tremendously," Melara said.

"Forgive us, Pro," Helastion said, "for presuming to know your truth better than you do and for allowing our own fears to cloud our judgment. We wish you only the very best."

They all said their goodbyes, then Melara and Helastion withdrew.

When they were gone, Stribjus burst into gales of laughter, cartwheeling around his friends, then coming nose to nose with Pro. "Look at you! Who's the warrior now?" he said. "On to Erinmar!"

"Let's stand in a circle once more, close our eyes and focus on our breathing. Imagine an enormous tree before you," said Loahn. "Allow that image to fill the landscape of your mind. We are standing before it. Its trunk is enormous. Now simply repeat Erinmar in your mind."

In her mind's eye, Pro saw Loahn walk right up to the huge tree, its trunk gnarled, its branches spattered across the sky. He put his hand on it. Pro sensed that the tree responded to the empath, almost tickled at his touch. The center of the tree's great trunk - right before Pro's eyes - shifted, shimmered, and vaporized, revealing a large door.

"So, this magic tree is the entrance to your world?" Pro asked.

Ancient Tree Entrance to Erinmar

"It is any tree actually," Loahn said. "Well, any ancient tree – they are keepers of wisdom and care. You place your hand, respectfully, on its trunk, listen, and wait. If you are listening intently, and the timing is right, the tree will respond with an invitation and a request. Only if you make a sacred oath to do no harm, will the tree grant you permission and the doorway to Erinmar will open. Do you want to try it?"

As they took the vow to do no harm, the tree allowed each of them to enter Erinmar through the grand entryway. Once they were all the way through, Pro was not surprised as she looked back to find the passageway had closed and the huge solid substance of the ancient tree's trunk was restored.

No going back. Only forward, through and into whatever is next.

With a warm smile Loahn said, "Welcome to Erinmar."

18. WELCOME TO ERINMAR

Pro felt her whole-body tingle. It felt wide awake and vibrant. Sun streamed in her bedroom window. As she sat up in bed, Pro was surprised that she felt refreshed. She grabbed her journal, making some quick notes and a couple of small sketches. When she realized it was 9 a.m. Monday morning, she thought, *Actually, I could still make it to work for most of the day.*

"No, no, no, no, NO!" she protested aloud. "You claimed this day for yourself, Pro and you are going to take it."

But the work –

"The work will still be there tomorrow," Pro reasoned. "Free from work, and from Astara you get to decide what it is you want to do."

Okay! Challenge accepted. Well, let's see. What do I feel like? Let me just breathe into that. Ha! Really? Breathe into that?

"You would be proud of me, M2! I remembered to breathe – and I didn't have to feel afraid or panicked to do it. YAY ME!" Pro laughed long and hard.

This is the calmest and most focused I've felt in a long time. I actually feel inspired. Now that I'm free of Astara, I want to paint it – to capture some of the incredible things I saw.

She went to her studio, made thumbnail sketches, and painted – a variety of domas, the Council of Light, saving Zor, Loahn's healing sleenaje… She even thought of some of her Astaran dreams, like the warrior in the field. Images and paint poured forth and Pro didn't try to stand in their way.

I have no idea if any of this is any "good" or not and I don't care. This feels... liberating.

After a few hours in the studio, she grabbed lunch and then took a nap, falling into sleep with a sense of accomplishment.

She yawned and stretched and as she opened her eyes, she saw two moons in the sky. It felt like dawn. Pro and her three friends were lying on a grassy hillock by a small lake.

It took Pro a few moments to get her bearings. The blue-greenish grass underneath her was plush and soft. A light blue rock softly caressed her head. The lightest blanket of pink and coral covered her. Waking up was the gentlest of experiences – like being in a bath scented with lavender.

As she became more lucid, she realized that Loahn was only a few feet away, meditating with his legs crossed and his palms up. Calm radiated from him with a soft rainbow glow that reflected the orange-purple sunrise blazing across the sky. She had never felt so safe and secure.

As Pro pulled back the blanket, it wafted into the air and floated away so delicately that the movement didn't even startle her. She smiled as she surveyed the sprawling, lush landscape. Stribjus and Zor appeared to awaken just as peacefully. Pro watched their expressions of wonder when their blankets floated away and the pale blue rocks they had been sleeping on began to roll across the ground – almost hovering like a mist.

"Those rolling rocks are Lumler," Loahn explained. "The pink and coral creatures you saw as blankets are the Eflurial – soothing creatures who are fueled by the dreams of those whose comfort they support. When one first enters Erinmar, the Lumler help visitors to trust the ground and find their footing, while the Eflurial bring peace and comfort, dissipating any anxiety or stress. Then they move on."

Pro found the whole idea of such species a little mind-boggling. Then she noticed something else. *This world is so still – so peaceful.*

"Welcome to Erinmar – my home," said Loahn. "We're up early, so we can take a bit of time as we travel to my parents' house. But before we venture to the village, I need to tell you some things about my world. Erinmar is a merging world. You will see a multitude of creatures and there is no hierarchy here. One species or combination of species is no better or more elevated than another.

Welcome to Erinmar

Each being has its own gifts and here they are shared freely, some might say too freely. The merging takes place with physical contact, which gives parties access to what the other has experienced. For most inhabitants of Erinmar this process happens unconsciously; they automatically attune to the feelings, thoughts, and presence of the other.

"You have actually already experienced some of that merging. The Lumler and the Eflurial were able to help you ground and center, lighten up and release stress because of their ability to merge and seek out the parts of you in need of nurturing. Similarly, the other beings in Erinmar have their own gifts to share and will be excited to learn from you through a kind of osmosis.

"Now, be aware, you may halt the merging process at any time. Some people forget that option as they explore this world and encounter so many species open to connecting with them. Creatures of all forms and species experience these mergings in a multitude of ways, ascribing various meanings to them. Some find it particularly jarring that every merging is in itself unique, rather than a prescribed technique or process they can control every step of the way.

"What many fail to understand is that in any merging here, those you merge with only have access to what you choose consciously or unconsciously to allow. These processes of merging are not intended to be invasive, but we have had a few guests who found the merging here overwhelming for them and they had to leave.

"One guest told me it felt like giving his power away, insisting, 'My secrets are my strength.' For another, the merging felt so good she was afraid that if she kept allowing it, she would lose herself completely. Though the mergings are completely non-sexual, another creature received them as so profoundly intimate and ecstatic that they were sure that experience must be reserved for just one partner in their life. Still another felt like the mergings were simply too good to be true. He never felt he deserved to feel so accepted for who he was, without proving himself and somehow earning a level of respect and appreciation. The process was too easy for him to accept it.

"I encourage you to practice saying 'No, thank you' or 'Stop' often – silently or aloud, to establish your own boundaries. You can also just put your hands in front of you - palms out – to request that a creature keep its distance. You have all witnessed that I have my own challenges in that regard, especially if someone I care about is in pain. The amulet Zor gave me has been a great reminder of my ability to draw my own boundaries. Zor, have you anything to add?"

"I do, indeed," Zor said. "Loahn and I have talked at length about his world and the mergings. At first the idea was repugnant to me, but he's been helping me know that it's safe to let down my guard – sometimes. My biggest challenge has been facing my mistrust of the whole concept of merging. What might happen if I let go of my combative convictions – my armor? I suggest we practice exploring our own boundaries with each other before we venture out into this world."

"I'm game. It sounds like great fun to me," Stribjus said. His propensity for finding fun in every opportunity baffled Pro.

I suppose the ability to charge away at lightning speed makes being open to new experiences much less daunting.

He launched into what seemed to be a grand version of a game she played as a child: Red Light, Green Light. He practiced keeping his distance, then taking a step forward and throwing his hands in front of himself. When he suddenly appeared six inches in front of Pro's face, she screamed "No," and he reappeared six feet away.

"I'm sorry, I'm sorry," Stribjus said. "I need to remember the experience with the Kermuffles and acknowledge that in my own way, I can be overwhelming for some people." He played with Loahn and Zor as well, exploring and testing not only his own boundaries, but theirs as well.   Then he was practicing with everything around them – trees, rocks, even flowers. At one point he was tiptoeing on the blue-green grass, asking permission to step.

Pro found herself practicing boundary-drawing at times quite cautiously, and then with more abandon.

If I can follow Stribjus' example and make it a game it seems much less intimidating, and even much less rude to say, "No!"

So, she gave herself permission to play, surprised to find how easy it could feel to both establish her own personal boundaries and to allow them to shift – to expand or contract. *Like a doma.*

Approaching boundary-drawing as a game, Pro found she was actually enjoying the process.

At one point, Zor looked apprehensive, yet as Loahn took her hand, Pro saw tension in her face and shoulders melt away. She heard Zor say, "I do think I have made peace with the idea of merging, knowing that I can draw my own boundaries as I need to. I think I am more nervous about meeting your parents. Just afraid that they will find my warrior background off-putting."

Loahn said, "They will love you because you are you. It is just a plus that you love me, and I love you." He smiled reassuringly. "Trust me, everything will be just fine."

I'm not so sure how I feel about this whole idea of merging, Pro thought. *Loahn has been merging with me to some extent since the moment we met. That's been okay... it's funny, I think I'm not so concerned about a kind of invasion of my privacy as I am a bit afraid of losing myself in someone else.*

Like I did with Ash, Pro thought, finding it a bit hard to swallow. *Lord, I really did that. Dressing more conservatively for his office parties, careful not to make any waves – to control what Ash called my wild child.*

Luckily, Loahn broke her introspection, "Does anyone have any questions?" He gave them a moment, but no one spoke up. "Great. Let's forge ahead then."

They set out for Loahn's village. Pro was grateful they were in no hurry. There was so much to take in. In the distance she saw yellow waters pouring over purple cliffs into a river that fed a golden-silver lake. As they walked by, the water rushed up to greet her, scaring her at first. Then she remembered to say "No!" and the yellow-silver wave subsided. It really works, she thought with a sigh of relief. Then Pro let out a shriek of delight.

"Look!" she said. "What is that? It's a fountain, right?"

"What?" Zor asked. "What did you see? I see a waterfall in the distance, but no fountain."

"No, it's not there now. But it was there," Pro said. "Or was it? Or have I just lost my mind?"

Then it appeared again, in midair, sprays of water in the sky that materialized in a cascading array of yellow, silver, green and pink. And then it was gone. Then another appeared over a different spot in the lake. This one shimmered silver, blue and gold.

"It's like fireworks made of water," Pro said.

"Ah! Those are Shiftlers," Loahn explained. "They are translucent and balloon-like, so they are not always easy to see. Their tentacles make them excellent swimmers and foragers. They dive down deep, swelling with water to five times their regular size. Then, they propel themselves into the air where they expel the water to create those cascades."

"They travel in groups we call sho-als," he continued. "Swimming around them is quite an experience. We will all go swimming sometime – but not right now, Stribjus," Loahn said, sensing the jokester's rising urge to bound into the water and play with the Shiftlers. "I want you to meet my parents."

"All right, if we must," Stribjus feigned begrudging disappointment, then burst into a smile, running lightning-fast circles around his friends as they traveled on.

They approached the home of Loahn's parents. It was apparently made of living trees, their branches entwined with vines. More lush vegetation formed a roof.

As Loahn was about to announce their arrival, a ten-foot-long furry eel-like creature with a cat's head slithered out and wrapped around Loahn's leg. Before his friends could panic, the creature nuzzled against his chest and licked his face.

Laughing, Loahn said, "Oster, hi! I know! I have missed you, too." He turned to the group, still nuzzling the critter, "Oster is a Scoo who helped to raise me," he explained. "They watched after me, helped me learn to walk and develop my senses. Because they are so warm and attentive, the Scoo help to raise all kinds of creatures. How have you been? Have you missed me?"

Pro could feel the vibration of the Scoo's response which prompted more laughter from Loahn.

"I'd know that laugh anywhere," a warm, rich voice rang out. "Welcome home, my son." The man who appeared in the doorway was so strikingly handsome that it took Pro a moment to realize he had no eyes. The part of his face where she expected to see eyes was simply smooth and sculpted. The man continued speaking. "How are you? How long has it been? And who are your fellow travelers?"

"Questions, questions, questions," the woman who bustled out of the doorway said, "before we have even had time to give our boy a proper greeting. Oster, make way, I'm coming in for a welcome home hug." The Scoo unwound to the ground. "Mmmhaaaaaahmmhhoooooommmmmmm," Loahn's mother intoned as they hugged. Loahn's father moved in until the hug grew to encompass all three family members – four counting Oster the Scoo, who surrounded the other three.

Prompted by the tones of Loahn's mother, all four of the huggers were humming various pitches, vibrating with sound as they hugged. Pro thought the rich ringing sounds they made created a wonderful kind of song as they hugged. It was sweet and soothing and playful all at once. All four of them were merging in a grand family reunion.

My parents never hugged. Their signs of affection were much less demonstrative. It's funny, I never thought about that. I just accepted that was the way things were.

As the hug drew to a close, Loahn spoke up, "These are my friends – Zor, Pro, and Stribjus. My mother, Cepella, and my father, Jolner."

Cepella exuded such a sense of safety and support that Pro saw the startled expressions of Zor and Stribjus melt into smiles as Cepella opened her arms to request a hug, humming as they accepted her embrace. Stribjus, to Pro's great amusement, hummed right along. When she came to Pro, while the magnitude of the humming hug took her aback, Pro relaxed into the warm welcome of her open arms and soothing tones. When it became too enveloping for her, Pro squeezed Cepella's shoulders and then stepped away.

I did it. I said, 'No thank you' and I didn't even need to say it out loud.

Jolner placed his hands over his heart and then reached them out to his son's friends. "You are most welcome here," he said. Oster greeted each of them individually, somehow sensing their comfort level and communicating through vibration and a kind of "eeeeeeekshaaa" sound. He nuzzled his furry face in Pro's hands. Pro felt Zor revving up to say 'No,' when the Scoo rose to just under Zor's height three feet away and inclined his head in a respectful bow. Then Oster played with Stribjus for two minutes, wrapping and unwrapping, squeezing and teasing.

In ten minutes time, they were all like one big happy family with a bonding that happened in such a comfortable, comforting way, Pro felt totally at home.

How could people I just met seem so familiar and safe? It feels like they're just inviting me to be whoever I am. Just because I'm their son's friend, they accept me totally.

Sensing her thoughts, Loahn said, "Actually, they are just completely accepting of who you are, Pro. And that has nothing to do with me, or your being my friend."

When she thought about it later on a walk by herself, the level of that open acceptance brought Pro to tears. She couldn't remember ever feeling just invited to be who she was, however she was in that given moment. There were always expectations. What did her parents, her teachers, even her friends or Ash expect her to be – need her to be?

Why have I been so afraid of disappointing the people I care about?

19. LIFE IN ERINMAR

In a very short amount of time Pro and her friends settled into an easy rhythm in Erinmar. While accommodations were found for all of them across the village, they gathered with the villagers for their evening meal, making new friends, sharing their adventures and discoveries. Breakfast was with Loahn's family.

Pro still dreamt of the Beckoner, but her call seemed less urgent somehow. In fact, the beautiful music seemed encouraging more than anything. One morning Pro asked out loud, "Have I become complacent and abandoned my mission? Shouldn't I be strategizing with Zor how to conquer Felagor?"

M2's voice reassured her, "You are gaining other skills and tools that will aid you in that encounter."

"And what about the Agency? How am I ever going to find that? I don't even know what it is."

"You will, you will. Some things take time. Give yourself the gift of time."

Easy for you to say. I have no idea how long I've been away this time or if I'll have a job when I get back – IF I get back. Do I even want to go back? With everything I've been through – in all these crazy places – while I have jumped back and forth arbitrarily, or so it has seemed, I've never once asked to go back home. I haven't even thought to ask. Why is that? Should I be worried?

Pro could feel M2 smiling as they said, "Only if worrying about it would be fun for you. The answers you seek will be given – and more. The answers to questions you do not presently know how to ask will appear. All in good time, Pro. All in good time."

As promised, after they settled in, Loahn took his friends for a swim in the yellow-silver lake. Being immersed in the shimmering waters was not like any swimming experience Pro had ever had before. ❧

I can feel the support of the water; it's like I'm one with it. Somehow, I feel its nurturing. It's as if the water supports my floating when I want to float and supports my diving in when I want to go underneath the surface. Loahn had said every merging would be unique. I guess this is what he meant.

Swimming with the Shiftlers was another brand-new experience. At first it reminded Pro of swimming with dolphins in Hawaii. Feeling them move around her then burst into the air and spill water down was so playful, Pro felt like a kid – joyful, present, and free. The whole day was magical. In fact, it seemed to Pro that something about Erinmar seemed to bring out the magic in everyone and everything.

I'm not really even sure what that means – to be magical. I do know I want to pay close attention and log my impressions so I can paint them later. Pro imagined a painting of herself merging with the lake, with Shiftlers cascading water down on her.

Stribjus had never swum before, but because he moved like a whirlwind, swimming itself was no problem for him at all. And besides, the beautiful yellow-silver water would never let anyone drown. Pro sat on the shore and made some thumbnail sketches of his antics for paintings.

Eventually, they all lounged on the blue-green grassy hillock by the lake. Pro drifted off to sleep.

When she awoke in her apartment, it was dark, as the clock assured her it was 8:45. After making some quick notes in her journal she grabbed some food from the kitchen and went directly to her studio. There was a lot more painting to do – of floating pink blankets and blue rocks that rolled like mists, of fountains of water over a silver-yellow lake and Oster the Scoo. After a few hours of painting playfully, she set her alarm and wafted off to sleep.

As she luxuriated on the blue-green grass that caressed her, she heard her friends' voices.

"Loahn, your family is so wonderfully warm and welcoming. It may take me a while to get used to their effusive displays of emotion, but I will work on that," Zor said, smiling.

"Or play with it?" Stribjus interjected.

Swimming with Shiftlers

"Mmmmmmmm," Pro sounded as she rolled over and opened her eyes.

Zor smiled. "Or play with it," she agreed. "And I will keep saying, 'No, no thank you,' when I need to."

"That sounds perfect," Loahn said. "Pro, you are back with us! Have a nice nap?"

"Um, hm," Pro nodded and smiled. "I had a dream about painting some of the wonders of Erinmar. It was luscious."

"Now that you are back with us, I have a surprise," Zor said, reaching into a bag she had brought and pulling out three pouches. "I have something for you." She handed one to each of her friends.

Pro, Loahn, and Stribjus opened the bags to find glimmering crystals, each a unique color, in a beautiful silver setting.

"It's jewelry," Pro said. "How beautiful."

Zor said, "They can be worn as necklaces or bracelets. They can even be displayed or tied somewhere. And they are, of course, more than lovely trinkets. They are an invitation."

"An invitation to what?" asked Pro.

"To return to Astara." Zor said. "It requires a willingness to receive peace within yourself. It is not just an escape hatch – it is a way in, a way through. That was a place I wasn't sure I was ready to claim until recently. Because I was raised to fight as a young girl, I was afraid embracing peace meant surrendering and giving up."

Zor explained further, "Whenever you truly wish for peace and healing, hold this amulet in both hands, and imagine Astara. Set an intention, open to receive its peace and healing, and you will be there."

It's important for me to remember that. The peace and healing of Astara are always available for me to access. All I have to do is open to the possibility and set a clear intention. Mmmmmm. Just the thought of that option helps me feel more secure.

"Zor, thank you so much. What an amazing gift," Pro said. I wish I had something for you in return."

"Trust me," Zor said, "the gift of your friendship is more than enough."

"Loahn, it is even possible to be an Inspirer and an emissary who visits other lands," Zor continued. "And Stribjus, if you want to, you could go back to Astara right now."

"Nah!" Stribjus said, "We just got here and after the welcome we've had, how can I not want to stay and play for a while?"

With that, Pro gave Stribjus a big hug and, to her amazement, they found themselves humming through it.

"Wait, I just thought of something." Pro reached in her pocket, held onto the crystal there and decided. *This is the perfect gift for Zor.* Facing the princess, Pro took her hand. "I have carried something around with me for years, hoping it would help protect my heart, as I was told by a wise old shopkeeper. But you have been showing me the courage it takes to open your heart. You inspire me. So, please accept this rose quartz heart."

Pro saw Zor start to protest, and continued, "You know it would be rude to refuse to let me do something like this to show my appreciation for you, right?" Zor nodded slowly and, to Pro's great surprise, shyly. "So, I guess you are just going to have to take it," Pro grinned.

After lounging in the grass for a while, Loahn and Zor dozed off holding hands with their foreheads touching. *It is so sweet*, Pro thought. She suggested to Stribjus that they go for a walk.

As they walked, Pro said, "Thank you, Stribjus – for helping me leave Astara and for coming with us to Erinmar. You didn't have to come, but I'm awfully glad you did. Ugh! 'Awfully glad'? What kind of expression is that?" Pro smiled as she questioned her own verbiage.

Since when did I become so hyperaware of the words I choose?

"Words are powerful tools," Pro heard in her head. It was M2. "Words impact how we receive an experience. 'I couldn't possibly do that' is very different from 'I shouldn't do that,' from 'I will do that.' Some words expand. Some words contract."

Like a doma, Pro thought back. *I suppose you're right. I never really thought about that before.*

Stribjus continued this new game, "Are you 'terribly' glad?"

Pro grimaced, "No, no – nothing terrible, please. Let's see. I know. I am terrifically glad," she proclaimed.

Laughing as they walked along, they came upon a meadow that reminded Pro of a wheat field, only this field was a deep luscious purple red, its vegetation low to the ground. And in the beautiful reddish-purplish field, a pale green fawn-like creature was dancing on two feet. *Or are they hooves*, Pro wondered. She had no idea.

The dance was captivating—a rhythmic homage to the sky and the earth with outbursts of staccato movements that resolved in long luxurious flowing lines.

She has such strength and grace. Why do I assume a graceful dancing creation is female? I have no idea how gender even operates in this world. Why do I keep making assumptions?

Gender concerns aside, Pro noticed the being's long fingers reaching through the air completing every gesture with an ease and an elegance that stretched out across the landscape up into the sky.

They watched for a long time, until the creature, hands recoiled under hooves and on four legs, bounded through the field right up to them.

"Hi, I'm Pimsal," the beautiful creature said, unfurling fingers from under a hoof and offering a hand.

Stribjus just kept staring – speechless, so Pro spoke first. "Hi, I'm Pro. And this is Stribjus."

Still wordless, Stribjus took Pimsal's hand tenderly and kissed it. Then they stared into each other's eyes.

Finally, Pimsal broke the silence. "I am guessing from your reaction to my dance, that you have never seen a Sweeker before."

Pro and Stribjus shook their heads.

"May I touch your shoulders, that you might understand?"

Stribjus nodded his head vigorously. While she was grateful to have such a clear invitation to merge, Pro was a bit more hesitant. Then she, too, nodded her head.

As Pimsal touched her, the rush was kinetic. Immediately, a strength surged through Pro's pelvis and her legs. She felt like she could leap miles into the sky. Hand-hooves adjusted rapidly to bound or grab and extend through space. *Wow! Is this too much? Am I losing myself? No, it's okay, Pro – just relax. You can do this. Just breathe into this experience. Breathe. All right. I'm all right. I can feel this connection and still be who I am. Ha!*

Oh, my gosh! This is an invitation to dance through life. Merging, Pro felt herself as Pimsal – dancing gratitude to the earth as her hooves dug into it, leaping joy into the sky, celebrating the majesty of a flower with a graceful touch. Her cells pulsed with a vibrancy. She had never felt so grateful to be alive.

Then the merge was done.

Stribjus finally spoke, "You are amazing."

"Of course," Pimsal replied without a trace of ego or irony, "but aren't we all in our own ways? Thank you for sharing your gifts with me. Stribjus, your juggling skills are incredible."

Pro could see that Stribjus was enthralled. Pro had never seen him flustered before. It was endearing.

"Pro, your paintings are powerfully evocative."

"Which reminds me, I should be running along. There is so much I want to paint. It was a pleasure to meet you, Pimsal."

"The pleasure was mine, Pro. I look forward to dancing to your paintings." Pimsal said.

Dancing to my paintings? The idea took her by surprise. *As if they are music.* It made her smile. "I would really like that," Pro said. "Bye for now."

As Pro ambled away, the energy between Stribjus and Pimsal kept pulling her attention back to the purple-red field. She saw them laughing. Then Stribjus juggled. When Pimsal began to juggle as well – at times using all four appendages, Pro was sure Stribjus had just met someone as whimsical, magical, and powerful as he was. It struck her that they were merging in yet another unique way. She made some quick sketches so she could paint moments of their first encounter.

As she went off to paint, Pro was aware of being alone, but far from lonely. It felt funny, in a way, to be on her own yet to feel more connected than she ever had.

Erinmar truly is magical. She glowed. *It's as if all of the creatures here bring out what is special in each other. AH! I get it! THAT'S the magic. No wonder I find each of my new friends here so magical.*

She made friends easily here, to her amazement. Not that she had a hard time making friends at home, but here the connections were often as deep and immediate as they had been with Loahn's family.

She felt a special bond with Oster, who basically had adopted her and made sure she had everything she needed. She hadn't had a furry companion since Pris died years ago. What adventures she and that dog had had together! Oster reminded Pro how much she missed furry playfulness and unconditional love.

Ash had a strict no-animals policy. "Too much trouble," he would say, putting an end to the discussion the moment she brought it up.

One morning Oster kept winding circles around her as she had breakfast, rubbing against her legs and popping up to look playfully into her eyes.

"I haven't seen you this excited since we first arrived. What is going on with you, Oster?" Pro teased.

"I think he has his heart set on taking you for a walk," Cepella said.

Pro laughed. "Okay," I guess we're going for a walk. See you later, Cepella."

Oster slithered and rolled and bounded circles around her as they walked through the village, at last coming to a large stone structure.

When he opened the door and led her in, she saw the huge space with rays of shimmering light. Only then did he merge with her, so she received his thoughts.

"This is your art studio, Pro. Loahn and I stocked it for you with all kinds of supplies. I hope you like it".

Pro burst into tears. "I love it! What an incredible gift. Thank you, Oster. It's amazing. And so are you." Beaming, Oster wrapped himself around Pro and they humming-hugged for a long while, tears streaming down her face.

That night Pro fell asleep full of gratitude. She woke up before her alarm clock – on Planet Earth – alert, refreshed and ready to go. As usual, she got to work early. As soon as Paige arrived, she went by Pro's desk. "Are you doing, okay?"

"So much better, thanks for asking," Pro replied. "I got a lot of sleep. I must have really needed it."

"I'm glad you're feeling better. I've got a new project for you. It looks like you are becoming our sci-fi go to. Your work on Falling Between the Lines was pretty good. You actually managed to make some graphic sense of all the bizarre shifts in that book. Good for you."

"Thanks, Paige."

"This new project is even trickier. It's called The Galactics. 'A team of shapeshifting superheroes travel to various galaxies realigning the galactic order.' Don't ask me – that's just the byline. I'm not the one who makes this stuff up."

"Sounds interesting," Pro said. "I'll dive right in."

"I want to challenge you," Paige continued, "to make bolder choices. You have some good ideas, but then it feels like you tighten up and pull back. No holding back on this one. Go for it! Give it a shot, and if you need help let me know." With that, Paige dashed away.

And there she goes, Pro thought, *off to torment some other poor soul. Thanks for reminding me that whatever I do is never good enough.*

Wait a minute! Hold on – that is NOT *what she said. Yes, it is a challenge, as she said, to step up my game. Is it possible for me to take that challenge as an invitation instead of as a putdown? Hmmmmm. That might take some practice.*

Reading through <u>The Galactics</u> that morning images popped into her head. She took notes and made sketches.

Well, if our superheroes are shapeshifters, I am going to have to find a way to make each one emblematic in some way – so we recognize them in whatever form they take. I need to keep digging for clues that make each one unique. Whew! This is a challenge. Bold choices! Thank you, Paige. Pro broke into a smile that lit up her face.

Before she knew it the day was gone. She arrived home tired but stimulated. *It wasn't a bad day. Now I guess I should address some of those phone messages I've been avoiding.*

"Are you okay," was the first thing Doria asked. "I saw you leave the reception, but I couldn't get away. I'm sorry, Pro. I had no idea Ash would be there."

"Not your fault. It was a tough weekend. Sorry I've been out of touch. How's it been going?"

"Great! Even better than I hoped for. A couple of art critics responded very favorably, and people have been showing up like gangbusters. I've heard several people comment on how much they like your work."

"I'm relieved to hear that. I wasn't feeling so great about it when I left on Friday. I'll drop back by when I can – busy week at work."

"Sounds good," Doria said. "Don't forget, we have a 'Meet the Artist' event on Sunday at 4. See you soon. Thanks again for jumping in on such short notice. Oh! I almost forgot – though it is in one of the several messages I left you – you will probably get a call from the owner of Fantasia Gallery. She was 'intrigued by your work' – those were her exact words."

"Oh, wow! Okay. I'll be on the lookout. Thanks, Doria. Enjoy the week. You did a terrific job pulling this all together."

Pro returned Thom's call and left a message: "Sorry I vanished. It was a bear of a weekend, and this week is pretty full. Maybe we can grab dinner this weekend. You could even come and see some of my artwork. I have a few pieces on display at a gallery right now. More soon. Take care."

She forced herself to listen to Ash's message – essentially a formal apology for… many things. *That one I don't need to respond to.*

Pro made a salad and reflected on the day. *Galactic shapeshifters? What do I do with that? I haven't had much experience with shapeshifting – imagine. Oh! But I know who has – well, who had… Jake.*

She went to her studio and rough-sketched an idea for a tribute to Jakey that featured five different versions of him from ripped jeans and a tie-dyed t-shirt, to punked out in leather at a coffee shop leaning in to earnestly encourage her to, "Not give a damn what anyone thinks about you," to dancing at Neon Spectacles on Halloween with spiked green hair in a yellow leather miniskirt.

You were really something, Jakey. Many things – truth be told. I want to honor that. And I have to make sure that your amber eyes light up in every version I paint. They always sparkled with a kind of somber mischief. Thank you for all of your gifts, Jake. I'm sorry the world was such a tough place to be. I know the feeling. Now, I need to lay down and drift off.

And so, she did.

20. PAINTING

Weeks passed in Erinmar as Pro painted and painted. *This feels so different from the ways I was painting at home for the job, doing the advertising thing or even the painting I was doing in Astara. In the healing world, the primary subjects grew out of my dreams and maybe even out of my mind as I tried to make sense of everything I'd been experiencing. But here in Erinmar – here something is very different. It feels effortless and fun and even loving. Loving? What an odd choice of words for painting.*

Pro found herself painting with a sense of – what was it – urgency? A fervor? A passion? Not exactly, though there were moments each of those feelings was alive in her. It was something else, some other quality she couldn't quite define. The more she tried to clarify it, the more elusive the term became. She couldn't pin it down or put boundaries around it, so she finally let go of trying to figure it out.

Once she did that, of course, it came to her, like a Crestlin – the small butterfly-like creatures that reminded Pro of irises, her favorite flower, with three flowing purple and yellow wings. The first time one landed on her shoulder, it tickled her ear as she felt it say, "Hello." Its sweet, soft wings reassured her with a calming 'voice' that made her feel safe and somehow valued just for who she was. *The creatures of Erinmar each have their own unique ways of doing that,* she thought one day as she painted atop the rainbow cliffs. It was one of her favorite places to sit and think and look out over the village and the beautiful ever-changing landscape of Erinmar.

🦋

Actually, it feels wrong of me to think of them as creatures, even though their species are unique and foreign to everything I knew before. To think of them as "creatures" makes them somehow strange, when it feels truer to say that they feel like friends – even those I only greet on my walks.

The thought trembled through her whole nervous system, tingling up her spine, touching some old, buried loneliness and setting it free. *Free as a Crestlin,* she thought with a smile.

The Crestlin couldn't be captured – and not because they were fleet of wing. They seemed to dematerialize and simply reappear somewhere else. That tendency made Pro think of fireflies and how when she was a child they only appeared when they lit up.

That sense of wonder infused her art now. In fact, she was painting with a joy and a passion that reminded her of being in college. She had a sense of purpose – that was the term that had eluded her. She was painting with a purpose, but not the goal-oriented drive her parents worked so hard to instill in her.

Well, that never quite took root, did it? This sense of purpose was filled with an easy knowingness – knowing who she was and that she was, indeed, living on purpose – without so much effort and angst.

Wow! Can my work actually be playfully purposeful?

Pro's painting started to resonate with the truth of the subjects she painted, filtered through her own perspective. Her work was luminous, as if the light of her heart shone through. That felt so different to her, she realized one day.

When I put my heart out there at home, it got trampled on, so I learned to protect it – armor it to some extent, though I was never able to completely wall it off, no matter how hard I tried to shut it down. But as I'm opening my heart here, with all of the acceptance and support I'm getting – Wow! It's like I am finding a new freedom in my painting that pours out of me and onto the canvas.

She painted her class at The Gridline, not a documentary representation of her students, but an abstracted version that crackled with the energy, effervescence, and joy they were learning to bring to their own art. That painting also made her more acutely aware that Fen was not simply troubled; she suspected he was being bullied. I have to find a way to help him. I don't know how yet, but I will know.

I have to find a way to help him. I don't know how yet, but I will know.

And, of course, she painted the inhabitants of Erinmar – her

❧ *Pro Paints at the Rainbow Cliffs of Erinmar*

new friends. Her paintings were celebrations of wondrous beings like the Whirlpa: the merfolk of indeterminate sexuality. She was told they were able to mate in a multitude of ways. She painted them in various settings: swimming with their four fins aflutter, using them like propellers to travel both on top of the water and through the air, and like webbed feet to walk on land. The triptych was a tribute to their mutability – their incredible ability to adapt to different landscapes and navigate them effortlessly.

They're shapeshifters! Ha! That's perfect!

Okay, how do they do that? I know a lot about modifying my behavior to various circumstances and to the needs of other people. I have been doing that my whole life. But what the Whirlpa do is different. What evolutionary process allowed them to be so open to adaptability without losing a sense of themselves?

Pro found great joy in painting her new friends and offering her portraits as gifts. She painted the elflike Grolfin, who mobilized on their webbed ears, and the tawny Kostlings that sprouted eight legs when they awoke. She captured the starfish-like Turfters at various stages as they uncurled from their rolling ball-like state. They were all portraits of magic and transformation in action.

Pro's painting of Pimsal, the fawn-like Sweeker, and Stribjus in midair captured the playfulness and warmth between them. The nighttime picture of them surrounded by Spilf, with their six wings and three tails that glowed bright orange, was unabashedly romantic. Pro was thrilled to see Stribjus so swept away and she delighted in capturing the bond growing between them. *It seems like the levity that used to be his armor has now become a gateway to deeper ties. Even their disagreements seem playful. I've never seen a relationship where two people – well, two individuals – just unlocked such joy in each other. I never would have imagined that was even possible.*

As Pro reveled in capturing her impressions of these amazing creatures and events on canvas, Loahn, with Oster, showed up at her studio one afternoon with a surprise – a Durnlinger named Drewfog. The 12-eyed yellow green Durnlinger were artists of a different sort. Their art was to absorb and share impressions of things. Their many eyes served a myriad of functions. They could "photograph" images and store them, shrink or enlarge them, project them, even embed them, etch them into practically any surface – on leaves, on cloth, on walls. Drewfog delighted in Pro's art as they catalogued it all and assured her the Durnlinger would be overjoyed to create an archive of her work. Anytime she gifted a painting, she only had to have the recipient trot, crawl, ooze or galumph over to the Durnlinger to have it recorded, archived, resized, and manifested on any surface they desired.

Showing all of her work to Drewfog made Pro take stock of how much she had actually done since arriving in Erinmar. She fell asleep that night glowingly content.

Awakening refreshed in her bedroom, she immediately wrote in her journal. *Is it bizarre that now I seem to be moving back and forth between worlds without any kind of jolt or disorientation? Probably. Pro chuckled. I think it helps that I'm painting in both worlds, so I don't feel like I'm losing track of who I am based on where I am. Whenever I go to sleep, I'm not quite sure what world I will wake up to. Pretty wild. And for right now that's working just fine.*

The depth of her artwork in Erinmar made Pro incredibly aware of just how commercialized everything in her world had become.

Ha! Working in advertising you would think I'd have noticed that my world has been basically one big commercial. But no, I just did my job. Maybe it's time to change that. Paige wants bold choices? Let's do it! It's Wednesday. Countdown to my six month make-it-or-break-it review. Oh, Lord… I mean — Whee!

The day flew by. She worked on ideas for <u>The Galactics</u>, forcing herself to take risks and sketch out ideas from a brand-new threshold.

It's just an experiment, Pro. You can judge yourself at every turn and rip up ideas along the way as you get frustrated with yourself. Yeah! That's always been fun, she thought sarcastically.

You want a challenge? Okay — the goal for today is fifteen colored pencil thumbnail sketches — five for each of the main characters. And… and whatever they look like, I will share them with Paige and get feedback. In fact, I will email her right now to see if she has time late this afternoon to meet. No turning back.

Even though it made her stomach churn like there was no tomorrow, she sent the email.

Pro's stomach was turning flip-flops as she walked to Paige's office for the meeting she herself had requested. *You do realize you're setting yourself up to get shot down, right? What was I thinking?*

Paige's reactions surprised her. "I have to admit it looks like you took my challenge to heart. Some of the ideas – not all of them, certainly – but some of your ideas are a radical departure from anything I would have expected to see from you. I like your concept of using a unique color palette for each of the main characters. It will give you lots of latitude to explore while they maintain their unique identities. There is some powerful energy flowing through a few of these."

Paige went on to point out what she considered the strongest elements that were surfacing for the three protagonists. She even asked Pro questions, like. "What stands out to you about each character? What makes us care about each one?" She concluded with, "I appreciate you sharing with me so early in the process. I think that takes some guts. I know I can get very protective and precious of my own initial ideas. You're off to a good start, Pro."

As she returned to her desk, Pro thought, *that is not the response I was expecting. Paige was not only helpful, but actually encouraging. I guess people can surprise you – if you give them the chance. Thanks, Paige.*

That evening Pro received a call from a number she didn't recognize. She almost let it go to voicemail, assuming it was someone else asking her to donate more than she already had, but something told her to pick the call up.

"Hello?"

"Is this Kathryn Proscher?" a woman's voice asked.

"Yes, it is," Pro replied cautiously.

"Ms. Proscher, my name is Sonya Mandevall. I'm the owner and curator of Fantasia Art Gallery downtown. I saw your work this past weekend and it intrigues me. In the bio you have posted, you state that these paintings are part of a larger body of work?"

"Thank you, Ms. Mandevall. I appreciate your response to my work. Yes, I'm working on a series of paintings called Dreamscapes."

"Let me get right to the point. I believe your work might be a good match for the artistic mission of my gallery. I'm interested in work that opens up people's imaginations – that transports them. Your paintings did that for me. Might I treat you to lunch tomorrow so we could discuss the possibility of you having a major exhibition at Fantasia Art?"

Pro froze. *Really? Is this a prank call? Remember to breathe, Pro.* "Well… Wow! I really don't know what to say."

"Then just say 'Yes, lunch would be fine.'" Pro could feel Sonya smiling. "No obligations – just a chat to get to know each other, share our thoughts about art, and consider some possibilities."

"Okay, then. Yes, lunch would be fine," Pro laughed. "You would need to come to me though. I have an hour for lunch from

11:30-12:30. I work for Clive Bennett Advertising Associates, in the old Atkins building across from Mercy Park."

"Coming to you is no problem. I know the area. There are lots of restaurants around there. Any allergies, or favorite places?"

Pro almost suggested Lotus Dreams, Elaine's go-to, but what came out of her mouth was, "Nope. Surprise me!" *Did I just say that? Isn't my life lately just one big surprise after another?*

"I can do that. I will make a reservation for us and text you the place. I look forward to meeting you, Kathryn. Have a Fantasia-filled evening."

I think I better sit down. Did she really say my own exhibition? Am I ready for that? Talk about a giant leap. Pro started to tremble and couldn't catch her breath.

Stop! Stop, stop, stop, stop, stop, stop, stop, stop, stop, stop.

"*STOP!*" The sound of her own voice burst Pro out of her downward spiral. "You don't need to jump to conclusions one way or the other. You are just meeting to talk tomorrow – that's all! Easy, right?

Right! Just ignore the fact that it might change my whole life.

"You can't know that. You can't," she reassured herself. "Just show up for lunch and take it one bite at a time." The thought made her smile sheepishly. "An inspired idea. That actually reminds me – I'm famished and eager to paint."

Let's do it! She threw together a platter of fruit, cheeses, and crackers so she could munch as she painted. *One bite at a time.*

Pro painted – and munched – for hours. Images from Erinmar leapt from her body onto canvas effortlessly, playfully. She had no idea what time it was when she slipped into slumber.

She awoke in Ernimar refreshed and eager to paint some more. There, Pro found her artwork at the studio moving into a new phase of increased meaning as she thought of each of the worlds she had been visiting. She decided to give thanks to each world as it inspired a painting.

Her painting of the Dark World she had first encountered depicted her like the central figure in Munch's famous painting "The Scream," as she recalled screaming 'STOP' and the creeping, crawling scorpions, bats and spiders that filled her with terror had all frozen and cocked their little heads at her.

The doorway/lobby painting, which took her away from that darkness, she now envisioned as a magic portal with more stories to be told.

Her paintings of "Four Paths" was whimsical. She thought of it like one of the *Choose Your Own Adventure* books from her childhood. In one painting, all paths led to the same destination and in another version they all led different places. As she painted them, she was sure that every one of them was, possibly, a path for her. Each of them – direct, jagged, curved, spiraled, and so on – held the potential to lead her where she needed to go.

M2's voice reassured her, "You are making your way, Pro."

Making my way? What does that mean, exactly? Forging my own path? Making it up as I go along? A path that leads where? To a whole array of worlds where I have to find what? The Beckoner? The Agency?

But no wizardly-wise reply came, except, "Be patient."

Though she was becoming increasingly aware that each world had held some kind of gift for her, she certainly didn't feel like she belonged in any of them, at least not for good. *Well, that doesn't ring true. In some ways it is, has been, I hope, for MY good – but not for always.*

Pro thought, felt, and painted her way through each one.

The swashbuckling guardian at the gate who demanded she assert her right to enter Thanton and claim her dreams was the centerpiece of one painting. It was only in creating the painting that Pro realized that the guard bore a striking resemblance to Quinn, the first art professor she had in college. She had had such a crush on him, and he had challenged her to step up and consider that she might actually have some talent as an artist. That thought had felt exciting and dangerous – and, like Thanton, full of opportunities for confrontation.

The thought of Thanton filled her with excitement, remembering how she had claimed her power in the midst of danger, bravado and gamesmanship. She painted the huge brawl of wrestling, swordplay, and fisticuffs.

In one version of Thanton, Stribjus was five different places at once, which seemed completely appropriate.

In a very different way the flying, floating world of Navlys had challenged her. The silks, in her panic, had taken her to terrifying heights. How had she navigated that? Oh, she remembered, *I had to learn how much to let go and how much to hold on.* She painted Loahn placidly floating in space beside her flailing aeronautics. Her Navlys triptych captured his serene wisdom, her terror and her pride at having successfully disentangled herself. In each of those paintings, M2 floated in the background, taking a different form each time.

And Vergon. She certainly remembered Vergon and Felagor the Terrible with its nightmare world of festering fears, doubts, and inadequacies where memories were weapons. She painted the monster from many vantage points—distorted images within a multitude of mirrors, arms and heads flying as they taunted and tormented, lashing out viciously.

Have I ever done that? She asked herself. I have to admit I have. It's why I am so afraid of getting angry. I have allowed it so rarely, that my anger frightens me. I guess we all have the potential to lash out and be hurtful.

In one version of the monster, an armor-clad warrior predominated, reminding Pro of Clive and the way he and his team swept in to transform Atkins Advertising.

Pro wondered if Felagor itself might be tormented. Why would the monster covet the Beckoner – hold her prisoner with such fierceness? Pro found herself imagining Felagor's loneliness, isolation, and pain and painted one version of the monster from that threshold. The black and blue hues in that painting were filled with sorrow, as if the monster was crying out in pain that was masked by its ferocity. She knew what that was like – burying the stuff that was judged bad.

What if Felagor imagined itself guarding the Beckoner to protect her? In that painting the monster appeared almost parental.

Her longest series captured the Kermuffles huddling together in fear all the way to their dancing with glee. She couldn't believe how she had taken charge of the situation, trusted her instincts, and worked with the Kermuffle Kquing. *I helped them to be playful – well, to bring out their playful side. It would be pretty arrogant to assume they had never been playful until I showed up.*

On one canvas, they were dancing in a myriad of pink bubbles. As she painted that canvas, she felt like she was at her fifth birthday party blowing bubbles in the backyard. It delighted her to realize that some of these Kermuffle paintings in Erinmar were actually paintings she had on display at ImagineArts Gallery.

She created many paintings of Astara, too. Its magical domas filled many canvases. The Council of Light, the crystalline walls and the fierce love and adamant overprotectiveness of Helastion and Melara all had their places in Pro's art.

One day when Oster visited her studio, Pro said, "It's so wonderful to be painting here. Oster, thank you for making it possible. I painted while we were in Astara, but those paintings were very different. I wish I could show them to you, but I had to leave them behind."

Oster coiled and jumped and immediately took her to the Durnlinger. Apparently, Oster related Pro's situation to them. The Durnlinger conveyed to Pro, "If you do not mind giving us access to the mental records of those paintings, we can merge with the part of your brain where those images are stored and transfer them for you to canvas, or whatever material or surface you would like."

"Really?" Pro said. "That's amazing. I would love that. Thank you so much." Within a few days the number of paintings in her studio had grown richer with various versions of her experiences. Pro studied the paintings from Astara beside those more recent creations in Erinmar.

They feel very different, she thought. *Why? What is the difference? It looks like the Astara series serve to document events more. Also, many of them have a dreamlike quality. Of course! They grew out of my dreams. But here on Erinmar, my paintings illuminate my subjects. I am transforming them, often with more than one interpretation, so they have more nuances, more feeling. In return, I am transformed by them. I never imagined my art had the capacity to do that.*

It was odd to Pro that these worlds seemed so much more real to her than the one she had grown up in. Since going down the drain, through her own personal sinkhole, she had just been scrambling to cope with whatever challenge she was thrown into. In Astara, and now in Erinmar, there was time to reflect, and she had... off and on.

Is all this just a series of dreams? Did I pass out in the office? Is my body in a coma somewhere in Mercy Hospital?

"Does it matter?" M2 asked her.

I don't think it does – at least not right now. As a wise being told me, I will know when the time is right. Pro felt M2 smile at that response, and she smiled back.

I have never had so much fun painting just for me, so I'm going to enjoy myself and trust that I'll know when it is time to move on. For right now, I just need to be as present as I can in whatever reality I happen to awaken in. Wait a minute! Who is this woman who is actually admitting it might be okay to not have complete control of everything in her life? That would be you, Pro. That would be you.

She was filled with peace as she fell asleep that night, and not at all surprised to wake up in her apartment two hours before her alarm - refreshed and raring to go.

Great! I can paint for an hour or two and still get to work early.

The morning was filled with worlds of paint. Capturing images of Erinmar before she went to work inspired Pro to take even more risks bringing the shapeshifting characters of The Galactics to life. She was having such a good time immersing herself in her work she was glad she set an alarm for her lunch date with Sonya at Le Petite Patissier. Lunch, too, flew by and it took her breath away – in a good way.

What Pro remembered Sonya saying was, "I really enjoyed what you created for this exhibit. I checked out your website and these pieces are quite different from your earlier work. I feel immersed in your magical worlds. How many pieces are there in this series?"

"It's really new, I'm not sure at the moment." *Lord! I haven't thought of that at all.* "But I am very excited about the series. It's a new direction for me. I plan to paint a whole series of worlds – hence the title Dreamscapes."

"I would like to see more of your work because to be frank, what I have seen so far I find inspiring, and I don't use that word very often. When things have calmed down for you, come visit the gallery and see what we do there. I think the kind of work you're doing would be a good fit for Fantasia Art. In fact, the series you're talking about sounds perfect for us. I would like for us to keep in touch and explore how my gallery might support your work. You could show a few pieces at a time and when the series is finished, we could feature a whole exhibition of your work. Your worlds could take over the gallery for a few months. How does that sound?"

Pro's mouth dropped open and she had to keep remembering to close it – and to breathe. "That sounds incredible." *And more than a little terrifying.*

"I want to encourage you not to sell any of your new work just yet, Kathryn. When the whole series appears, they could potentially jump in value. We'll have a chance to roll out your series a little bit at a time as you develop it – like sneak previews of coming attractions. I know I'm getting ahead of myself, but I have a great feeling about this connection. I hope I'm not overwhelming you.

Pro smiled. *Oh, no! NOT AT ALL! Really? My whole series? Sneak previews? A venue where my work is encouraged and supported? Why would that be overwhelming? Breathe, Pro. Just breathe.*

Pro caught her breath enough to speak, finally. "To be honest, it's wonderful to hear someone so excited about my work, Sonya. Oh! And it's Pro. My friends call me Pro – short for Proscher."

"I know I come on strong, Pro," said Sonya, "but I get a vision and I run with it. Keep in touch and come on down to the gallery when you can."

Pro's head was spinning like a top as she rushed back to the office.

Oh, my God! That was mind-blowing! Did that really happen? Is this even possible? What an opportunity – and what pressure.

Pro wanted to laugh and cry and scream and skip and run and dance her way back to CBAA. She managed to calm herself enough to just walk – and to keep on the sidewalk.

You're going to screw this up, you know, a voice inside her said.

Pro heard her father's voice as she entered the building, "If it sounds too good to be true, it probably is. There are no free rides, Kathryn."

She arrived in the lobby consumed by sadness and fear. The big clock there told her she had five minutes to get back to work.

She leaned on the table in the lobby to catch her breath. As she looked up at the haunting mural, she was sucked into the mélange of colors. The cacophony of images and sounds that swirled around her – her parents and Ash and Miss Massachusetts, Zor and Loahn, Professor Tilson and Stribjus and Jake and Felagor. Sinkholes and steam holes bursting with judgements whirled her around.

She awoke from her nightmare covered in sweat – in Erinmar. *I can't think about all of this. It's too much. I just need to paint.*

Oster appeared at her door that morning, greeting her with a nuzzle and playful carryings on, escorting her to her studio. The Scoo could always sense exactly the kind of support she needed.

Oster, you are wonderful, she thought, *touching her forehead to her friend's. I feel much lighter now. Thank you.*

At her studio in Erinmar, Pro embarked upon a new series, revisiting moments from her past. Her parents, her sister, her nanny, her boyfriends, were popping up in her paintings.

In one painting, a small girl and a dog splashed around in a fountain of Shiftlers, with their cascades of multicolored water, while a nanny reached out in helpless panic. It was playful, even whimsical.

In another, her sister Patricia appeared as the flight attendant she had always dreamed of being, a companion piece to "Patricia, the perfect wife and mother."

Even Ash appeared in her paintings – before Miss Massachusetts. Ash laughing, Ash dancing with her in Hawaii – walking on the beach holding hands.

Elaine showed up as well with all of her wise-cracking straightforwardness and warmth, in her own personal doma of wisdom. Pro painted Elaine looking straight out, right through the onlooker's bull, with a raised eyebrow, a piercing gaze, and a wry smile that refused to become a smirk.

Her tribute to Little Jakey appeared as well. Images of various versions of him leapt off the canvas.

Is painting my past just nostalgic for me? I don't think so. No, I'm certainly not romanticizing my past – painting it as all rainbows and roses. There are plenty of dark moments here: arguments, admonishments, run-ins, abandonments. It's like my own artistic sleenaje.

That thought amused her to no end. It also filled her with a sense of accomplishment and confidence. *That really rings true. This whole process of painting is exactly that – a sleenaje. I am transforming old ways of thinking about myself and even the people and events in my life. I can see those changes reflected in my paintings.*

Painting her new boss, the mover and shaker – confident, willful and headstrong Clive – made him more accessible, more human. She painted various versions of him. In one, his giant head filled the canvas. In another he looked like a little boy dressing up in oversized suits with bright shirts and loud ties. She painted him holding a pink slip and cocking his head. *Now why have I been so afraid of him?*

In a way, it makes sense. I'm not in the office – I don't have to confront him – and I don't have to face all of the times over the years I've been too scared to say what I felt… oh, Lord.

As she painted all of these aspects of her experience, Pro had the feeling that she was somehow reclaiming them as her own and even getting some sense of how they were connected. *Connected? To what? What does that even mean?*

She had felt connected to Ash, hadn't she? And certainly, at least at times, she had connected to her painting, though with the demands of her job she had little time for her own creativity, so busy was she pouring it into the demands of other people.

I'm feeling more connected to me, to different parts of me, even as I notice all of the wonderful connections being made around me and with me — defining my OWN questela as a connection between brain, body, and heart.

Maybe that's what's different.

21. CONNECTIONS

Zor and Loahn were spending a great deal of time together and as they did, Pro and Zor grew closer as well. Pro was surprised to find that Zor confided in her like a best girlfriend. "I can't even begin to describe all of the things I'm feeling," Zor shared with Pro one softly sunny afternoon. "Is it insane that I feel giddy? I've never felt giddy before in my entire life."

"We went swimming last night in the yellow lake," Zor continued. "The Shiftlers were especially active because one of the moons was full last night, so we played with them and floated under their air waterfalls. It was magical."

"As he held me in his arms in the water, it felt like the whole world was buoying us up. And later as we lay on the soft blue-green grass holding hands, he leaned over and kissed me so tenderly I could hardly bear it. I have never felt so vulnerable and safe at the same time. Is that insane?" Zor asked.

"I think it's wonderful," Pro said, squeezing her hand. Zor gave her a big hug and, to Pro's surprise, started to hum. While she was witnessing the changes in Zor, a humming hug was the last thing Pro expected.

How can she embody strength and gentleness at the same time? Pro thought. *I have no idea, but she's doing it beautifully. I want to be able to do that. Up to now I couldn't even imagine it was possible.*

"One other small thing," Zor added seriously. "Loahn asked me to marry him – again. And this time I said yes." They both squealed and threw themselves into a humming hug that seemed to last forever.

Zor continued, "This morning, we went to tell Cepella and Jolner, who had already sensed the shift, of course. They absolutely beamed their approval, as did Oster, and the humming hugs we shared then I thought would really never end. Cepella and Oster are already planning the engagement celebration, which apparently here in Erinmar is a huge event for the entire village. So, I don't know what we're in for, but it's sure to be amazing."

"Cepella told me that the engagement celebration needs to take place next week, 'Before the entire village decides to celebrate without us.' Her words."

Zor and Pro couldn't stop smiling – and laughing at the notion that the whole village would have its own celebration in honor of the happy couple... without them.

The next week flew by, filled with village-wide preparations for the engagement party. Pro designed invitations, which the Durnlingers printed on a plantlike material that held organic inks beautifully. The master-printers assured her these would disintegrate the week after the party.

The entire village was a flurry of activity and excitement in preparation for the big event. Tents were set up by the lake so that the Whirlpa, the Shiftlers and other water folk could pay their respects and join in the festivities. The entire area was festooned with garlands and flowers, tables for food and stations for drink.

The day arrived and the festivities began in the afternoon. There was food and laughter and toasting, but the highlight was the engagement dance. Loahn had warned his friends that they would all be taking part but assured them there was nothing to fear. The dance was repetitive and Cepella and Jolner would guide them through it. At Zor's insistence they were taught the basic steps in advance.

The pattern of movement itself was quite simple. Two partners began some distance apart and then acknowledged each other – with a nod, a bow, a curtsey, or whatever sign of recognition struck them in the moment. Then each partner made a small circle around themselves in either direction. Next, the partners rushed towards each other and then back.

Finally, the moment arrived. The villagers gathered around a huge open circular area. Jolner and Cepella walked to the center and greeted all of the guests. And then the dance began.

🦋 *The Engagement Party*

Each time Loahn's parents circled themselves, it was clear to Pro they were dancing much more than steps. They were claiming their own spaces. Though he had no eyes, Jolner navigated his way through the dance with the same sure-footedness Pro had come to take for granted from Loahn. Cepella, of course, bursting with joy, was the epitome of a humming hug. They approached each other and then withdrew, reminding Pro of a minuet she had learned in grade school.

It's an invitation to be seen and received, to choose how you want to connect and share.

In phase two of the dance, after moving toward each other, the dancers paused, then circled one another. Next, they promenaded side by side, then parted to inscribe two large curves, which delivered some of the dancers back to their original partners and others to someone new. The repetition of each movement reaffirmed the merging of the dancing partners.

Entering phase two, Jolner went to Loahn and Cepella went to Zor and invited them into the dance, repeating the same sequence with their new partners. The pattern extended out from there as Loahn came to Pro, inviting her into the dance.

Pro felt the impact of his request. As he stood before her and she gazed into his blind eyes, which saw so much, her heart opened with the warmth of deep friendship.

Loahn is extending an invitation to me, and I get to choose to accept or not. I don't have to automatically say yes just to be polite. I could choose to sit this one out and join the dance later. How many ways have I been afraid to step into a dance of new possibilities before – terrified I would make a mistake or get it wrong? I am not missing this opportunity. Why, thank, you I would love to dance.

Pro smiled warmly at Loahn as she began to move. Encircling herself filled her with an awareness of her own personal boundaries before she moved toward Loahn.

As they encircled each other for the last time, smiling, they both promenaded to invite Oster for the next partnership and as she made her first circle with Oster and Loahn, Pro noticed that Stribjus and Pimsal were partnering as were Zor, Cepella and Jolner.

More and more participants were invited in, with pairs, trios, and larger groups forming and then reconfiguring. Pro noticed those who were establishing themselves as couples would tend to gravitate back to each other more and more throughout the dance, yet Jolner and Cepella, and even Zor and Loahn for that matter, did not dance solely with each other. M2 took part as well. Pro felt the magician watching, sensing their thoughts as they smiled down on the celebration of merging.

I have never thought of repetition in quite that way before, but that's what it is. The repetitive movement seals the bond between the dancers, celebrating their merging – however playful, affirming, or challenging the interaction might be. Every connection is its own unique event. Wow! How wonderful!

Pro had always been intimidated by dancing – always afraid she would screw up somehow. However, here, because it didn't matter what part of the dance someone was on, and the patterns of the limbs were not prescribed, there was no way to get the movement wrong.

This whole celebration feels like one gigantic liberating dance. It really does! Everyone is free to move into and out of the dance patterns whenever they choose with whomever they choose. Sitting, visiting, swimming, eating are all just various aspects of a much larger dance. What an exciting way to think about living, Pro thought as she danced with Stribjus into the lake.

Pro did her best to connect with every being she had painted. It felt like a lovely way to thank them for sharing who they were with her. All of Erinmar joined in. The Lumlers rolled through, and the Eflurial wafted down and back up and around in their own version of the dance.

At one point, Pro found herself at the center of a large circle by herself. For just a moment part of her thought she ought to be embarrassed, then she simply let that self-judgment go as she smiled and whirled. It was then she noticed that she did, indeed, have a partner. A Crestlin hovered around her and danced with her. She was sure it was the same one who had greeted her when she first came. At one point as it hovered in front of her, the lights made its wings of white and pale blue turn pink, and the image of that pink slip Clive had held in front of her face flashed across her mind.

For a moment both of those realities interfaced, and Pro felt the love and support of the Crestlin even as she was aware of the unspoken threat of the pink slip. Pro started to recoil from it, bracing herself. Then she gazed at the Crestlin, softening, relaxing – finally reaching her hand out to her flying friend. The juxtaposition of the images made her smile as she circled herself once more. Pro acknowledged the beautiful Crestlin gratefully as it flew to her shoulder. Then, as the circle around them reconfigured completely, she went on to dance with Drewfog the Durnlinger.

Pro couldn't remember ever having a night filled with so much goodwill, playfulness, sharing, and love. *This is a whole new level of connection. And it feels so easy. Can love – not just romantic love – but Love with a capital "L" – be so easy, so accepting? I guess so*, she thought with a big grin as she laid down to sleep. *It certainly was tonight.*

Peace enveloped her like a warm soft blanket, an Eflurial of gentleness, peace, and joy.

When she opened her eyes and found herself in front of the painting at CBAA, she panicked. *Oh my God! How long was I out? Did anyone notice?*

Co-workers were bustling by her. She looked at the clock.

No, that's impossible. All that time that passed in Erinmar and I still have two minutes to get back to my desk? That makes no sense. But I'll take it.

Pro shook her head at the mesmerizing painting, dashed back to her desk and into <u>The Galactics</u>. Submerging herself in the worlds of the shapeshifters made the afternoon fly by. Multiple versions of the three lead characters emerged and merged, creating depths and dimensions that helped her calm the excitement and fear around her lunch with Sonya. The nuances she was creating in the eyes of Acheron, the holy one captivated her. *Good work, Pro. Someone could get lost in those eyes.*

That night her sleep was deep and peaceful and for the first time since she had come to Erinmar, she dreamt of M2 and the Beckoner together. M2, the Miraculous Magician, never said or even thought a word. *I don't think they think in words.* But Pro clearly felt the pride M2 exuded as they smiled – proud of Pro, proud for Pro. She allowed that loving acknowledgement of the depth of her growth and understanding to wash over her.

As she heard the Beckoner's voice calling her, it felt like a great yearning reaching out. It was calling her into a courtship dance of empowered peace and love. She had no idea what that phrase meant but when she awoke, she remembered the dream with great clarity, and she knew it was time for her to leave Erinmar.

My time here – there? – here? – does it even matter? - has felt suspended. My painting has been so prolific and my experiences so vast at times it has seemed like surely years have passed. At other times everything has blurred by in the blink of an eye.

The celebration had gone on and on through the night. Jolner and Cepella had invited the extended family to gather at midday for a light meal. Loahn, Zor and Stribjus were there, of course, along with Oster and Pimsal. Their sharing throughout the meal was a delightful revisiting of the events of yesterday.

When they finished eating, Pro said, "I had a dream last night and I heard the Beckoner's call again. It was so compelling – like nothing I had ever felt before. It was like being called home. The Beckoner is calling out to me, and I know she's the key – she can make sense of this whole crazy adventure I've been on. I have to go. I have to find her."

As she expected, there was an uproar, but not of admonishment. It was clearly an outpouring of love and support.

Jolner said, "We honor that you need to do what is yours to do."

"You know there will always be a place for you at our table," Cepella chimed in. "You are family. You are a part of us now. And I will set that very place for you whenever we gather here so you might know you are with us and that you are loved."

"Of course, we will join you. The wedding won't be for months and months. There is plenty of time for us to go with you and get back," Zor said to Pro. Then she looked at Loahn.

"Yes, of course," Loahn said.

Stribjus said, "Count me in." Then he looked at his new love and said, "Before you ask, Pimsal, you can't go with us. It is too dangerous, and I couldn't bear putting you in peril. I will be back in a flash." He grinned.

"No," Pro said. "It's time for me to find the Agency. I don't know who they are, but I know I will find them, and I know the Beckoner is the key. I have to do this."

"But you'll need protection. I should be the one to go with you." Zor insisted. Zor touched Loahn's cheek. "I love you more than I have ever thought possible, Loahn. And your love gives me more strength than I could ever have imagined. That strength will empower me to kill Felagor and return to you."

Loahn smiled tenderly at Zor's proclamation. "My dearest heart, you can't prove your love by killing."

"And this is not your task, Zor," Pro said. "All of you have sacrificed so much for me. I have learned so much from you and grown so much. You've put yourselves in harm's way – for me. You have stood between me and my greatest fears, between me and death. And this is mine to do – alone."

Zor started to speak, but Pro stopped her. "Zor, I don't know if you know I can be every bit as stubborn as you can."

"I've seen it," Stribjus jumped in. They all smiled.

Stribjus came to Pro, took her hands, looked in her eyes and said, "We will miss you – terr-i-fically." Everyone laughed, then a hush fell over them all as the finality of Pro's decision echoed through the house. Oster slithered around Pro's right arm and put his furry head on her shoulder.

It was Zor who broke the silence. "You don't have to leave right away, do you?"

"Everybody will want to say goodbye," Loahn said. "Everyone in Erinmar has adopted you, in case you haven't noticed."

"I have noticed that." Pro said with a smile. She considered for a moment. She thought about the Beckoner and M2, then replied, "No, of course I don't have to leave this instant. I will take a few days to finish any paintings and close up my studio. I think today I will visit some of my favorite places like the lake and the rainbow cliffs, then spend the bulk of my time in my studio where everyone is welcome to pop in to visit and say goodbye." Tears were rolling down her cheeks.

"I will miss all of you – terr-i-fically," she said. She smiled and rushed out of the house to sit by the lake. The silver-yellow water lapped at her feet to comfort her. The blue-green grass caressed her as she fell asleep.

When she awoke, she found herself staring into Acheron's eyes, back at her desk in the CBAA office.

Oh, God! What the hell is happening to me? Do I need to talk to Dr. Lambdowski about some kind of medication? No, that's crazy. It's okay, Pro. You have gotten a lot done and the afternoon is pretty much gone. On to the next adventure. She smiled. My life is beyond bizarre, but I have to admit – it's pretty good.

Then she remembered.

Oh, my gosh! The Gridline. I've been so busy I haven't even thought about today's project. My mind has been filled with galactic shapeshifters, among other things. Wait a minute. I have another idea around shapeshifting we could play with. Do I have time? I'll need to get it set up before they arrive. I can make it. Is there anything I need to pick up? Nope – no time, we'll wing it with whatever I can find in the space.

At The Gridline, Pro created a large found object sculpture in the middle of the room of chairs, boxes, water bottles, an extra easel, anything she could find. She grabbed a couple of ground cloths and covered the whole thing just before the students started arriving.

"Grab an easel and position yourselves in a circle around this big thing in the center of the room, along with plenty of paper and whatever art supplies you choose to work with today."

Once everyone was in place, she continued. "Today is an exercise in perspective – but in a different way than you might be used to. As I lift the ground cloths off of my found object sculpture, please stay at your easel. Do not walk around the piece. Paint or draw only what is right in front of you. As always, your representation of what is in front of you may be as straightforward and photographic as you would like or make it abstract! Just base it on your feelings if that's what strikes you. Are there any questions?"

Miraculously, there were none. "You'll have about an hour, then we will discuss your work."

The hour passed quickly as the students threw themselves into the assignment with gusto.

"Okay, great work!" Pro said. "Now before you take a look at each other's work, I want you to close your eyes for a minute and let your mind just imagine what the other sides of the sculpture might look like."

"Our minute is up. So, take a stroll around the room and see what your classmates have created." Pro gave them a few minutes to absorb what they were seeing, before she asked, "So, what do you notice? Does all of your artwork look the same?"

"No, not at all," Jessica said.

"They're all completely different," Carlos chimed in.

"Why is that do you think?" Pro asked.

"They have to be different," Fen said, "because we each saw only our own point of view. We didn't get to see what anyone else saw."

"And the other side didn't look anything like I expected it to," added Louisa.

"Does this tell you anything about art? Or about life?" Pro asked.

"Well, it is easy to think what I'm seeing is the whole picture," Henry said.

Anita said, "And we can only paint or draw from our own viewpoint – even if it is abstract."

"Wait – so, if someone doesn't understand why we painted something the way we painted it – whatever it is, that doesn't make us wrong and them right," Fen added.

"And it doesn't make them wrong either," Katie said. "We're just looking at things in a different way."

"Wow! I'm still learning that, so you're way ahead of me," Pro said. "Give yourselves a huge round of applause, then let's get things put away – including all the parts of my beautiful sculpture. We're done for the day!"

The room exploded with clapping, cheering, and high-fives.

She managed to catch Fen before he ran off. "Hey, Fen, are you doing okay?"

Fen sheepishly replied, "It's been a rough time, Miss Proscher, but I'm getting better."

"I'm glad to hear that. If you need to talk, I'm here. And, you know, sometimes painting or drawing, journaling, or talking out ideas when times are rough can help."

"That's a good thing to remember, Miss Proscher. Thanks for looking out for me. Have a good night."

"You, too, Fen. Take good care of yourself, okay?"

"Thanks. I will. I'm getting better at that, I think." He gave a shy smile.

"So am I, Fen. So am I. It's a process – for sure. See you next week."

Pro journeyed home exhilarated. *Oof! The kids did such great work. And I helped them get there. It's odd. I've never given myself credit for the impact I'm making. I've been proud as all get out of them, but not of myself. But that's changing. Sonya said my work was inspiring. Inspiring. What more could I ask for?*

At home, Pro grabbed some snacks, then sat in her studio. Paintings from Erinmar, imprinted on her brain, flowed through her fingers effortlessly onto canvas. She painted Stribjus and Pimsal dancing and juggling in the red-purple field of Erinmar and she started painting the warrior triptych from her dreams in Astara.

After a few hours she laid down on the couch and dozed off. She awoke preparing to leave Erinmar.

The next few days passed in a heartbeat. Pro's studio was constantly full – with all kinds of visitors thanking her for her beautiful paintings, helping her to pack things up and store them. To her surprise, delight, and sometimes embarrassment, they were also sharing what they loved most about her.

The morning of her departure arrived, and the entire village gathered outside of her studio to see her off. M2 even appeared to witness and support the unfolding magic. The villagers of Erinmar did not seem surprised at all to see the wizard, Pro noticed. The Miraculous Magician was welcomed like an old friend, but only briefly. This was clearly Pro's moment and none of them had any desire to pull any attention from her.

Before Pro could say anything, Loahn stepped forward and said, "We have a surprise for you!" The crowd cheered. "You have to put on this blindfold," Loahn continued.

As she was being blindfolded, Pro heard Jolner's voice say, "We have one last journey for you to take before you leave Erinmar."

With a friend at each shoulder and Oster wrapped around her left ankle helping guide every step, they went on a long walk.

"Where are you taking me?" Pro asked.

"You'll see." That was Stribjus, Pro was sure. She could hear lots of voices behind her. It sounded like the whole village was following them.

Finally, they came to a halt. Someone took her hand and placed it in front of her on a wall. It was rough. Instinctively she knew she was by the rainbow cliffs. How perfect that they should take her to one of her favorite places to say goodbye.

Her blindfold was removed, and she found her hand was on a picture etched into the side of the cliff. That picture was surrounded by other pictures of her friends here in Erinmar.

She gasped. *They're my paintings.*

Then she realized they were way beyond her hand, or even her line of vision. She stepped back a few paces to see more and more of her own artwork. It stretched as far as she could see to the left, to the right and upward. Her eyes welled with tears, so wonderfully overwhelming it was to witness the expanse of her own art.

Oster spoke and Loahn translated, "The Durnlinger have been working in shifts non-stop since they heard you were leaving. They wanted to archive as much of your work as they could find – to resize it, organize it, and etch it on the side of the cliff, which is delighted to host this tribute to you, Pro." The crowd cheered and cheered.

Pro moved further and further away from the cliff. The scope of the project overwhelmed her. *Did I really paint that much?* She kept backing up, noticing the Durnlinger had done something more. Across the cliff wall, her art collection coalesced, forming one massive, sprawling image. The darks and lights lined up to create the face of a stunning woman. She was absolutely beaming – and magical. For the briefest moment Pro thought it might be Zor.

When Pro realized the face was her own, she burst into tears. Never in her whole life had she thought of herself as anything but perhaps mildly attractive. This portrait, however, was undoubtedly her – and she was radiant. One of the Durnlinger must have taken it at the engagement celebration. There was so much camaraderie and joy and love in that face.

"This way you will always be with us," Loahn said.

Zor added, "and this is the way we will always think of you."

"Terr-i-fically beautiful and joyous and shining," chimed in Stribjus.

Pro couldn't stop crying. She had never seen a tribute quite like this. *And it is all for me.* Her heart had to expand to receive all that had been poured into the creation of the giant mural.

Wow! Oh, wow! It's like an avalanche… of what? Appreciation, certainly. And admiration… but there's more. There's so much joy here – and love. For the first time in her life, she was not only unafraid, but honored and excited to be seen and heard.

Zor wrapped an arm around Pro's shoulder and said, "Let's go to the grassy hillock for your final sendoff. Are you doing all right?"

With tears still streaming down her face, Pro smiled and said, "Never, ever better."

Pro and her friends laughed and led the entourage to the blue-green hill where Pro had first awakened in Erinmar. On the way, they stopped by the yellow-silver lake where the Shiftlers put on a grand display of waterworks to honor Pro. Colorful cascading waterfalls materialized all over the lake, then disappeared. It was magical.

Finally, Pro stood atop the hillock looking out at all of her friends. She let herself bask in the huge outpouring of love, soaked it up, and radiated it back out to the adoring crowd. For just a moment she felt like a rock star. She found the thought both amusing and humbling.

"I have so much to thank you all for," Pro said. "This mural is the most remarkable thing I have ever seen. How can I begin to thank you for that?" She went on, "Thank you for welcoming me so open-heartedly into your world, into your lives, for making me feel so accepted, appreciated, and valued – not just for my artwork, but for who I am. You have taught me so much about myself and about friendship, boundaries, connection, and love. I am eternally grateful! Please know that you will always be in my heart no matter where I go. And who knows where my journey may take me? I might very well come back and live among all of you. 'Til then, be well and take care of each other as you all do so graciously. All my love."

A cheer went up in the crowd that rang throughout Erinmar and went on and on and on. Then the crowd withdrew, dispersing until only her small circle of friends remained. Jolner, Cepella, Oster, and Pimsal stood off to one side, while Loahn, Zor, Stribjus and M2 stood close-by.

Stribjus came forward first, producing a small yellow cloth that kept changing colors as he turned it over and over. Pro thought it was a wonderfully playful reminder not to take herself – or life – TOO seriously, because things are always going to change. "Whenever you remember to laugh, to play, to lighten up – I am with you," he said, placing the cloth in her jacket pocket.

As Stribjus stood back to try to control his tears, Zor came to Pro and offered her sword. "But won't you need it," Pro said.

Zor shook her head. "I can always manifest a sword when I need to. Whenever you stand up for yourself, for who you are and what you believe in – I am with you."

M2 came forward next and stood in front of her. As Pro automatically brought her attention to her breathing, she felt waves of light pour through her that were calming, energizing, strengthening, and loving all at once. "Whenever you remember to breathe and flow, I am with you. And Pro – you know every bit as much about being magic as I do." Pro heard his thoughts and smiled in gratitude.

Then Loahn placed his hand on Pro's heart. His presence reminded Pro to honor and celebrate EVERYTHING – ALL of her feelings. Loahn pulled at the yellow cloth Stribjus had placed in her pocket and kept pulling and pulling. Huge swaths of cloth came out, billowing – literally covering the grassy hillock with four different colors, one for each of the companions. Pro felt lost in the flurry of billowing cloth, until she emerged a moment later at its center. And out of each one of the colors of fabric the companions appeared and said, "We are all a part of you – we always have been and always will be."

The cloth engulfed her once more as Pro heard The Beckoner's call.

Somehow the Beckoner's voice called her into consciousness. She stirred, gently coming out of slumber to find herself on her couch. She had no idea how long she had been asleep. *But, hey, the concept of time seems to be more and more fluid in my life. It's dark out and the clock says it is ten o'clock, so we'll go with that.*

She grabbed her journal. As she wrote and drew for more than an hour, she couldn't keep track of all of the feelings bubbling up inside.

Okay, this makes no sense. My emotions are all over the place. I feel like a boomerang. I feel a kind of completeness, but then immediately I feel emptiness. There is immense joy and overwhelming sadness. I feel strong and brave and incredibly vulnerable and fragile. Maybe I am really falling apart. But why? Things seem to be going so well. Okay, my six-month review is tomorrow, and they might let me go. Then what will I do? I have no clue, and okay – that thought terrifies me. On the other hand, the lunch with Sonya was amazing. Is it really too good to be true – that someone actually sees me and my work and gets me? Am I just deluding myself? Reaching too high? Setting myself up to fall into a sinkhole so deep I can never make my way out? I want to cry and scream and laugh all at once. Is there a word for that? I think there is – nervous breakdown. Yeah, I know, that's two words – cut yourself some slack, Pro. Is there a word for the opposite of Questela – where the head, body, and heart are at war with each other?

She had some warm almond milk with cinnamon to try to calm herself down. It didn't work.

Maybe I should paint some more before I go to bed. What am I thinking? My mind is much too jangled to focus.

She brushed her teeth and laid down. *I hope I can get back to sleep. Right, like that's going to happen. I'll just be tossing and turning all night.*

She threw the covers over her head and immediately fell into sleep.

22. FACING FELAGOR

As the cloth covered Pro again, she was engulfed in darkness. In the depths of that darkness the Beckoner's voice grew louder. *Or does it only seem louder to me because of the darkness?* The cloth was lightweight, but it was so voluminous that, as she plowed her way through, it billowed in a colorful dance. When finally, she was able to remove the cloth, it disappeared in a flash of light that momentarily blinded her. As her eyes adjusted to sunlight, she wasn't sure where she was, only that she was no longer in Erinmar. She was also aware that she was totally alone.

Pro looked around to get her bearings. Zor's sword was at her feet. *But where AM I?* The surroundings did look familiar, but she wasn't sure why.

As she realized exactly where she was, her stomach churned. *Oh, no! OH, NO! I've been transported to the entrance of Felagor's lair. How did that happen?*

She was in Vergon. She broke into a cold sweat. Her skin crawled. The terror rising from the pit of her stomach knocked the air out of her. *I knew I was journeying back to face Felagor, but I thought I'd have time to strategize. Yet, here I am...*

It's all right, Pro. You can do this. This is where you were headed. Someone – M2? The Beckoner? – just saved you the trouble of a long journey.

"Thank you?" as she said it aloud, she realized it came out as a question.

Am I really ready for this? Okay. Just calm down. Breathe… Breathe… B r e a t h e. We can do this. Okay, I'm not sure who I mean by 'we' or what I mean by 'this,' but okay.

It did occur to Pro that she was not making any sense, but at the moment that was the least of her worries. As she calmed herself with her breath, she forced herself to remember what first venturing into Felagor's lair was like. *It was volcanic. There were blowholes of steam and yellow slime, and the occasional sinkhole, of course.*

Oh! And there were voices. There were voices from my past and they were yelling and screaming at me. They were dead set on making me doubt myself. And I did. They made it so hard for me to think clearly, I wanted to just cry and run away. But I'm stronger now – I know I am. And what people from my past said or thought about me has no power over me now. They don't know who I am NOW.

Yes… this feels good… but what if this is just bravado? Am I just trying to convince myself that I've changed?

No. I HAVE changed, and I have grown since I was here last. I've made strong decisions and stood behind them. You CAN do this, Pro. It's what you came here to do – it's time to face Felagor.

Pro wasn't sure if those thoughts were her own, or echoes from M2. For a moment that concerned her, but then she realized – it didn't matter. What mattered was that she could feel the truth ringing through those statements.

It was odd for her to realize she thought about that encounter in those terms. *To face Felagor. Why not 'to attack Felagor,' or 'to conquer Felagor?'* Then Pro realized, *there's a difference between showing up prepared to do battle and itching for a fight. I will do what I need to do.* She made fists and beat them downward, claiming her strength.

I am not the same. She picked up Zor's sword. She played with it a bit, testing its weight and the heft of it. She widened her stance to gain more balance. Then she swung the sword a few times, noticing that with each flourish she was gaining confidence and strength.

"Ha!" she shouted as the sword sliced through the air. "Ha! Ha!" She remembered from fencing class that making sound helped her feel more grounded – or, as the instructor had put it, 'more in her own power.' That was certainly the case now. In fact, she had never felt more present in her body – strong, grounded and capable.

I really do feel strong. I hope it lasts. "Let's do this," she said out loud.

Now, before I enter the caves, what do I need to do? I need to claim my strength as I breathe. I'm doing a good job of that now – let's keep that going. As I breathe, I also need to keep clearing my head. If I hear voices, I need to remember they are not real. But that is not enough. What else can I do? Oh, I know! I can hum.

She remembered the wonderful humming hugs of Loahn's mother and how calming and centering they were. Pro smiled. *I like that idea – not only will the humming remind me of Erinmar, it's making my own sound rather than listening to those other voices.*

Then Pro heard the sound of the Beckoner, and she knew she was ready to enter the caves of Vergon.

As she entered, the heat immediately blasted her skin. Her nose filled with the acrid smell and she forced herself to breathe deeply through her mouth, so the smell was less overwhelming. There were the blowholes of steam she remembered. She had the vague impression that shrieks emanated from one, while voices from her past burst from others. She refused to listen. As they got louder and louder, she hummed softly to herself.

Yellow slime spewed from a blowhole. It took Pro by surprise, but she managed to dodge it just in time. She came to a spot where the caves branched off. She heard Felagor's deep guttural roar off to her right. She felt its rumble in her stomach. For a moment it almost knocked her off her feet, but she widened her stance and regained her balance. As she followed the rumbling roar, she was careful to circle around a sinkhole like the one that had almost ensnared Zor. Her heartbeat quickened. *We can do this*, she thought, coaxing her heart to slow down before it burst from her chest.

She tried to focus on the source of the rumbling – to let it guide her to the cave where Felagor was lying in wait. That very thought sent shivers up her spine. Then the sound seemed to be coming from behind her and she found herself in a cavern with three paths. *No*, she thought. *It's coming from the center cave. Wait, now it seems to be coming from everywhere. Ugh! This is exasperating. What am I supposed to do?* But then she stopped herself and she thought of M2.

"Just breathe," she said aloud. "Breathe, calm down and focus." She felt M2 smile.

Just listen, she thought. Or was that M2's voice? *I'm listening, but there are so many voices I can barely hear myself think.*

"Ican'tDOthisanymoreIcan'tDOthisanymoreIcan'tDOthis. . ." raced
through her head.
**"You're not a little girl anymore – You've GOT to
learn to control yourself."**
"Pro? You think you're a PRO? Hahahahahahaha!"
"Watch your step. I have
my eye on you." **Who the hell do you think
you are?"**

For just a moment she wanted to scream – to run – to do anything
to drown out the voices from her past. But almost immediately she
stopped herself. *That is just old programming,* she thought. *Time to tune
to a new channel.*

Listen for the truth. The rest is illusion. Listen for what is real. Pro's
thoughts and M2's voice intermingled.

*I remember the first time we were here Loahn said we needed to tune in to
the life force. He said the other paths were dead ends. I have to listen for what
feels true and right for me.*

Then she heard The Beckoner's voice – ringing clear and true.
Pro focused all of her attention on that beautiful singing. Breathing
deeply, she was able to tune herself to the Beckoner's call, so the
other voices receded ever so slightly, but it was enough. The
Beckoner's voice was coming from the cave to her left.

Yes, it was the path to the left where Loahn had sensed a life
force the first time we were here. I remember he said the others were
dead ends. Pro pressed forward.

She heard the voices calling out to her, but the moment they
started to shake her, she remembered to breathe, gripped the sword,
and focused on the Beckoner's call. Then the voices fell away. But
she could hear Felagor breathing. She felt it in her heart – in her
blood.

Or am I just sensing that?

But she knew it didn't matter. The Beckoner's call was getting
more pronounced. She was almost there.

And then she saw the shining, shimmering jewel. The singing
crescendoed. The music soared into the stratosphere and then dove
into a deep, warm well of alto-infused tones. The sound washed
through her, vibrating her cells to life, soothing her soul. She had

never felt such a sense of peace – so calm yet energized. She felt herself bathed in the cascading voice of the Beckoner.

Pro still wasn't sure where the sound was coming from, but she saw the jewel sparkling and changing colors with the modulations of the Beckoner's glorious song. She could see the sounds – now pink, then azure blue, then tangerine changing to canary yellow as the voice rose and fell. The colors and sounds were perfectly synchronized. *They must be the very best of friends,* she thought. Then suddenly, she understood. *You ARE the Beckoner, aren't you? The voice and the jewel are one.* Even as the thought rang through her, the shimmering of the voice and the sparking of the jewel seemed to smile at her.

"I'm very pleased to meet you," Pro said out loud. In response the Beckoner shone bright golden light and emanated a warm, throaty mid-tone that rang through Pro's body.

Pro took it all in – the sound, the color, the magnificence of the Beckoner. She felt so at peace that her mind went back to the friends that had made this journey with her, the friends whose love and support gave her the courage to be here now in this moment of wonder. With her new friends Pro felt so accepted, cared for, and at peace – so at home with herself.

That's strange... why, then, would the Beckoner feel like home to me now? And what does home mean anyway? I feel them with me – Zor, Stribjus, Loahn, and M2. Is this home? It certainly didn't feel like any of the places where she grew up. Maybe home isn't exactly the right word I'm looking for.

I know what it is – it's a sense of belonging – of being exactly who I am in this very instant. There is nothing to prove. Just being me is enough. Enough for what?

It doesn't matter. I am right where I need to be. I feel... magical.

Pro's sense of contentment was shattered in an instant - Felagor loomed before her, its massive dark presence blotting her view of the Beckoner. There was silence. Pro felt her stomach clench and suddenly it was hard for her to swallow.

Keep breathing. Keep breathing. Find your center – that calm place you discovered when you were up in the air in Navlys. And remember how supported you felt by the ground in Erinmar. Let it support you now. Come on, Pro. You can do this.

From the mass of darkness, heads and arms slithered out of the beast Felagor's core and hovered in the air. As the heads peered at her, Pro felt overheated, and yet she shivered with cold. Butterflies flew every which way in her unsettled stomach as heads leered at her and fingers taunted her, daring her to move an inch. The heads and hands moved toward Pro and then backed away in a taunting, mesmerizing dance.

Slowly, Pro raised her sword. Yes, the sword was hers now – it belonged to her. Pro fought to keep her wits about her and not be drawn into the maze of faces and fingers. She held incredibly still – poised to strike… if she needed to.

Then the heads became familiar faces: her mother looking frustrated and stern, her father flustered and exasperated, her sister Patricia resentful and jealous, and, of course, Ash, oozing disappointment.

Dropping the sword, Pro threw her hands in front of her eyes.

"These are only snapshots from the past," Pro heard M2 – or was it her own voice – say. "You are much more than your past, Pro."

"I AM much more than my past," Pro shouted out loud as she re-claimed her sword.

Okay, okay. I need to be present in THIS moment, with the Beckoner, and with my friends' incredible support.

Pro could hear their voices inside her head, "We are all here with you facing Felagor. You do not have to react."

Tears began to trail down Pro's cheeks. She was surprised to notice that they gave her strength. She smiled and almost burst out laughing. *These are not tears of weakness, disappointment, inadequacy, or even fear. These are tears of gratitude for the love and support I have.*

Her stomach was calming down. Pro felt her shoulders release and her breath go deeper. Even her feet felt different, as if they were sending roots deep into the earth, increasing her sense of balance and her confidence. Pro stood strong, refusing to react to the taunts of Felagor's heads and hands.

"I am not willing to play your games anymore, Felagor," she said aloud.

As she spoke her truth, the hands and heads pulled back and Felagor shifted. Out of the dark mass rose the warrior who reminded her of Clive in their first encounter. Pro stared into the monster's eyes. They blazed bright amber as the creature glowered right back at her, ready to cut her down. In those eyes she saw Clive once again challenging her to prove her worth. Pro raised her sword to attack when the Beckoner began to sing once more. The beautiful music stopped Pro in her tracks, and she knew she was going to be struck down by Felagor's shadow warrior. The glorious strains of the Beckoner brought her such peace, she resigned herself to the fatal blow she knew was coming.

It was then that she realized Felagor, too, was motionless, as if the monster was also filled with the shimmering sounds that Pro felt coursing through her blood, her breath, her being. The Beckoner was calling out to both of them.

But she sounds different this time. This is not a call of "Come find me," or "Come save me," Or even of "Here I am." What is it? What's different? Pro locked eyes with Felagor.

Then she felt more soundwaves pour through her – cleansing, warming, refreshing, and reassuring her all at once. She felt the soothing waves touch her heart and she knew. It's a call for understanding.

Pro and Felagor kept scrutinizing at each other. Then, at precisely the same moment, they both cocked their heads. When Pro cocked her head, she felt something in her shift. She found herself no longer peering at Felagor, but looking into the brute, who had shifted yet again. The mirrors that had so haunted and derided her in that first battle were facing her. However, this time Pro was looking into the depths of Felagor as she gazed into the mirrored surface. There, she saw her own reflection and, beyond it, other manifestations of the beast.

She remembered the paintings she had made of Felagor while she was in Erinmar. She saw in the creature's darkness the loneliness and isolation she had painted. As that image awakened in her, Pro felt a stirring deep inside. It surprised her that she felt no pity for Felagor, but a deep understanding.

I know loneliness and isolation. And you know, don't you? You know we share that. Her thoughts rang out louder than words.

Then the image she had painted of the parental Felagor filled her head and she saw that, too, in the creature's depths. She saw the profound love it had for the Beckoner, the sense of responsibility, the vigilance it had as her protector.

I see the love, the weight of the responsibility you feel toward her. The care you take as her protector – even your willingness to appear to be a monster in order to keep her safe. These thoughts, too, were stronger than any words and Pro knew that Felagor was receiving their impact.

She could feel the creature – the protector – softening, even as it was expanding. She saw the mirrors and around it the fierce warrior and around that the heads and arms. *Oh, my God! These aren't just different sides of Felagor; the creature is all of these things – as well as the lonely soul and the parental protector.* Then Pro made a move that surprised even her. With a huge breath, she took her sword and laid it down on the ground. She felt Felagor look deep inside her and heaved a tremendous sigh. *Is that relief? Letting go? Is it giving up? Is it mine? Felagor's? The Beckoner's? All of ours?*

The stirring inside Pro was churning now, expanding, as the singing swelled. Her solar plexus heated up as she saw herself in Felagor's many facets.

Then Felagor shifted toward Pro's left, which afforded her a clear view of the Beckoner sparkling and shining. She felt the song reverberating through her, sounding through every cell. The song, she realized now, was an invitation. She opened to receive it. It felt to Pro like her core was on fire.

Am I about to self-combust? The modulations of the Beckoner's song pulsed through her as its colors shimmered pale blue to lavender to fuchsia to deep purple. *It's okay. I'm pretty sure it's okay.*

As Pro felt her own atoms vibrating and shimmering, she slowly opened her jacket to receive even more. Looking down, Pro saw a hole in her solar plexus – a huge deep velvet opening – like a galaxy.

Holding her jacket open, she turned ever so slowly to her right, inscribing a full circle that reminded her of the engagement dance of Erinmar. She was letting the Beckoner's song wash over her – through her.

As she turned, she realized she was making herself vulnerable to Felagor, but a part of her that started to surface – to warn her to protect herself – calmed and gave itself over to the song – not hypnotized, just comforted.

As Pro turned back to Felagor the protector once again – she no longer thought of it as a monster or a creature – its head was still cocked, looking deep into the galaxy within her. Then Felagor turned its gaze to the Beckoner – shining and glowing and singing. Pro watched as Felagor, ever so gently, reached out to the Beckoner, picked it up and held it close.

The gesture was so gentle, so sweet that Pro smiled as her heart opened even more. She couldn't imagine taking the Beckoner away now. Now she understood so much more.

What happened next, Pro never would have anticipated.

Felagor offered the Beckoner to Pro. The offer took her aback. It was overwhelming to think that she even deserved to hold the Beckoner. She wrapped her jacket around herself, struggling to pull herself together.

This is a lot to take in – it's amazing. So, does this complete my journey? No – wait a minute. I'm not done. I still haven't found the Agency. It's what M2 said in the beginning, "You have to find the Agency." And I still don't even know what Agency I'm supposed to look for.

Okay, let's think this through. All along I thought there was some kind of external organization I had to find. But what if I look at this whole mission – to "find the Agency" from a different threshold? What if the Agency isn't outside of me at all?

What if THIS is the Agency? It's the determination I had to find WITHIN MYSELF – the boldness to take action. What if this is the SENSE of agency I had to discover.

I know the truth. It is MY truth. Whatever happens now, even if I burst into a million pieces like a supernova, I know this is what I came here to do.

Then Pro began to cry, great easy tears of joy in awe of the Beckoner – of Felagor – of the journey she had made to get here.

So, what was the point of this journey? What have I learned along the way? SO much. Too much to begin to wrap my brain around. It's like every picture I painted held its own lesson. All to lead me to my own agency – my own SENSE of agency.

Pro thought of the cliffside portrait of the beautiful woman – her portrait – made of all her little bits of creation.

What exactly have I gained? I know I have more confidence, but it's not just that. I've learned to value myself and all those little pieces that make up who I am. I've discovered that I am worthy of claiming the magic that I am.

Pro humbly bowed her head, opening her jacket once more to reveal a (w)hole galaxy within her. Felagor lovingly placed the shining jewel that was the Beckoner in that very spot – with her heart – and Pro became the song.

As she merged with the glorious music, every molecule of her being vibrated with life force.

It feels – no, it used to feel like it was so hard to just be me. But I didn't even know what that was. I was always so full of other people's voices. I had to always think about what they needed me to do or to say or to be. Or I would think about what I needed to say to sound stronger or more intelligent or more giving.

Wow! I've never imagined before that it could actually be not only easy, but joyful to just be me.

THAT'S what I'm a "Pro" at, she realized, laughing. That's the gift that no one can give me or take away from me – if I'm willing to claim it – the ability to just be ME.

Then Pro fell into her wholeness – HER music. She stepped into herself, as her melodies swelled and shimmered and rang through her.

I can see it and feel it all now. I am all of my paintings, all of the worlds I have experienced. I am Felagor and the Beckoner. I am the doorway and the mural. This is home. This is belonging. This is MY experience. This holding on and letting go, this shining – this is my wholeness – my truth.

As she honored her own value, her own wholeness, Pro felt exhilarated – no, that wasn't it. She felt like a star, burning bright in the night sky, expanding her light across galaxies, and it was absolutely magical.

A sound like water being siphoned up a tube engulfed her, and she lifted off the ground, spinning upward.

🦋

🦋 *Spiraling Up the Drain*

23. WELCOME FORWARD

Water streaming on her face startled her, but only for a moment. As Pro showered, she couldn't stop smiling.

I'm actually beaming. Why does it feel like the first day of school and I'm exhilarated? My six-month review is today. YAY! Hahahahahahahaha! I can't believe that doesn't scare me at all. Is that just denial? My parents would say that's exactly what it is. BUT I am not my parents, or Ash, or Professor Tilson, or Clive, or anyone else who has their own ideas about what I should do – or be.

Pro grabbed her journal, writing and sketching a huge thank you to the worlds she had visited and the friends she had made: M2, Zor, Loahn, Stribjus, the Beckoner, as well as countless others – even Felagor!

I'll be back to visit – I promise.

Ah, My dream journal! I have to hand it to you, Dr. Lambdowski. This dream journal was really a terrific idea. But it isn't just a 'Dream Journal'. With the sketches and ideas I am filling it with now, it's much more than that. I think it is The Magic Journal: A place with space to claim, chronicle, and celebrate the Magic that I AM – with playfulness and gratitude.

The rich yummy hum that filled Pro turned into a deep belly laugh, then into a grateful sigh.

After journaling and sketching for what seemed like hours, or maybe just minutes, Pro looked at her clock. *I still have another hour and a half before I have to wake up. Wait! I AM awake, right?* She thought about it for a minute. *Ha! I am. Totally. Hmmm. Shall we go back to sleep?*

"Are you kidding?" she said aloud. "There is work to do – worlds to paint. I'm going to have my own gallery showing. Whether Sonya sponsors it or not, it will happen."

And that doesn't just feel like bravado. It feels like the truth. Wow!

Pro rough-sketched two works she knew would be important and magical. One was the portrait of a beautiful woman painted on the side of a rainbow cliff. The other was titled "To Felagor." Then, as she considered how the whole journey began, she rough-sketched a triptych she titled "Sinkhole Dreams."

Let's see, the first panel will be "Sensing the Sinkhole" – filled with danger and potential. The second panel is "Possible Paths" as the woman in the picture visualizes turning back, going around, leaping over, or diving into the sinkhole. And the third is "Stepping Out with a Knowing-ness Into the Unknown." Hmmm. It sounds like my life. Yes!

She hummed and danced her way through preparing for work, making a point of dressing up and wearing her blue jacket for her six-month review.

I don't know that I have ever felt this light and playful and trusting before, she thought as she sailed to work, stopping at Starbucks for her morning chai. *Trusting? What does that even mean? Trusting of what? Well… that I will be just fine – whatever happens. Whatever happens today or tomorrow or…*

❦Pro arrived at work and stood before the mural looming over her in the lobby of Clive Bennett and Associates Advertising.

Even that looks different to me. It really is a beautiful painting. Why was I so intimidated by it before? Before, its boldness seemed so challenging. Now it just feels like an invitation to play and explore.

It's like pink bubbles running up and down my spine. The thought brought a smile to her face as she remembered the Kermuffles and how she had helped them overcome their tremendous fears.

And I did that, Pro thought. *I DID THAT! With lots of help. Okay, let's get to work.*

She arrived at her desk to find messages on her computer from Paige and Clive's secretary, Clarissa. Before she even looked at them, she sent a quick message off to Elaine, "Lunch today – my treat."

Now I'll address the summons from on high, Pro thought playfully. Paige asked her to send everything she had so far for <u>The Galactics</u>, including her earliest brainstorming versions before lunch.

❧ *The CBAA Mural: Worlds*

Clarissa's memo informed her that her six-month review would be in Clive's office that afternoon at four-thirty

Great! I get to sweat it out and fret all day.

Wait a minute – old programming, she thought with a big grin. *I don't have to go there anymore. NO! I refuse to go there. Really? To Clive's office? Ha! No, silly, to fussing and fretting that things won't be some certain way. If Clive is crazy enough to let me go, then this isn't the place for me to be. And if my job is secure, then I get to choose how long I want to stay.*

I'm not sure if Mother would be appalled at my thinking or proud of me. And, you know, that doesn't matter either. Look out, world – Pro, the rebel!

No, not a rebel – a woman who no longer automatically reacts to keep everyone around her happy – a woman who is proactive.

At that thought she laughed so hard she could hardly breathe. *That's what it means to be Pro! I like it.*

Launching back into <u>The Galactics</u>, new ideas poured in for ways to blend and illuminate the many facets of the main characters. By eleven-fifteen she had completed close to a final draft of the first of the three galactic dimension shifters, Acheron, her favorite, and was halfway through the second character when she sent numerous files off to Paige.

She met Elaine in the lobby, and they headed off to Lotus Dreams. Elaine's first remark was, "Whoa! You look radiant. You aren't pregnant, are you?"

"Hey, I'm finally learning how to take care of myself and I'm not sleeping with anyone, so no, I'm pretty sure I am NOT pregnant, but thanks for asking. And thanks for noticing."

"So, what's going on? Did you already have your six-month review? I thought it wasn't 'til late this afternoon."

"Oh, I haven't had it yet, but I wanted to have a celebratory lunch with you anyway."

"So, you're that confident you have this in the bag?" Elaine asked.

"No, not at all. What I do know is that I'll be just fine – whatever happens at four-thirty. I really do know that."

"That's fantastic, Pro. I knew that a few miles back. It's great to see you believing in yourself. So, what happened?"

"It's a long story, but I can give you some highlights."

It was the first time she had ever witnessed her friend speechless, until finally Elaine said, "And you are painting these worlds and these fantastic creatures that you met? I can't wait to see them."

"I have four on display at a gallery right now," Pro said.

"And you never told me? I would have been there for the grand opening. At any rate, I have to see them. I'll go this weekend. Will you be there tomorrow? Give me the details and you have to let me take you out to dinner."

The afternoon flew by. At four-fifteen, Pro sent off more files to Paige, put away everything on her desk, and put on her jacket.

Here we go!

"Hi, Clarissa. I have a four-thirty appointment," Pro said.

"Come on in, Pro," Clive's voice rang out from his office before Clarissa could reply. "Have a seat."

Once Pro was seated, Clive dove into talk about Atkins and loyalty and CBAA and how different it was conceptually and that some people were able to make the transition and others weren't. Then he got to the point.

"It was obvious to me from the outset that your work was solid. Old Atkins had good things to say about you and your work portfolio backed up his confidence. So, I never had any doubts about your work ethic or your dependability. As I saw you wrap up old projects, I could see your attention to detail and your eye for color and line. The big question was how would you adapt to this new culture? It's a big shift, I grant you that. CBAA is known for cutting edge work and it's important to me that we keep that edge. Paige and I had a long talk about you early this afternoon. She talked about your attitude and your dependability and reservations she has had about whether you could make the leap to join us. Then she showed me the files you sent her today." He paused.

Okay, I'm sure it's for effect and I have to admit – it's pretty effective. I have no idea what comes next. I don't know why I'm not nervous as hell. I'm just breathing through this, M2, she thought, playfully.

"You really surprised us both, Pro. Your ideas for this project are striking and inventive and bold. Can you sustain that? How can any of us possibly know? So, there is really only one thing to do…"

Clive stood up and Pro stood up, too. He picked a pink slip up from his desk. She remembered from six months ago the moment Clive wielded the pink slip very clearly. And now she was reliving it – but it didn't feel the same at all – SHE didn't feel the same.

Whatever is coming – bring it on.

He gazed at Pro, examining her face, looking deep into the strength in her eyes and cocked his head.

The cocked head. I've seen it so many times through this whole crazy journey. Why? Why does it keep showing up? Just for fun, she cocked her head back at Clive, then started to chuckle. *Is that all it is? Can it really be that simple? It's just a slightly different perspective. And it changes everything. Now I know what I need to do.*

Rather than handing it to her, Clive took the pink slip. Relishing the moment, he slowly started to rip it up when Pro snatched it out of his hands. She folded it twice more, made a few quick tears then unfolded the paper to reveal a series of butterflies. Pro looked at Clive and smiled quizzically. Then she took the butterfly pink slip, brought it together in her hands and threw them open.

To Pro's delight, the butterflies flew up and around her. *Are these butterflies real?*

Can Clive see them? I guess it really doesn't matter at all. And then, Pro giggled.

While Clive managed to refrain from bursting out laughing, he could not hide his amusement. He opened both of his hands to Pro as if to say, 'Okay, then. Welcome to the family.'

He grinned at her and walked back behind his desk. With a big smile on his face and shaking his head, he said "See you Monday, Pro."

"Probably," Pro grinned back as she left his office and headed back to her home base.

Well, that was fun!

Her co-workers eyed her furtively. They knew that meeting was big. Elaine came out of her office and looked at Pro. Smiling drolly, Pro gave a very small thumbs-up. Elaine silently clapped her hands. Pro imagined stories would be flying – like butterflies – next week. *It'll be so much fun to share my paintings with Elaine this weekend, dinner, then Girls' Night Out – the drinks are on me. Sorry, Thom. We'll get together next week.*

Pro laughed and thought of Stribjus somersaulting and juggling, grinning at her. *We really made use of our sense of humor through that whole experience,* she chuckled to herself.

She made fists and beat them downward, claiming her strength – congratulating herself for taking initiative and taking action. She saw Zor fighting with glee as she stood by Pro in Thanton. *Your strength is a great inspiration, Zor.*

Pro stopped and listened and felt inside for how that encounter went. She was tickled at how she had trusted her instinct and how calm she felt then and now. She thought of Loahn meditating and radiating peace to her flying silk aerial escapade. *I am not up in the air, all wrapped up in a problem I don't know how to handle. I claim that peace for myself now – in BOTH holding on AND letting go. Blessings, Loahn.*

Pro remembered to breathe and thought of M2's watchful presence. *Thank you, M2. I understand now that your wisdom and guidance are always with me.*

Oh! And Felagor – much thanks to you for teaching me that things are not always what they seem and when facing what might appear to be a monster, there could be a better way than charging into attack mode.

Beckoner, what can I say? Thank you for calling out to me and leading me to who I am.

She felt all six of her friends smiling, beaming their love and support. Had she dreamed them? Perhaps. Did it matter? Not a bit. For her, they were far more real than Ash and Miss Massachusetts.

Pro grabbed her bag and headed out. In the lobby, she paused to drink in the mural once more.

"Thank you. You have been a part of this – this growing – this coming into my own – this journey. And on we go!"

Pro felt like she was flying. Once outside, she crossed the street to the small park. There, she stopped and took a moment to drink in the world around her – the bustling city where so often people did not take time to breathe, listen inside themselves and be with what they were feeling.

I lived that existence for a long, long time. Cocking her head, she thought – *not anymore.*

Pro looked at the world around her and acknowledged its gifts with her arms open wide. She smiled and made the Kermuffle 'sparkle-hands' gesture to the busy city around her.

Then, Pro took a big deep breath, put her hands to her heart and thrust her arms forward – ready to move forward, ready for whatever was next. She felt the Beckoner's song reverberate through her, generating light within her. She saw two beautiful butterflies dance around each other. As they flitted by, she made a rich deep humming sound.

It was a bit warm, so Pro opened her jacket. Then she noticed the lining.

🦋 *Butterflies and Possibilities*

She had a vague memory of liking the lining when she bought the jacket almost five years ago to celebrate her new job, and though she wore it often, the jacket lining hadn't caught her attention for years. Now, the dark blues and silvers – moons, planets, comets, and stars – shimmered in the sunlight, giving birth to a spell of rich laughter.

There is a universe of possibilities and it's all right here – around me and in me.

This feels incredibly different. I feel incredibly different. No more simply reacting, she vowed – *to my parents or Ash, or Clive.*

I am owning my life right now. I am being magic. Ha! This is the next step. The thought thrilled her, filling her with excitement and hope.

Do I know exactly where this new direction is leading me?

Nope… no idea… and that's just perfect. This is my first step into the great mystery that is my life – and it starts now.

THE JOURNEY IS ON!

ABOUT THE AUTHOR

Michael Ellison, Ph.D., is committed to using theatrical, educational, and energetic tools for personal and systemic transformation. With a Ph.D. in Theatre from The University of Minnesota, Michael has coached, taught, performed, and shared his transformational body/energy work across the United States, in Canada, Denmark, Germany and in the Philippines, where he worked with Lea Salonga.

As an associate professor at Bowling Green State University (BGSU) for 23 years, he revitalized the Humanities Troupe to create and perform pieces dealing with important social issues such as racism, sexism, and homophobia. As a teacher, coach, inspirational speaker and energy worker, Michael specializes in helping people "be more fully present."

An energy practitioner for more than 30 years, Michael has studied Reiki, Awakening Your Light Body, and Crystalline Consciousness Techniques which he utilizes in his work in the arts as well as with individual clients, assisting them in releasing blocks to personal transformation. He helps people to "get out of their own way" - to ground, center and open to new possibilities for claiming who they are, moving forward from a new threshold with fresh perspectives.

For more, visit michaelellison.net

ABOUT THE ARTIST

Melanie A. Stinson is an award-winning writer and artist as well as an energy and bodywork therapist. Melanie's magical weavings, wearable art, oil pastels, photographs and digital art have been exhibited throughout Northwest Ohio as well as online. With a background in ballet, modern, and improvisational dance Melanie has served as a dance analyst and as director of membership for New York City Ballet.

Melanie believes in the power of dance and art (non-verbal art forms) to transform people's lives, providing healing and inspiration. She has taught creative arts and creative movement to a broad range of people from toddlers to adults. A certified Reiki Master Teacher and Crystalline Consciousness Techniques Energy Master, Melanie has also studied Rosen Method techniques, Laban Effort/Shape and authentic movement as well as other healing modalities. A writer of children's stories, poetry and dance-related screenplays, her Reiki-infused art collage story "Being Magic" served as the inspiration for "Being Magic: A Journey to Wholeness."

For more on Melanie's art, visit melaniestinson.com

www.ingramcontent.com/pod-product-compliance
Lightning Source LLC
Chambersburg PA
CBHW051149030726
47504CB00004B/1113